A Perfect Love

Heavenly Daze Book Four

LORI COPELAND
ANGELA HUNT

THOMAS NELSON
Since 1798

NASHVILLE DALLAS MEXICO CITY RIO DE JANEIRO BEIJING

Published in Nashville, Tennessee, by Thomas Nelson. Thomas Nelson is a trademark of Thomas Nelson, Inc.

Published in association with Alive Communications, Inc., 7680 Goddard Street, Suite 200, Colorado Springs, CO 80920.

Thomas Nelson, Inc., titles may be purchased in bulk for educational, business, fund-raising, or sales promotional use. For information, please e-mail SpecialMarkets@ThomasNelson.com.

Scripture quotations in this book are from the Holy Bible, New Living Translation © 1996. Used by permission of Tyndale House Publishers, Inc., Wheaton, Illinois 60189. All rights reserved.

This is a work of fiction. Names, characters, places, and incidents either are the product of the authors' imaginations or are used fictitiously. Any resemblance to actual persons, living or dead, events, organizations, or locales is entirely coincidental.

Library of Congress Cataloging-in-Publication Data

Copeland, Lori.
 A perfect love / Lori Copeland and Angela Hunt.
  p. cm. — (Heavenly Daze series)
  ISBN-13: 978-0-8499-4343-0 (trade paper)
  ISBN-13: 978-1-59554-552-7 (mass market)
  I. Hunt, Angela Elwell, 1957– II. Title.
  PS3553.06336 P47 2002
  813'.54—dc21
2002023466

Printed in the United States of America

08 09 10 11 12 QW 5 4 3 2 1

O perfect Love, all human thought transcending,
Lowly we kneel in prayer before thy throne,
That theirs may be the love which knows no ending,
Whom thou forevermore dost join in one.

O perfect Life, be thou their full assurance,
Of tender charity and steadfast faith,
Of patient hope and quiet, brave endurance,
With childlike trust that fears nor pain nor death.

Grant them the joy which brightens earthly sorrow;
Grant them the peace which calms all earthly strife,
And to life's day the glorious unknown morrow
That dawns upon eternal love and life.
—DOROTHY FRANCES BLOMFIELD GURNEY,
1883

Prologue

*W*inter, the locals tell each other, is the measure of a man, and January is the month by which we measure all others. By the turn of the year, the summercaters have long been gone, the leaf people have vanished, and the island's few Christmas visitors have returned to their business on the mainland. By January, winter has settled onto the coastal towns too: The tourist shops have closed, the streetcars have ceased their trolling, and the bed-and-breakfast owners have drained their pipes, boarded their windows, and flown to Florida. The Heavenly Daze folks, however, don't leave. It's as if the idea never occurred to them.

By January the lobstermen, like our own Russell Higgs, have stacked their traps and piled their buoys. Like brightly colored bowling pins, the buoys lie scattered over the brown lawns, waiting for play to commence. On some days Russell will gather a few traps and venture onto the sea, for fishing is a year-round operation here, but January, his wife, Barbara, reminds him, is just as apt for repairin' as it is for lobsterin'.

Heavenly Daze, the locals say, is some different in winter. After observing more than two hundred of the coldest seasons on this little island, I can attest to their observation. In winter the island is quiet, more subdued. The light fades from the day by 4 PM, and gone is the sparkle that gilded the summer ocean. Sea smoke covers the water now, shifting over the surface like lace over a worn gray blanket.

Welcome back to our little island off the coast of

Maine. If you've never had the blessing of visiting Heavenly Daze, you should know that many years ago, a child of God known as Jacques de Cuvier begged the Lord to safeguard the inhabitants of this blessed place. In answer to that loving prayer, the Lord dispatched me and six others of the angelic host. Our mission is quite simple: We protect and serve those who live in the seven original buildings on the island of Heavenly Daze.

I am Gavriel, captain of this small company, and I guard the church. Occasionally I don human flesh and visit my angelic brothers—Micah, Abner, Caleb, Yakov, Zuriel, and Elezar—but most of the time I observe quietly and relay messages from the Throne of the Most High. The human inhabitants of our island, you see, don't realize that the curtain separating the earthly and spiritual realms is more like gossamer than iron, and everything that happens on Heavenly Daze is dear to the heart of the Lord God. He, of course, is dearly concerned with everything happening everywhere, but after spending more than two hundred earth years on this same stretch of soil, I must admit that I take a particular interest in this island and its people.

I know the glory of God fills the universe, and entire nations of people sing his praises. But to me nothing sounds as sweet as the crackling winter voices of the people in our little town.

Come join us for a jubilant January on the island of Heavenly Daze.

—Gavriel

Chapter One

$\mathcal{F}$eels more like mud season than winter out there. My skin's not even stickin' to the windowpane." Cleta Lansdown, coproprietor of the Baskahegan Bed and Breakfast, pulled her palm away from the dark window to scoop up a pair of eggs-over-medium from a layer of hot bacon grease, then slid them onto a paper towel–covered plate. Her family—husband, Floyd; daughter, Barbara; and son-in-law, Russell—sat behind her in varying degrees of alertness.

Four AM, and every last one of them except Russell should be in bed. But Barbara got up because her husband, a lobsterman, liked to be on the water at sunrise, and he insisted that she keep him company before going out. So Cleta got up because when Barbara was half-asleep she couldn't boil water, let alone cook, and Floyd got up because he couldn't resist the aroma of bacon in a frying pan.

Barbara yawned and reached for a piece of toast. A snarled cowlick poked through a layer of plastic green rollers on her head. Cleta eyed her daughter worriedly. The girl looked tensed up this morning. She'd always had a delicate constitution—never been like other girls her age. But Barbara wasn't a child any longer; she'd be twenty-three next month. Twenty-three. Where had the years gone? Why, it seemed like only yesterday that Cleta had carried a tiny, pink-faced bundle up the front steps of the Bed and Breakfast with Floyd holding tightly to her arm. It had taken thirty-six hours to bring their child into the world, and it seemed as if only thirty-six minutes had passed until she was grown . . .

With one eye cracked open, Barbara slathered butter on her toast. She looked at Russell, her husband of three years. "Pass the jam."

Russell grunted, his unshaven features dark as a drunken sea merchant on his first night home. "Better lay off the sweets, hon. You'll lose your girly figure—"

"Just pass me the jam, Russell." Barbara threw him one of her "or-else" looks. Or was that the dry-up-or-I'll-smack-the-snot-out-of-you glare? Cleta shook her head. She'd lost track. Barbara was full of moods lately.

Setting the plate of eggs in front of Floyd, Cleta cautioned him to eat only one. "They're full of cholesterol," she warned.

Through his thick glasses, Floyd eyed the forbidden fare before his gaze shifted back to her. "Then why are you cooking them for me?"

"Just hush up and eat."

Obediently Floyd picked up his fork and pulled one egg onto his plate, then cut into the runny yolk. "Don't know why we can't have some of those fancy dishes you make for the summer complaints. Caramel-apple French toast, egg casserole, orange muffins." He stared at the piece of burnt toast he was holding. "Some of that nice granola with dried fruit and nuts would be good about now—"

"You're a nut." Cleta sat down at the table and reached for the cream pitcher. She glanced at her daughter. "What's wrong, Doodles? Aren't you feeling well this morning?"

"Mother." Barbara glared at Cleta, blueberry jam rimming her tremulous upper lip. She slammed her hand on the table, splashing coffee from Floyd's cup onto the green Formica. "Don't call me Doodles. How many times do I have to remind you that I'm a grown woman?"

"Well, don't get your Fruit of the Looms in a bunch!" Floyd growled, reaching for a napkin to mop up the spill. Cleta dashed cream in her cup and stirred, trying to keep quiet. She'd called Barbara "Doodles" from the day she was born. So had everybody else on the island, until Barbara announced she was an adult and had outgrown the silly name.

Pffff.

Adult?

Twenty-three was still wet behind the ears.

But she'd zip her lip, because Floyd hated it when she and Barbara quarreled during a meal—and that happened more than Cleta cared to think about. Barbara was cranky as all get-out lately.

Stirring her coffee, Cleta frowned and glanced at her son-in-law. Had he and Barbara been quarreling again? She'd overheard them yelling at each other a few times, but usually the trouble blew over within an hour. Cleta tried not to interfere in her daughter's marriage, and she'd warned Floyd to stay out of the kids' problems. But it wasn't easy. Once or twice she'd forgotten her place and jumped right into the middle of a fray, but that was Barbara's fault. The girl wouldn't stand up for herself, and although Russell was a good boy, he wasn't perfect—in fact, he was downright inconsiderate of Barbara at times. He could be thickheaded, and had a tendency to put work before the Lord, usually preferring a seat on the water to one in the church on

Sunday morning. He was as independent as a hog on ice. A true lobsterman.

Need she say more?

He had no reason to complain. Lobstering had never been better, so he had nothing to fly off the handle about. Old-timers swore they couldn't remember a year with a higher yield—last year Maine lobstermen trapped a record 56.7 million pounds—almost twenty million pounds more than the one hundred–year average. Russell bragged that on a typical day he had kept only one in every eight to ten of the orange and green mottled tail-snapping beauties in his trap. Though limited to eight hundred traps, Russell made a handsome living, but Cleta didn't know what the kids did with their money. Russell often talked about getting one of those new Ford double-cab diesels, but since automobiles weren't allowed on the island, Russell admitted he wouldn't have much use for such a vehicle. He'd have to leave it at the ferry landing in Ogunquit, and too much funny stuff went on over there in the summer . . . he'd likely venture across one day and find his truck vandalized or something.

Other than Russell's traps, his clothes, and his boat—the *Barbara Jean,* a three-year-old, thirty-foot double-wedge hull with a single inboard diesel—he owned nothing. The fiberglass boat, purchased last year from a Portland lobsterman's widow, had nice, low hours with a small forward cabin and windshield, open-decked cockpit aft, and up-to-date equipment, including radar, VHF radio, and a depth sounder. The rig sure beat the little dory his great grandpa Higgs worked out of in the late eighteenth century.

Russell and Barbara used to talk about getting their

own place when they had children, but children seemed to be a touchy subject these days. The fact that Russell and Barbara remained childless after three years was downright baffling, since Floyd often threatened to turn the water hose on the pair when he caught them smoochin' in the parlor like a couple of heathens. He also referred to Russell as the "resident mooch" until Cleta made him stop.

The boy had been improving, though. Since the Christmas Eve service, a wonderful time of sharing for the entire town, Russell seemed to be looking at church in a new light, and the next Sunday found him perched in the family pew, where a God-fearing man should be. Cleta had been praying for such a change, and it warmed her heart to see the boy mature a little.

She enjoyed the kids living upstairs. She loved spending time with her only child, and she and Barbara had always been close. The house seemed as empty as a storm cellar on a sunny day without her, and Barbara wasn't well, no matter what Russell said. She was delicate—always had been. Men didn't understand delicacy in a woman, but a mother did. Especially Cleta, who'd had her fair share of ailments without the comfort of a mama's hand. Her own mother had been as cold as kraut; Cleta couldn't remember ever receiving a hug from the severe New England woman.

Cleta's closest friend, Vernie Bidderman, owner of Mooseleuk Mercantile, got right peeved with Cleta when she compared her raising to Barbara's. Vernie accused Cleta of not cutting the apron strings, an accusation that couldn't be any more off the mark. A parent had every right to worry about her child, and a parental obligation to be concerned. Cleta wasn't going to be like her mother and not give a fig about her child's welfare.

"Bull." The last time they'd had this conversation—last week or so—Vernie had crossed her arms and stared down her nose at Cleta. "We've been friends since before you conceived Barbara and I'm telling you it's time to give up. You can't continue to direct, control, and interfere in your daughter's life."

"As if I would!"

"You would. You do."

"Why, that's a big fat lie, Veronica Bidderman!" Cleta slammed the bag of sugar she was about to buy onto the counter. If Vernie was going to be ornery, she'd go to Ogunquit for her supplies.

"It's the truth, Cleta." Vernie picked up the sugar and set it back on the shelf. "You'll never give up criticizing and trying to run that girl's life until you're made to stop."

Words bubbled up like lava from a volcano. "Barbara's my child. What would you know about children?"

Cleta felt the sting of guilt after that remark, knowing the barb went deep. Stanley Bidderman, Vernie's husband, had run off twenty years ago and only returned last month. His untimely departure had left both Biddermans childless and resentful.

"You're only jealous of how close Barbara and I are," said Cleta.

Vernie took a deep breath. "I won't deny that I would have loved to have a daughter. But though I don't, I still have eyes, and I see a suffocating parent who doesn't know it's time to turn loose. It's time, Cleta. Let your daughter go."

Cleta choked on the words that rose in her throat. Why, Vernie had some nerve! Cleta and Floyd were only helping the kids get a good start. What parent wouldn't do the same? And she and Floyd were certainly willing and able. Why, during the winter they would rattle around in their old house like clothespins in a milk bottle without Russell and Barbara.

Vernie sniffed. "Barbara's a grown woman."

"And your definition of a grown woman is—?"

Vernie crossed her arms over her ample chest. "Anyone old enough to get married and vote should be responsible enough to pay their own rent. Russell makes more than you and Floyd, Cleta. Face the truth—you're keeping the kids dependent because you don't think they're capable of handling difficulty if it comes along. But running interference for Barbara will stunt her ability to figure things out on her own. And Russell—well, I'm surprised Russell's put up with you as long as he has. If he wasn't such a good boy he would have walked out two years ago."

Cleta's face flamed. "Walked out! On Barbara?" She sputtered. "Thank you very much, but I'll do my shopping in Ogunquit this week. Nobody there is going to tell me how to raise my child."

Vernie shook her head. "Shop wherever you like, Cleta, but you'd best listen to me before it's too late. Set your child free. Offer Barbara the opportunity to meet life on its own terms before she turns on you."

Cleta studied the shopkeeper from lowered lids. "You've been ordering those psychology books on the Internet again, haven't you?"

Vernie eyed her sternly. "Cleta."

"What?"

"Learn to knit or something, but butt out of Barbara's and Russell's life."

Vernie's stinging censure still rang in Cleta's ears. Well, Cleta had all she could handle without taking up knitting, thank you very much. She was a proud business-woman who kept her guests happy and satisfied. During the tourist season she rose every day before dawn to bake sausage-and-egg casseroles, slice fresh fruit, and supply hot muffins warm from the oven. She brewed expensive fla-vored coffees like crème brûlée and tiramisu, and served her gourmet muffins in lined wicker baskets with sweet churned butter. Such niceties kept the guests returning to the Baskahegan Bed and Breakfast and the inn operating in the black.

Knitting, indeed.

She'd leave that up to Birdie Wester, and Cleta would see to her own doings whether it suited Vernie or not.

Clearing her thoughts, Cleta picked up the plate of bacon and waved it under Barbara's nose. "You're eating like a bird this morning. Have some meat."

She watched, pleased, as Barbara sleepily pulled four pieces onto her plate.

"Well . . . I'm not very hungry."

There it was—the whine.

Floyd complained about Barbara's whining, but who wouldn't sound a wee bit edgy at this hour of the morn-ing? Of course, Cleta was used to the early hour, and so was Floyd. He couldn't sleep past sunup if Cleta tied him in the bed, but Barbara was a good sleeper, and had been since infancy. Left undisturbed, Barbara could stay in bed until midafternoon, and often did. But then the poor thing had a terrible time going to sleep at night. Barbara didn't come alive until Leno was on, then she'd get interested in movies on the Lifetime movie channel; sometimes it'd be three or four o'clock in the morning before the child could unwind enough to sleep. Russell was ready to get up about the time Barbara was ready to turn in. If children ever came along . . .

Cleta shook her head. Barbara wouldn't know day from night if she had a baby who got her up at all hours.

She eyed Floyd, who was slurping his coffee. "What's on your docket today, Floyd?"

"Thought I'd go down and fire up the truck. Then I got to study."

Cleta drew a deep breath. Floyd had been taking a correspondence course in mechanical engineering for the past several weeks. Though she was glad he'd found something to do, his studies had reinforced his annoying fixation on things mechanical.

Her husband had a virtual love affair going with the community fire truck. As faithful as the sunrise, he went down to crank the engine once a day in order to keep the motor in top shape. There hadn't been much call for the fire truck lately—none, actually, since last October when a gull snatched Pastor Wickam's toupee and the awful hairpiece landed in a pine tree.

"Got to keep 'er running smooth." Floyd reached for the saltshaker. "Do you know what a vehicle like that would cost nowadays if we had to replace 'er?"

Cleta didn't venture a guess because she knew. Floyd reminded her and the entire town at every monthly meeting.

"Nine hundred fifty thousand dollars," Floyd supplied.

"Hmm," Cleta said around a mouthful of toast.

"If that one goes on us, we'll never get another."

Cleta sighed, then, like a good wife, mumbled her line. "Did we pay that much for this one?"

"No. Got this one at a steal but only because it was ten years old. Still paid over three hundred thousand bucks."

Cleta rolled her eyes toward the ceiling. "That much?" She hated this conversation, but they had it nearly every morning. Why couldn't Floyd find a new topic?

Her husband nodded. "Needs new rubber, though."

"Ayuh. New tires. So you've said." Again and again and again . . .

"Daddy," Barbara whined.

"I know, I know." Floyd leaned over and pinched Barbara's cheek. "You gals don't like to talk business so early in the morning. But you have a fire with bad tires and see if you don't change your mind, little missy."

Russell pointed toward the plate in the center of the table. "Pass the eggs."

Sighing, Cleta handed him the plate.

≈

As sunlight streamed through the tall window of her bedroom, Barbara leaned against the window frame and stared past the dock toward the sea where her husband worked. Was he thinking of her as he baited and tossed out his traps? If so, was he missing her, or enjoying the peace and quiet away from this house?

Unable to face the disloyal thought, Barbara reined in her gaze, settling on the mulched flower beds that lined the front walkway. Those flower beds were Micah Smith's pride and joy, though he had little to do with them in the winter. In summertime, the Baskahegan Bed and Breakfast was the town showplace, gardens of annuals and perennials in full bloom. Beds of old-fashioned apothecary rose dotted the spacious lawn facing the Atlantic. The flowery fireworks of scarlet salvia, the eccentric mop tops of bee balm, and mounds of cloverlike globe amaranth lined the red brick walks with friendly greetings for the tourists.

"Look," some woman would inevitably exclaim as she bent to fondle a siren-red clump of Lawrence verbena. "Have you ever seen anything more heavenly?"

Micah loved flowers, and Barbara was fond of saying he possessed a green thumb plus four green fingers. No one could wield a trowel, fork, shovel, and rubber pail with such astounding effect. But island winters were merciless, and once the leaves and flower beds were raked and the outdoor furniture stored in the shed behind the B&B, Micah had little to occupy his time other than leading music at the church and enjoying coffee and doughnuts at the bakery with Abner. That morning habit, Micah declared years ago, was proving disastrous to his waistline, so he wanted to earn his keep by housecleaning in the winter months.

When Cleta had protested that cleaning wasn't Micah's job, he only smiled and said he liked to feel needed. So now the forty-somethingish gardener helped with the vacuuming and cleaning in winter, attending to each guest room with as much dedication and precision as he gave his beloved flower beds. Like clockwork, he cleaned twelve rooms—thirteen if you counted the attic bedroom, used only for overflow—five guest rooms and three baths upstairs, and the Lansdowns' bedroom, kitchen, parlor, and bath located downstairs. Each Monday morning Micah started at the top of the house and worked his way down, rarely finishing before noon on Thursday. The high-pitched whine of his vacuum cleaner reverberated along the sixteen-foot ceilings until Barbara declared she was going to frow the cord.

In the church, the house, and the garden, Micah was a perfectionist. He didn't just sprinkle tender plants or vacuum the center of guest rooms. He pulled out heavy chairs, beds, and nightstands with the same diligence he sowed, weeded, and fertilized every inch of the lawn. The lively man went about his mission like a sugared-up General Patton, hellbent on annihilating dust mites, powdery mildew, black spot, and rust. Occasionally his trained eye would catch sight of the dreaded rose mosiac fungi and life wouldn't be worth living around the B&B until he'd stamped out the blight.

Now Micah and his Hoover were bearing down on Barbara, roaring down the carpeted hallway.

"If it's no trouble, I'll do your room and be out of your way soon!" Micah shouted above the siphoning noise. The Hoover mowed through a path of resistance, catching the hem of a window drape. The fabric corkscrewed up the shaft, the wall screws straining to hold the curtain rod. Micah quickly stepped on the power button and shut off the machine. "Not a problem," he said, turning the vacuum on its side.

Tightening the belt of her robe, Barbara walked to the

doorway of her bedroom and leaned against the framing. Oblivious, Micah patiently proceeded to undo the snarl.

She would have heaved the cleaner out the window and told her mom to buy new drapes.

Sighing, she folded her arms and caught her reflection in the antique hallway mirror. What happened to the dewy-eyed twenty-year-old girl Russell had married? She was nowhere in evidence today. The image that stared back at her had allergy-puffed eyes behind thick glasses, no makeup, and thin lips. The swinging, sassy haircut Russell had thought cute a year ago now hung like linguini against her pale features.

She leaned forward, making white indentations on her cheeks with her thumb and forefinger. Water retention from too many nitrates. She really should lay off the bacon.

"Micah? Why would any man in his right mind marry me?"

The gardener, absorbed in salvaging the drape, glanced up. His brown-eyed gaze softened. "What a question, Barbara. Any man would be proud to have you for his wife."

"Oh, stop it." She leaned against the banister and stared at the ceiling. Micah always had a kind word for her—especially when she didn't want to believe him. "Look at me! I'm an ugly, overweight, water-retentive wretch, and I don't see how Russell stands me."

Forsaking the vacuum, Micah propped his hands on his bent knee and smiled up at her. "What a way to talk. The Lord made you in his perfect image. Are you questioning his purposes?"

"No." Barbara averted her eyes from the look of kindness on the gardener's face, feeling somehow ashamed of her neediness. He was right; she shouldn't feel so down on herself, but how could she help it? Men didn't care what they looked like; but for women, looks were important. Looks were what caught a man's attention in the first place, and after you caught a man's attention you had to charm him, and flatter him, and make him feel special. And once you married him, you had to please him, and care for him, and eventually, give him a baby . . .

And in that lay the problem. Lately Russell had been insisting it was time they started a family and found a place of their own. Barbara had been stalling, hoping that the announcement of a baby would ease her way out of her family home, but there'd been no baby thus far.

She supposed she was at fault. She wasn't in any hurry to leave home, even though she'd been a married woman for three years. Mom and Dad were . . . well, Mom and Dad, and she loved them with all of her heart. But lately she felt uncomfortable here, even smothered, and she couldn't explain this feeling to anyone.

What was wrong with her?

She tried to be enthusiastic about the prospect of having a baby and leaving home. Each month built to a climax of hopeful suspense—was she or wasn't she pregnant? There were breathless days when her monthly cycle failed to begin on time, and sometimes, when she was late, she spent days in a kind of hopeful bemusement, refusing to take even a simple aspirin in case the miracle had happened.

But those days were inevitably followed by the awful waking up to a low abdominal ache and the sure knowledge she wasn't carrying a child. Russell always stirred when he heard her crying, and rolled over to take her into his arms, whispering that he loved her and they would be parents when the time was right. They had to be patient and wait on God's timing.

Cleta and Floyd only looked at each other with "what's wrong now?" expressions on their faces when Barbara came into the kitchen with dark circles ringing her eyes. Disappointment, thick as sea smoke, hung in the air for a few days before life settled back to normal and the cycle began again.

"Is something bothering you, Barbara?" Micah's concern pulled her from her thoughts.

Sighing, she gripped the banister behind her. Outside the window, bright sunshine streamed through the lace curtains—deceptively misleading for January. Just as her young body was deceptively misleading, offering the promise of babies and a home when there was none.

"It's personal, Micah."

"I don't mean to pry."

"No, it's not that I don't want to tell you. You're like family, after all. It's just that I don't want to embarrass you."

The gardener smiled softly. "I don't think you could embarrass me, dear girl. I have seen more things on earth than you could imagine and—"

"I don't know why I can't have babies," Barbara blurted out. "Russell and I try . . . but it doesn't happen. Russell wants a son so badly."

Micah tilted his head slightly. "Babies come when the Father sends them. When the time is right, you will conceive."

Barbara had heard that same assurance stated in a hundred different ways:

Be patient.

In God's perfect timing, it will come.

Don't be in such a hurry; enjoy your carefree days. Children are a lot of responsibility.

Have you thought about adoption?

Cleta had been less than encouraging. Oh, Mom wanted a grandchild, but she made it clear there was no hurry. Children were a lot of responsibility, she said, and once babies started coming Russell would want a place of his own and that was the silliest idea this side of heaven. Barbara and Russell were just twenty-three and twenty-eight. "Goodness," Mom would shake her head, "You have your whole life ahead of you—what's the rush?"

Barbara was beginning to think Cleta wanted them to stay at the B&B forever. She sighed, her eyes roaming the hallway. She loved this old house. She especially loved the bedroom she and Russell had made their own. Together they had picked out the drapes and bedspread. One Saturday afternoon they had laughed and kissed as they hung the masculine blue and green plaid fabric, vowing they would keep it forever. Later they had laid in bed holding each other, secure in their love.

They'd always had a good relationship, but lately Barbara sensed a strain. Though Russell loved Floyd and Cleta—as much as one could love one's in-laws—he made it clear he didn't want to live in their home forever. He'd compromised with Barbara by agreeing to remain at the B&B until she got pregnant, but what would happen if she didn't conceive a baby before Russell lost all patience?

And she couldn't blame him for being impatient. She'd really let herself go in the past year, and why not? Russell was gone all the time on the boat, while she was left here with nothing to do but sleep, eat, and watch television. She didn't have her own house to care for, and her mother and Micah took care of most of the work at the B&B. When she tried to help around the house, Mom warned that her delicate constitution wasn't up to hard labor.

And Mom had a fit just before Thanksgiving when Russell broached the subject of he and Barbara renting a house or apartment in Ogunquit. Even Floyd had added his two cents to that brouhaha, saying that renting was only a waste of good money. Cleta would spend all day on the ferry crossing over to see Barbara, so they might as well save the wear and tear on everybody and let Barbara stay where she was—leastways until kiddies started coming. If Russell had money to burn, however, he might give some serious thought to donating a new set of tires for the fire truck. That would be money well spent.

Upon hearing that, Russell had left the house in a snit, slamming the door behind him. Barbara had bolted for her room, and that concluded the subject. Nobody had wanted to bring it up again.

Barbara looked down at the sympathetic gardener. "I'd be happy to wait for the right time, but the right time may be too late," she confessed, driven to reveal her deepest fear. "I'll be lucky if Russell sticks around that long."

"That is the silliest thing you've said so far." Micah rose, shaking his head. "Russell's a patient man, and he isn't in this marriage for babies. He loves you, Barbara, deeply. It seems to me you aren't being sensitive to his needs."

She stared in honest amazement. What needs? Russell didn't have needs; not like hers. He could walk through the Wal-Mart baby department and not get weepy. He could stand and sincerely rejoice when friends announced pregnancies while Barbara ran for the guest bathroom in tears. It wasn't his makeup that had to be redone, his eyes patted with cold water to reduce the swelling, or him pasting on a bright smile of bravado for the remainder of the evening.

Russell didn't understand a woman's need to cradle an infant, nourish it, give it life. He was willing to let nature take its course while Barbara wanted results now. She didn't fear the weight gain, varicose veins, heartburn, or the stretch marks she heard other women complain about. She would welcome a change in her body. Yet pregnancy never happened, and she was starting to fear that it never would.

"Have you talked to Dr. Marc?"

Micah's gentle inquiry drew Barbara from her thoughts. "Not yet—Mom says there's nothing wrong with me. She tells me to be patient."

"What does Russell say?"

Shaking her head, Barbara crossed her arms. "He would like to have a place of our own by the time we have a baby, but there's no reason we couldn't get pregnant now. His business is doing well, but the longer we stay here, the better off we'll be financially. That's why we haven't pushed the issue."

But Russell was ready to seek medical help; she could hear it in his voice when the subject came up. She didn't want to take fertility drugs—she wasn't up to having a passel of babies. Just one would do—one cute little boy or girl with Russell's brown eyes and long lashes. Russell would have to be the one who consulted the doctor, though—she would be too embarrassed to go. Besides that, doctors frightened her.

Other than having her tonsils out, she'd never had anything more than a cursory physical examination. Before Barbara's wedding, Mom had indicated with a strained look and a knowing eye that a gynecological exam involved more than a quick glance down one's throat and a peek into one's ears. Barbara wasn't sure she wanted to discover how much more was involved. She'd heard Barbette Graham talk about the night Georgie was born. Amazing, what some women talked about.

"Are you ready to tackle parenthood?" Micah asked, squeezing her arm in reassurance.

Barbara raked her fingertips through her hair. Was she ready? Or was she feeling pressured into motherhood? She often thought she could handle a baby, then Mom would remind her how hard it was to run a household and raise children. Sometimes Barbara didn't know what she wanted; often she wanted to be left completely alone. No pressure. No monthly anxieties. No talk of icky exams and prying doctors. When the time was right, a baby would happen if it were meant to happen.

She tossed her head and gave Micah a repentant smile. "I'm sorry. I'm talking your head off, and you have work to do. I guess I'm just in a pink stink this morning."

Squeezing his shoulder in thanks, she moved past him toward her own bedroom. Here she was complaining again. She needed more to fill her time—something to force her to take an interest in life. But Mom cleaned the house and Micah did the gardening. Dad took care of the Fire Station and Russell was out on the boat from sunup to sundown. What was she to do with her time? She'd read every book in town, tried crocheting and hated it, half-heartedly joined the Women's Circle quilting circle but found no real joy in working with a needle and thread. She couldn't think of a single thing that held her interest.

Micah knelt down and returned to the vacuum cleaner. Glancing back at his gentle features, Barbara wished she could be like the soft-spoken gardener, bathed in contentment.

Micah glanced up, caught her looking at him, and smiled. "I can see you're feeling better already."

Barbara came forward to drop a kiss on the man's head, then went into the bedroom to get dressed. She wasn't going to spend the whole day moping around the house. It was a beautiful day and she planned to make the most of it.

She picked up the phone and dialed the Clip and Snip salon in Ogunquit and made an appointment with Nadine Lott for Saturday afternoon. After hanging up she looked through the directory, found an ophthalmologist, and made an appointment for the same day. She had always wanted contacts . . . and Saturday might be a good day to take the plunge.

She could always cancel if she chickened out.

Chapter Two

$\mathscr{B}$arbara grumbled under her breath as she opened the side door of the Heavenly Daze Community Church and began the walk down the steep stairs to the basement fellowship hall. The Women's Circle had been making quilts here on the second Thursday of the month for as long as anyone could remember, for not only was quilting a satisfying activity, but the morning was a prime opportunity for keeping up with everyone and everything on the island. Today, however, Barbara was in no mood for gossip, giggles, or good deeds.

The Circle's major project was a quilt to be raffled off at the annual spring bazaar at the beginning of the tourist season. Every fall the women met to choose materials and patterns; the actual quilting took place in winter. Service in the Women's Circle, the women maintained, was a fine opportunity to show Christian love, for a portion of the raffle money would be donated to a worthy cause, but experience had taught Barbara that the monthly meetings were also a fine opportunity for the exchange of gossip. She had promised her mother that she'd take part in the quilting again, but her motives had more to do with self-preservation than Christian charity. Any woman who didn't appear ran the risk of being the topic of conversation in the sewing circle.

"Winslow is sprucing up the parsonage bathroom," Edith was saying as Barbara stepped into the room. "A beautiful new green border—scripture entwined around birdhouses."

Cleta sent her a puzzled look. "What kind of scripture do you put in a bathroom?"

Edith didn't miss a stitch. "Consider it pure joy, my brothers, whenever you face trials of many kinds."

Vernie took her place at the quilting frame. "High time you redecorated. That old paper needed replacing years ago."

Edith opened her sewing kit. "Oh, it's just a border. I'm not complaining, but it will be nice to have a change. Stanley's offered to help. Those two men should have the project knocked out in no time at all."

Vernie narrowed her eyes at the mention of her husband's name. "I don't know, Edith—maybe we ought to see if there's enough money in the church budget to have the job professionally done. You know how some men can get things screwed up."

"Oh, Winslow's real handy with that sort of thing."

"So is Stan," Vernie added, but Barbara noticed the endorsement sounded strained. Stanley Bidderman, Vernie's husband, had been living in the mercantile's guest room since Vernie caught the flu in late December. The entire island knew he was trying to woo his wife and earn her forgiveness—if forgiveness for walking out and staying gone for twenty years could ever be earned. Stanley kept venturing into Ogunquit to buy little gifts for Vernie, and Barbara thought his efforts were sweet.

Russell hardly ever brought her gifts anymore.

Bea looked up from behind her spectacles. "Good thing the weather's pretty. That'll be nice for the men—

they can open a window if things get stuffy in that little bathroom."

"Unusual weather," Cleta added. "Makes me nervous. I say we'd better enjoy it while we can. Barbara, honey!" Spying Barbara, she stood and pulled a folding chair into the empty space beside her. "What took you so long?"

"Nothing." Barbara nodded at the other women, who were all looking at her.

"Feeling all right today?" Dana Klackenbush asked.

"Fine."

Barbara slid into the chair next to her mother and plucked a needle from the large white square in the center. The work in progress was a Log Cabin quilt. Most of the women had worked like dervishes at home, piecing together various straddles into dozens of log cabin squares, then Birdie and Bea had stitched the squares together into a queen-sized quilt top. The sisters had added the batting and a nice calico backing, then stretched it into their grandmother's antique quilting frame. Once the actual quilting was finished, Birdie or Bea would apply the edging, then wrap the quilt in butcher paper until spring.

Barbara cut off a length of the sturdy quilt thread, then threaded and knotted her needle. Only those women with well-callused fingers made good progress now, since one could only tell that the needle had pierced top, batting, and backing when it pricked a fingertip—over and over again. The women of the Women's Circle prided themselves on beautiful quilts with tiny, evenly spaced stitches, and God bless the woman whose stitches didn't pass inspection.

Barbara ran her left hand under the quilt square in

front of her, then bent her head to concentrate on her work.

"Seems half the town was down with the flu week before last," Edith commented.

"Ayuh," Vernie responded, "I still have a bit of cough. Suspect it will linger a spell."

General conversation continued as the ladies bent to their work, fingers flying and eyes intent upon their stitching. They discussed the unseasonably warm weather, Christmas, New Year's (when Floyd had ripped the fire engine siren at midnight), and Annie's tomatoes.

Dropping her needle, Vernie stretched and rotated her shoulders. "Edith, is that a new hairstyle?"

"Yes, it is. I decided I was tired of looking at the same old me in the mirror. So I called Nadine at the Snip and Clip and told her I wanted something new."

"Well, it looks good," Cleta said. "A perm?"

"Ayuh, but not one of those tight ones. I wanted something loose and—" A charming blush colored the pastor's wife's cheeks—"a little frivolous."

Cleta grinned. "It makes you look years younger. Maybe I should give Nadine a call."

Vernie stood, then tapped Barbara's shoulder on her way to the coffeepot. "How's the lobstering these days, Barbara?"

"Doodles isn't feeling very talkative today," Cleta said, smiling at Barbara. "Are you, hon?"

Barbara shook her head.

Edith tucked her needle into a quilt square. "Well, I don't know about you gals, but I'm ready for a break." Standing, she looked toward the refreshment table, where a plate of cookies waited beside the coffee machine. "Are those fresh goodies, Birdie?"

"Oatmeal and raisin," Birdie chirped from the other side of the quilting frame. "Abner made them, so they're extra good. He says he's not going to tell me what he used to make them so moist. I suspect applesauce, but he made them while I was out, and he delights in keeping me guessing. He does the same thing with the molasses cookies."

Edith bit into one of the treats, then rolled her eyes. "Heavenly!"

"I thought so. Wish I could cook like him."

The women laughed.

"Speaking of Salt Gribbon," Cleta began.

Birdie blushed. "Were we?"

"No, but I want to," Cleta said, grinning. "How are the wedding plans progressing?"

Birdie smiled down at her work. "Very well, though we've had a few disagreements about how formal an occasion it should be. If Salt had his way, we'd stand on a rock outside the lighthouse and say our vows with only Pastor Wickam present. But I want a little more than that. Not fancy, mind you, but I'd rather have people throwing rice than sea gulls circling overhead."

The ladies exchanged amused looks.

"April can be chancy weather-wise," Bea pointed out. "Getting married on a rock is definitely not a good idea."

"We ladies would like to help decorate the church," Cleta offered.

Barbara stitched, saying nothing while the conversation ricocheted from the bride's colors of peach and teal, to tapered candles versus the fragrant, chunky variety, to bows on the pews or simple greenery.

Edith lowered her voice. "How's Salt's son doing in that rehab place?"

Despite her own misery, Barbara leaned forward. Everyone on the island had been astounded when Salt Gribbon's son, Patrick, appeared at the Christmas Eve service. Over the holidays the young man had played with his children, made peace with his father, and agreed that he needed help. After a short investigation, Salt and Birdie had found a wonderful rehab center for alcoholics, and Patrick was currently undergoing therapy and treatment.

"He's doing fine, I think," Birdie said, keeping her eyes on her stitching. "He's not allowed to call but once a week. But we're praying for him, Salt and I. The kids are praying, too, and we have every confidence he'll be out in time for the wedding."

"I hope your wedding won't conflict with the Puffin Days bazaar," Vernie said. "And while we're on the subject, let's think about what we're doing. The quilt has proven to be a good moneymaker, but we need something different. Can we think of some new event, booths, or games to make Puffin Days more profitable and more fun?"

"Profitable is good," Olympia said, "but we need to think of some way to keep the kids from being so rowdy! I don't know where the parents were, but last year by the time Puffin Days was over my flower beds had been trampled so badly they all had to be replanted. I simply dread the thought of all that destruction this year."

"Maybe short fences would help," Edith suggested. "Those white plastic things that can be put down and taken up easily."

Birdie snorted. "I don't think fences would keep those little heathens from running across the flower beds."

Edith shrugged. "Might slow them down a wee bit."

Dana Klackenbush punched her needle through the quilt, then yelped as she pricked her finger. "Sorry! But I was thinking that maybe we could do a better job of advertising that the day-care center is open all day. We could offer a special rate for, say, three hours, so the parents could explore the island and visit the booths without having to watch their little ones."

Birdie glared over the tops of her specs. "It's not the little ones who cause the trouble. It's the middle-sized ones."

"And the big ones," Bea echoed. "Teenagers." She shuddered.

Dana lifted her hand. "Okay—we'll have a special party for teens and preteens at the north end of the island. I'll bet Yakov would be willing to take the older kids down there." She glanced at Barbara. "Maybe Russell would help him? They could play some music, maybe serve pizza—"

Edith clapped her hands. "That's a grand idea! What a ministry to the older kids, who are usually bored silly anyway. Winslow will help, I know he will. He loves teenagers." She pointed to Vernie. "Be sure the information is on the flyers we'll be sending out, OK? We'll have a 'teen scene' down at the lighthouse."

Barbara smothered a smile as Vernie blinked at the pastor's wife. "A teen scene?"

Edith grinned. "Why not? Oh, maybe we can think of a better name for it, but yes, let's do it."

Vernie waved a hand in Edith's direction, then took her seat back at the quilting frame. "Whatever. Okay—what booths do we already have? The pottery booth is always a good draw. We need to enlarge that area so more people can get in to see Zuriel's stuff. And Charles Graham's paintings should have a more prominent place, maybe closer to the dock than last year."

Bea agreed. "The bake sale is always a good money-maker. Cookies do well, anything people can carry away."

"I was at a festival last fall," Olympia commented, "where one woman made a fortune allowing tourists to go through her home. I'd be happy to open Frenchman's Fairest again this year, but Caleb really isn't up to leading the tours. Can one of you suggest a servant who might be willing to lend a hand?"

"Micah might be able to help," Cleta offered. "And it seems fittin', since you're my across-the-street neighbor." She winked at Vernie. "I can't picture Micah boogieing down at the teen scene."

"If I send Yakov to help with the teens and pre-teens," Dana said, "I'll need some help with the wee ones at the house. You can't leave bed babies alone while you tend to toddlers." She turned toward Barbara. "What about you, hon? Would you be free to help with the babies?"

Barbara froze, conscious only of the fact that her mother's busy hands had stilled as well. Like blood out of a wound, silence spread from Barbara's place and spilled over the quilt. Unable to stand the tense silence, Barbara lunged out of her chair and ran toward the restroom, a sob escaping her throat.

In the bathroom, she ran the water, splashed her hands, then wet a paper towel and pressed the damp material to her cheeks. Slipping off her glasses, she held the cool towel to her eyelids and told herself to relax.

She had to get a grip on her emotions. These women were her friends, hers and her mother's. They weren't the enemy, and right now they were probably thinking she had slipped a gear.

She had to face them; she had to give them some rational explanation.

When she reentered the room, her mother was still frowning at Dana.

"I'm so sorry," Dana whispered, catching Barbara's eye. "I—I didn't think."

"It's all right," Barbara said, nodding. "I'm just having a bad day." She bit back a bitter laugh. A bad *year* was more accurate.

The women turned to their work, but conversation didn't start up again for a few minutes. Barbara picked up her needle and concentrated on her stitches until Edith spoke up.

"We've all experienced God working in our lives, but we sometimes forget that not everything is laid out all plain and simple," the pastor's wife said. "We say, 'God works in mysterious ways,' and that's right, but it's a trite saying. We can't always comprehend how he works, and we find it hard to have faith in what we can't see or understand. But one day we will be able to look back and see how things came together in just the right way. God's perfection."

The women all nodded.

Bea rethreaded her needle. "That's hard to keep in mind, but it's the truth."

Barbara finally found her voice. "Dana, I'd be happy to help with the bed babies."

Cleta looked up in surprise. "If you're not up to it, Doodles—"

"I'm up to it, Mom." She smiled at Dana. "I want to do it. And I'm OK."

From the corner of her eye, Barbara saw her mother shake her head, then return to quilting with quick, jabbing movements.

Sighing, Barbara concentrated on a long row of stitches. On the walk home, Mom would try to talk her out of helping Dana with the babies. But she wasn't going to be deterred. Maybe she couldn't have a baby, but that didn't mean she could avoid every baby shower and every drooling grin. If God didn't mean for her to have children, she had to accept the good with the bad.

Still, it hurt. Why couldn't she have babies when other women got pregnant without half trying? Was God punishing her for something? No, he didn't work that way . . . at least, she didn't think he did.

And while she'd like to find some reason for her infertility, deep down she suspected she wasn't ready for the responsibilities of motherhood. Why, she couldn't even stand up to her mother without feeling guilty. What made her think she could take care of a child? She couldn't even make up her mind about getting a new hairstyle, and the thought of seeing a doctor made her woozy. So how would she ever be able to handle a sick child in a medical emergency? She'd never be able to do it.

Vernie's crackling voice cut into her thoughts. "Did you see the way Dr. Marc's son was looking at Annie Cuvier at the New Year's Eve party? We'll be having another wedding before too long if I'm not mistaken."

Barbara exhaled softly. Annie and Alex would probably fall in love and have beautiful, smart, talented babies. Dozens of them. They'd eat luscious homegrown winter tomatoes while Barbara grew old and useless, remaining at home with her Mom and Dad. Russell would get sick of the situation and take off like Stanley Bidderman did, leaving town without a word of explanation, while Barbara sat in her empty bedroom and cried—

"Ow!" Barbara pulled the needle from her fingertip, then stuck her finger in her mouth.

Cleta pressed a hand to her shoulder. "Do you need a Band-Aid?"

"I'm fine." She thrust the needle back into the fabric.

Bea picked up the thread of conversation. "Did you see Isabel Potter's new baby? She's the lady who manages the butcher shop on Shore Road. Beautiful little baby. Surprising after thirty-nine hours of labor. Most of 'em have a pointy head after all that."

Cleta perked up. "Thirty-nine? Why, I thought thirty-six hours was bad. I thought I'd die." She laughed. "Once I heard about this woman whose water broke on the way to the hospital. They had to yank her out of the car so she could give birth on the side of the road."

Olympia's nostrils flared slightly. "My sister-in-law knew a woman whose child was coming prematurely. They took her to the hospital and sewed the birth canal shut so the child couldn't come out for another week or so. That poor woman must have suffered agony—"

Tuning out the stories, Barbara concentrated on her stitches.

≈

Awash in sympathy, Cleta watched her daughter. Barbara had to be hearing every word, and such things weren't proper topics of conversation for a young woman of her sensitive nature. Barbara didn't need to be hearing about babies and doctors and sutures. She didn't need to be thinking about anything but growing up and being happy.

While the others might disagree with her, Cleta knew Barbara was better off staying at the bed-and-breakfast where Cleta could watch over her. It had always been that way, and it should always be that way—at least until Barbara was older.

"I wish we had some more fund-raising ideas for Puffin Days," Vernie said, returning to the original topic. "Maybe the men will have some suggestions about how to fill the community chest."

"Floyd won't have any new ideas." Cleta sighed. "He's only concerned about getting new tires for the fire truck. The old ones are worn to the steel belt, but the city budget won't stand the purchase of new tires. He's fussed over it for months now."

"Winslow is trying to find money in the church budget for new hymnals," Edith said. "It's embarrassing when the tourists have to read over our shoulders to sing the hymns."

"Money." Olympia clucked softly. "Never enough when you need it, is there?"

Cleta glanced at Barbara as a question rose in her mind. Did Russell have enough money to move out? He kept his business affairs to himself, but even though he'd purchased a boat, he was bound to have a little something set by . . .

She bit her lip and buried a loose thread between the batting and the quilt top. Money was a touchy subject even in the closest of families, so perhaps she shouldn't mention finances to her daughter . . . unless the need arose.

☙

As the quilt circle broke up, Barbara followed Cleta up the stairs and waited on the graveled parking lot while her mother locked the church door. She huddled in her jacket, breathing in the clean scent of the sea and wondering how it would feel to kiss her mother on the cheek and walk away toward a home of her own, where Russell would be waiting. She could walk in and kiss him in the living room if she wanted without anyone squawking, they could eat anything, anytime they liked . . .

On the other hand, it was nice to go home and not have to worry about dinner. Her mother would take care of everything.

They crossed the parking lot together, Cleta jabbering about something Vernie had said, Barbara only half listening. After entering the house, her mother dropped her keys on the kitchen counter and moved to the refrigerator to start supper.

Sighing wearily, Barbara climbed the stairs, then went to her room and stretched out on the bed. The afternoon had been tiring. She'd known the subject of babies would come up—it always did, 'cause women and children went together like love and marriage. She knew the other women were probably wondering why she and Russell hadn't had kids yet, but, fortunately, lots of young couples these days waited a while before having babies.

Trouble was, she hadn't wanted to wait. A honeymoon pregnancy would have been fine with her.

She closed her eyes as exhaustion seeped through her brain. She was tired of thinking about babies, tired of worrying about Russell's disappointment, tired of breathing in her mother's suffocating closeness.

She was tired of everything.

Chapter Three

On Friday morning, Buddy Franklin signed his name at the bottom of the application, then lowered the pen and stared at the scratchings on the page. References? He'd listed his sister and brother-in-law, whose address he'd been sharing for the last several months. He had also listed Vernie Bidderman, who owned the Mooseleuk Mercantile, and Floyd and Cleta Lansdown, owners of the Baskahegan Bed and Breakfast. He suspicioned that neither the Lansdowns nor Vernie thought much of him, but they would be too polite to sound off about his shortcomings to a virtual stranger from the bank.

He crinkled his nose as he stared at his neatly printed block lettering. The loan officer might think it odd that the only people qualified to provide a character reference for Buddy Franklin lived on Main Street, Heavenly Daze, but he couldn't do anything about his lack of connections. He had lived the life of a will-o'-the-wisp until his brief career in the Navy, and the Navy was the last outfit on earth that'd be willing to suggest that the Key Bank of Maine provide Buddy with nearly four hundred thousand dollars at 7 percent interest. He hadn't managed to save any of his Navy wages, but had spent his paycheck like a drunken sailor even when he was cold-stone sober. When he'd finally been discharged, he'd had nothing to show for his brief and unfortunate naval career except three new tattoos: Mother, Kiss My Biscuits, and Don't Take Bilge from Nobody. With his parents dead and the ancestral home in Ogunquit sold, he'd had no choice but to appeal to his sister. Dana had taken him in with one stipulation—as payment for his room and board, he had to promise to attend church. And he had, on several occasions.

Buddy made a face as he skimmed the rest of the loan application. He knew his prospects were so poor the amount in the rectangular box at the top of the form might as well have been a million dollars. But Kremstock Industries, the outfit that owned the Lobster Pot, wouldn't take less than four hundred grand for the place. As the only operational restaurant on Heavenly Daze, tourists packed the brick building from April through October as they gobbled down lobster, clam chowder, and the Lobster Pot's specialty, Heavenly Harbor Crab Cakes.

Ayuh, the place was profitable, but managing it had been more difficult than the owners imagined. Since none of them lived in the area, they'd had to rely on local people to run the place, and since all the Heavenly Daze folk had their own businesses, the Lobster Pot managers and staff had always commuted from Wells or Ogunquit. On those rare days when the rough weather kept the ferry from running, the Lobster Pot couldn't open, and a closed sign in the window created unhappy customers.

Last summer the folks at Kremstock had hoped to solve their problem by hiring Buddy to manage the restaurant, but in less than six weeks he had managed to annoy all of his cooks and servers. By Columbus Day, at the end of the tourist season, all six remaining employees tossed in their aprons, collected their wages, and beat a path out the door, telling Buddy they wouldn't be back come April.

Management, Buddy figured, wasn't his style . . . as

long as it was someone else's restaurant. But if the place belonged to him, surely things would be different.

Satisfied that his loan papers were at least legible, Buddy folded the page and slid it into the preprinted envelope. The bigwigs at the Key Bank of Maine were about as likely to give him four hundred thousand dollars as they were to send him to the moon. This application was almost certainly a useless gesture, but it would earn him a few months grace in his sister's eyes. As long as Dana and Mike thought he was trying to be responsible, they'd stay off his back about getting a job and finding a place of his own.

Buddy closed his eyes as he licked the envelope. Dana and Mike would never understand him; they had been cut from different cloth. Ever since he was a kid, Buddy had known he was a loner. He didn't fit in anywhere, and the only person on Heavenly Daze who seemed to understand that was Yakov Smith, the man who lived in the attic apartment and helped Mike run his business.

Yakov understood, Buddy suspicioned, because he was sort of a loner, too.

From the window of his bedroom on the third floor, Yakov leaned on the sill and watched as Buddy hunched inside his coat and walked west on Main Street. Butch, the Klackenbushes' bulldog, pranced at his side, eager to go out with a member of the family.

As Yakov studied the pair, he noticed the edge of a rectangular envelope protruding from Buddy's pocket, and he knew the envelope contained the loan application— indeed, the entire family knew, because Buddy had talked of nothing else for the last week. Ever since New Year's, when Mike sat Buddy down for a man-to-man and told him he needed to find some sort of fittin' work, Buddy had turned his occasional references to the Lobster Pot into a full-fledged campaign, going so far as to venture into Ogunquit and pick up a loan application at the Key Bank of Maine.

Just last night, as the four of them sat at dinner, Buddy announced that he had nearly finished filling out the forms. "I've listed several of your neighbors as references," he said, looking at his sister with an uplifted brow. "I'm hoping that won't be a problem."

Dana shrugged and passed the mashed potatoes. "I think everybody here likes you, Buddy. But maybe you should have listed some people who knew you from one of your other jobs."

Buddy didn't respond to that comment, and Yakov knew why. Earlier, on a quiet afternoon when Yakov found Buddy waiting for the ferry, the young man had explained that he'd never held a job for longer than six months. "Wanderlust, that's what I've got," he had said, squinting out at the horizon. "I don't know how long I'll be staying here, either. I think I was born under a wanderin' star."

Yakov didn't know how long Buddy intended to remain on Heavenly Daze, but as long as Dana kept supplying roast beef and garlic mashed potatoes, he suspected that Buddy might find himself content to remain in one place.

"If you get the restaurant," Mike asked, slicing his roast beef, "are you going to keep it pretty much as it is?"

Yakov smothered a smile as he accepted a basket of yeast rolls from his hostess. Earlier reports that Buddy was thinking of turning the renowned Lobster Pot into a taco stand had horrified the townspeople.

"Folks seem set on keeping it a lobster place," Buddy answered, a lump of bread distending his cheek as he talked. "Whatever. But I was thinkin' of givin' it a name with more pizzazz."

Dana picked up her fork. "That's a nice thought, Buddy. What would you call it?"

Buddy bit off another hunk of bread, chewed thoughtfully for a moment, then swallowed. "I dunno. I figure me 'n Russell Higgs can go into business together. He'll bring in the lobsters, and I'll cook 'em. And then we can call the place Lobsters R Us."

Mike nearly choked on his dinner, and Yakov had to lower his gaze lest he laugh aloud. Fortunately, Dana was accustomed to her brother's wacky ideas. "I'm sure Russell wouldn't mind selling to you," she said, her words punctuated by the clink of her silverware as she forked up a mouthful of mashed potatoes. "But he can't be your only supplier, Buddy. What will you do if Russell doesn't go out for a spell? Or his boat breaks down? Or what if he brings in more catch than you can sell? It's nice of you to think of Russell, but he's been a lobsterman for a long time. He may not want to become a partner in the restaurant business."

Mike chortled a laugh. "'Specially one called Lobsters R—" He froze when his wife shot him a chilly glance.

"Don't give up, Buddy, even if the loan doesn't come through," Dana said. "I know the owners won't want the restaurant to stand empty this summer. Perhaps you can get a job there anyway, waiting tables or cooking."

Buddy made a face at that, and Yakov left the dinner

table with a clearer picture of how things stood in the household. Dana desperately wanted her brother to succeed, but even she didn't seem to think he'd actually get a loan to buy the Lobster Pot. Mike gave lip service to Buddy's dreams only because he was in love with Buddy's sister, and Buddy seemed not to care terribly much about anything, particularly if it concerned hard work.

But now the young man was walking the loan application to the mailbox, even though Yakov knew the loan's approval would require a heaven-sent miracle. And he'd received no word that a miracle was forthcoming, or that Buddy had even prayed for one.

Lowering himself to one knee, Yakov rested his arm on his thigh and dipped his head to peer out the window. From here he had a good view of the southern end of the island, from the smooth southwestern shore to the rocky ridge at the east. Directly across the street he could see the stately Frenchman's Fairest, home of Olympia de Cuvier, the island's only direct descendant of Captain Jacques de Cuvier.

Yakov smiled when he spotted movement in an upstairs window. Caleb, the house's resident angel and butler, was cleaning windows in an unused bedroom. As Yakov studied the wrinkled face of his angel brother, he saw the lined mouth curve in a smile. Without being signaled, Caleb had felt Yakov's gaze, and now he broadened his grin and lifted his cleaning rag in a wave. Yakov waved back, delighted that his brother found joy in serving the newly widowed Olympia. But why wouldn't he? The angels loved all those the Father loved, and felt their deepest joy in obedient service.

Now Caleb was moving his lips, speaking in the tongue of angels. Yakov concentrated, blocking out the earthly sounds of the house around him, and heard his brother's voice.

"Is Buddy on his way to the post office, then?"

"Ayuh," Yakov answered, in the tongue inaudible to all but angelic ears. "He has taken the loan application with him."

Caleb's forehead creased with a frown. "Will they approve it?"

Yakov shrugged. "I do not understand how men decide these matters. But Mike says the bank requires collateral, good references, and a strong employment history. Buddy Franklin has none of those things."

Caleb's head tilted slightly. "Has he asked the Father for help?"

"He does not know the Lord . . . at least, not yet. His head is filled with dreams, and his heart is heavy with loneliness."

"Perhaps, in time, he will find the Way. I know you will help guide him."

"I will do my best, but he does have free will."

"We will pray, then, that the Lord's will be done. For he does not want any of them to perish."

Yakov nodded in farewell as Caleb finished his cleaning, then moved away.

Rising from his crouched position, Yakov turned and surveyed his cozy attic room. He'd been living with the Klackenbushes ever since their arrival on the island three years ago. In obedience to the Lord's command, he had arrived on their doorstep and asked for room and board in exchange for help around the house, and Mike had been quick to accept the offer. The house had been run-down when the Klackenbushes moved in, and the newlyweds had neither the expertise nor the funds to complete a major restoration. But out of the generosity of their hearts they had given Yakov this attic room, and together the three of them had worked to repair and restore the house, establish the Kennebunk Kid Kare Center, and make a home in the community of Heavenly Daze.

Yakov had thought he had the easiest job of all the angels until last summer, when Maxwell "Buddy" Franklin came home to the State of Maine and begged his sister for a place to stay. Not wanting to oust Yakov, Dana turned the front half of the old carriage house into an apartment for Buddy. He lived alone in there, apparently content, emerging only for meals and an occasional trip to the mercantile for candy or comic books.

Yakov's Yiddish-speaking friends would have called him a shlemil, a simpleton, but Yakov didn't think the man a fool. And in Buddy he recognized a challenge. Though the newlyweds were far from perfect, Mike and Dana both knew the Lord. Buddy, however, was as lost as a sea captain in fog. Worst of all, he seemed to have no interest in spiritual things.

Believing that honest work boosted a man's self-esteem, Yakov had asked Mike if Buddy could help around the house. Mike rejected that suggestion with a scornful laugh. "You don't know Buddy Franklin," he said, shaking his head. "Dana loves him, but even she has warned me that he's a disaster waiting to happen. If it's valuable, he'll lose it. If it's working, he'll break it. If it's broken, he'll destroy it. No, I think we'll all be better off if we leave him be and let him find his own way in the world."

Moving closer to the window, Yakov peered down the windswept road and wondered what direction Buddy Franklin would go.

≈

As the soundtrack from *Dances With Wolves* poured from the stereo, Mike Klackenbush wrapped his hands around his coffee mug and stared at the flickering computer screen. His Van Gogh prints had been doing well this week, particularly the *Still Life Irises* and *The Customs Officer's Cabin, Morning Impression*. One of the Iris prints was now selling for forty bucks, not a bad price if one considered that Mike had purchased two hundred of those canvas prints for less than a dollar each . . .

A flash of movement caught his eye, and he reflexively turned toward the window. Buddy shuffled by, his hands in his pockets, his shoulders hunched against the steady wind. A bit of white paper protruded from his pocket—the loan application, no doubt. A sheet of paper that was about as likely to secure a loan for Buddy as a four-bit print was to secure a million bucks for Mike.

Sighing, he leaned back in his chair, sipped his coffee, then lowered the mug to the covered diningroom table, his makeshift computer desk. Buddy wasn't a bad guy—Mike could have done a lot worse for a brother-in-law. Buddy was just . . . six feet two inches of nothing special. The man had no ambition, no drive, no common sense. The sharpest thing about him was the bend in his brow, and everyone from little Georgie Graham to sharp-tongued

Olympia de Cuvier had taken Buddy's measure within five minutes of meeting him.

"Face it," Mike drew his old sweater closer about him, "the man is a born mooch. You and Dana will be supporting him for as long as he wants to stay."

Mike straightened as his computer chimed with an incoming e-mail. After clicking on the inbox, he read the query from an interested eBay bidder: "Is this print on canvas or paper? And how big is it?"

Biting back a caustic reply, Mike urged his fingers to diplomacy: "This print of *The Yellow Chair*, by Vincent Van Gogh, is on acid-free canvas. It's an 11 x 14 print, as is clearly stated in the ad, you moron."

Grinning, he looked at his reply, highlighted "as is clearly stated in the ad, you moron," then clicked delete. No sense in angering a perfectly good potential customer. After all, people didn't always read the ads, and the folks who did read didn't always pay attention to the words.

After scanning his reply, he clicked "send," then settled back to watch Buddy's retreating figure through the window.

Dana would never kick her brother out. Mike had already racked his brain for plausible reasons they might ask Buddy to leave, and none of them would hold water with Dana. He couldn't insist they needed their privacy, for they allowed Yakov to live in the house with them, and he'd never been a problem. Furthermore, Dana would say, after three years of marriage they were no longer newlyweds.

He couldn't protest that they needed room for children, because he and Dana had decided to wait until they'd been married at least five years before considering the idea.

As a certified elementary schoolteacher, Dana loved kids, but she also loved sending them home at the end of the day. Her hours were devoted to wee ones in the summer, when tourists deposited their children at the Kid Kare Center before taking off to tour the island, and during the remainder of the year she tutored Georgie Graham. At Christmas they had discovered there were two other school-age youngsters on the island, so in mid-April, when Dana declared a halt to her winter vacation, her classroom would be occupied by three students: Georgie, and Bobby and Brittany Gribbon.

No, Mike conceded, rubbing his chin, Dana wouldn't want children for a while. He had considered making a case for Buddy's departure by claiming a need for the entire carriage house, but even with the space divided there was plenty of room for Buddy's small apartment and the storage of Mike's eBay materials. Besides, the entire point of Mike's new business was to move stock in and out as rapidly as possible. If only one could do the same for brothers-in-law—

He smiled as a sudden mental picture filled his brain. An eBay ad, complete with a digital picture of Buddy, titled: One worthless brother-in-law, No Reserve, Guaranteed!

Guaranteed to take up space.

Guaranteed to eat five meals a day.

Guaranteed to stick like a burr.

Bidding begins at $1, so don't delay!

Who was he kidding? You could plate Buddy in gold and not get a single bid from anybody who knew him. Dana kept saying he'd change when he found a girl and wanted to settle down, but there was no chance of Buddy finding a girl on Heavenly Daze. The only single girl of marriageable age was Annie Cuvier, but she and the doctor's son had cast goo-goo eyes at each other all through the Christmas holiday, then they'd gone off to wherever they went when they weren't visiting the island.

No, Buddy was going to be his problem, his and Dana's, until the good Lord sent a miracle. In the meantime, however, Mike was not going to let his profligate brother-in-law get under his skin. He was going to prosper and make something of himself. Now that he had a computer, he was going to make some real money and show Dana that she had married a man who could support her.

Another e-mail chimed into his mailbox. Mike clicked on it, read that an auction had successfully closed, then clicked on the necessary links to send his standard message.

"Hello!" he began, "and congratulations on winning this auction! If you'll send me a money order or electronic payment, I'll get your beautiful art right out to you."

He filled in a few details, clicked "send," then zipped over to the eBay Web page to check on the list of his auctions. At the moment he had more than one hundred items up for sale, and he tried to keep them balanced so a few ended every day. Otherwise, things got hectic as auctions neared their close, for people always e-mailed him at the last minute with questions and payment details.

He folded his hands as the page refreshed and he saw that the bid on the Iris print had moved up another five dollars. Wonderful.

He had been a struggling graphic arts student when he met and married Dana. An Ogunquit girl, she'd been happy to move to Heavenly Daze, and when her mother died a few months after their wedding, Mike had been astounded to learn that Dana and Buddy were heirs to an estate held in trust (apparently the widow Franklin had known that Buddy couldn't handle any sizable inheritance). The trust fund now provided Buddy and Dana with two thousand dollars a month. The amount wasn't a fortune, but it did enable the Klackenbushes to live frugally and happily. They worked on the house themselves, Dana earned a small income through the Kid Kare Center, and for three years Mike had been content to help Dana with the school and work on restoring the historic house. He was especially proud of his work on the downstairs bathroom, the one used by all the kids in the day-care center. A septic line problem had limited them to one flush per hour until a few weeks ago, when Mike had rented a rooter and rooted the pipes clean.

But then he'd been bitten by the Internet auction bug. The first nibble came last summer. He'd been browsing the mercantile's magazine rack for some new home-improvement material when he spied Vernie working on her computer. She was exploring eBay, the world's largest Internet auction site, searching for collectible porcelain houses. While Mike watched, Vernie placed a last-instant bid and took a house right from under another bidder's nose.

Intoxicated by the adrenaline rush, Mike watched Vernie place another bid, and another, and then he placed a bid himself, on a new pair of binoculars. He lost that auction, but it wasn't long before he was dropping broad hints about wanting a computer for the Kennebunk Kid Kare Center. After all, computers were educational, Vernie loved hers, and the Grahams were getting one . . .

He wanted a computer so badly he thought about buying one, wrapping it, and writing "To Mike, From Guess Who?" on the card. But Dana came through, presenting him with a state-of-the-art machine complete with zip drive, nineteen-inch monitor, and rewritable CD drive. After Christmas he set it up in the dining room and sat at the table for three straight days, teaching himself how to work all the bells and whistles.

Then he got serious about his business. From a wholesaler at www.wholesaleart.com he bought a box of art prints on canvas, and then, after they arrived, he listed each one on eBay, careful to describe each individual picture in glowing terms. By the end of his week as an eBay seller, he had tripled his initial investment, and Dana's bewildered look turned to pleased surprise.

Now he was determined to put his profits back into the business, to buy more prints in bulk and resell them for ten and twenty times his investment. Yakov, who had expressed his willingness to help in any way possible, handled the auctions that had closed—he pulled and recorded checks and money orders from the incoming mail, and then rolled and packaged the prints in cardboard mailing tubes. So far, in only their second week of operation, Michael's Fine Art had brought in more than $1,500 . . . which was probably more than Buddy Franklin had earned in his entire civilian life.

Mike rubbed hard on his mouth, trying to erase the proud smile that had crept to his lips. A man shouldn't feel pride, especially when it sprang from comparison to a relative, but he couldn't help it. Buddy was a wastrel, a do-nothing, a mooch, and a bum. But as long as Dana didn't insist that Mike involve him in the art-print business when the bank refused his loan, he could stay in the carriage house. After all, he was family.

The computer flickered for a moment, then a rectangle flashed on the screen, informing Mike that his dial-up connection had been broken. Would he like to redial?

Confound that phone line! Mike gritted his teeth, then lifted his gaze to the ceiling. Dana had probably picked up the upstairs phone. Having only one phone line had never been a problem before, but now he could see that he would have to have another installed. His business depended upon having a stable and secure Internet connection, so as soon as Dana hung up, he'd call the phone company and arrange for the installation of another line.

After all, if used for business, it'd be a tax-deductible expense.

Chapter Four

*F*eeling proud and sassy, Tallulah de Cuvier wriggled through the doggy door of Frenchman's Fairest, then trotted out to the front lawn. Though the air was chilly, the sun shone bright and clean from the east, coloring the sky pink and gold.

Tallulah sniffed, parsing the scents of wood smoke, humans, and sea birds. Butchie the bulldog had walked here recently, probably to mark the post supporting the historical marker outside Tallulah's house.

That dog had never had any manners. He peed in the most obvious places, ate garbage, and had even been known to eat squirrels and sea gulls . . . Tallulah shivered at the thought of such atrocities.

Sitting on her haunches, she watched the sun as it lifted through a hazy sky, then pricked her ears forward. Ferry time.

Springing to her feet, she trotted to the dock, where Russell Higgs was washing gadgets in a smelly liquid. Tallulah breathed in a whiff of the stuff in his bucket, then jerked her head back and barked. Russell bent to scratch behind the mutt's ears. "That's gasoline, Tallulah. Best keep your nose out of it."

With pleasure. She thumped her tail.

Russell bent lower, and—ahhhhh—continued scratching. "Where's your buddy Butch this morning?"

In bed, where the lazy slug spends most of his time. Butch wouldn't get up early for a side of beef, but me, this ole

girl would pile out of her warm box on a nippy January morn-
ing for the mere scent of a fresh cruller.

She gave Russell her best smile, then lifted her gaze
toward the horizon. There was the ferry, right on time. By
golly, she was going to Ogunquit and she was going to have
a cruller, her first in a month on account of Caleb's sudden
concern for her weight. This morning Caleb had forgotten
to latch the doggy door, and Tallulah had made a break for
it. She felt as though she'd been in the Betty Ford Cruller
Center the last few weeks. She strained to peer over her
trimmer backside. Shoot. Her hindquarters didn't look that
much thinner, but she'd rather have the crullers.

Rising to her feet, she watched Russell bathe little gid-
gets and gadgets in the bucket of liquid stink. The handsome lobsterman was nice. On good days he shared his
tuna-salad sandwich with her. Other days he walked up to
the house to eat lunch with his wife. Those two were real
interesting to watch. Always nuzzling and holding paws.

"So how are you this morning, Tallulah?"

Ah, Russell had time to do a bit of neighborin'. She
stood up on her hind legs, her front paws fanning the air.

"What's up, girl? Looking for a treat? You should try
my house—I didn't finish my breakfast. There was so much
racket going on I had to get out of there." The corners of
his muzzle drooped.

Well, he just needed a cruller. That'd fix whatever was
ailin' him.

Tallulah dropped to all fours and checked on the
ferry's progress. The big boat was moving slowly across the
water, cutting through the waves as if it had all the time in
the world. Didn't Captain Stroble know she was hungry?

"You got a boyfriend, Tallulah?"

Her head snapped up. Say what?

Russell grinned and wiped his hands on a cloth. "Surely you have a significant other?"

Tallulah didn't think much in life was significant . . . except for crullers.

Russell grinned at her. "Love is great, ole girl, when it's going right. When it's going wrong—well, let's just say it can be pretty rough. Do you know what I mean?"

Actually, she didn't have a clue what he was jabbering about, but she was willing to sympathize.

Leaping onto the deck of his boat, Russell kept talking. "Babs and I get along great most of the time. I love her and I know she loves me, but living with her folks kinda puts a strain on the relationship."

Not knowing what else to do, Tallulah thumped her tail in commiseration.

"Don't get me wrong—Floyd and Cleta treat me well. Cleta spoils Barbara more than she should, but I don't mind. I work long hours, and Barbara would get lonesome if she didn't have somebody around." Russell dropped a tool and bent to pick it up, then rested for a moment. "The thing is, Barbara and I need our own place. We need privacy—room to breathe. Cleta's always there; she makes breakfast, lunch, and supper. If we watch TV anywhere besides our bedroom, we have to watch the TV shows Cleta likes, and we associate with Floyd and Cleta's friends." He looked at Tallulah. "For months Cleta nagged me about church on Sunday, and I was grateful to have work as an excuse. Not that I have anything against God or the preacher—I'm on good terms with both, really. But Cleta was driving me nuts, so I took the boat out just . . . well, to be ornery, I guess. But not long ago I realized that being stubborn with family is no way to make a life together."

He reached out and scratched Tallulah's ears. "Some folks would say we've got it made. We don't pay rent; Floyd won't even hear of us paying for groceries. Cleta and Micah do the cleaning and cooking, so Barbara and I live like royalty."

Tallulah tilted her head. Then what's the beef?

"I'm not ungrateful; I just want a place of our own. And kids. Maybe a boy, and then a girl."

Russell's voice drifted away, and he looked sad.

Then Russell reached into a sack, pulled out a cookie, and tossed it toward her. Springing lightly forward, Tallulah caught the treat in her mouth.

Yummm. Oreos.

She crunched the cookie. Chocolate-centered Oreos. Oh, bliss!

"Is that Tallulah?" Dr. Marc came down the hill wearing a lightweight jacket and no hat. The man moved quickly for a guy of eight—well, he was nearly sixty in human years, and the guy hardly ever panted.

Russell waved. "Morning, Doc!"

The dock jiggled beneath Tallulah's paws as the nice doctor stepped onto the rough planking. "Caleb sent me out here to fetch this little lady back into the house." He put his hands on his hips as he stared at Tallulah. "Thought you'd make the ferry, did you?"

Oh, cats. Tallulah tucked her tail between her legs. Maybe if she pretended to be repentant, the doctor would feel sorry for her and let her go . . .

No such luck. His big hand swooped down and caught her around the middle, then lifted her from the dock. Tallulah wriggled her feet, but the doctor had a firm grip on her belly.

"By the way, Russell," he said, settling Tallulah against his chest as he turned to face the lobsterman. "I have a leaky faucet I'd like you to look at. It may need a new seal, but I've never been good with plumbing."

"Sure, Doc, as soon as I get a minute I'll stop by and fix it for you." Russell wiped his hands on an oily rag. "I've been meaning to have a talk with you anyway."

"Oh?" The doctor's smile faded. "Something wrong?"

Russell glanced away as a blush crept up his neck. "I don't think so—but you'd be the one to say."

The doctor lifted a brow. "What's up?"

Russell appeared to be studying the toes of his boots. "It's not something a man likes to discuss."

"Don't let modesty stop you. I can assure you, there is nothing I haven't seen or heard."

"It isn't modesty—it's just sort of hard to talk about."

Tallulah felt her heart do a double beat when the doctor sat down on a box. She turned her eyes toward the horizon, where the ferry was still coming, but the doctor set her on his lap and looped a finger into her collar.

She sniffed. He didn't trust her. Imagine that.

"I came from a large family," Russell said, stepping closer to the dock. "So I'm used to giving in a lot—I suppose that's the problem. I give in to Barbara because I love her."

"Large family, huh? How many siblings?"

"Twelve, counting me. Having kids was never a problem in the Higgs household. Trying to keep the numbers down—now, that could be a problem."

"You come from around here?"

"Raised about thirty miles north. I had already graduated when I met Barbara; she was still in high school. We met at a football game. She was kinda shy, bein' an only child and all, but she had a great sense of humor, and she was able to laugh at herself. I like that in a person."

The doctor didn't answer, but only nodded, encouraging Russell to keep talking. Tallulah wiggled a bit, testing the strength of Dr. Marc's grip, but he held her tight.

Russell ran his hand through his hair. "Others don't know Barbara the way I do—not even her folks. She has a heart of gold, and she isn't selfish, not like you'd think an only child would be. With other people she's quiet, but with me, well, she's Barbara. And I love her to death."

"Sounds like you have a good marriage."

"The best. Married three years now." Russell scuffed the toe of his boot on the deck. "The only fly in the ointment is this baby thing."

Tallulah heard the doctor take a deep breath. "Baby thing?"

"Well, you know—we try, but nothing happens. Month after month Barbara comes up barren. Cleta's not much help, either. She wants to keep Barbara under her thumb, and she knows once Barbara gets pregnant we'll be looking for a place of our own. She has scared Barbara out of her wits by feeding her all kinds of horror stories about childbirth."

"That's a real shame, and unfair of Cleta. Maybe she doesn't realize what she's doing."

"Oh, she realizes—you don't know Cleta the way I do. Barbara is her life and she won't let go, even though Barbara's a grown woman."

Tallulah looked up as the doctor's voice softened. "Many mothers have a hard time letting their offspring fly the nest."

"We've tried everything, Doc. Barbara buys these medical books about what to do if you're not conceiving— why, I've even . . ." Russell shifted his weight. "Well, I've taken to wearing boxer shorts instead of briefs, but it hasn't made a difference. A lot more comfortable though."

The doctor nodded. "So I've heard."

"Anyway, I've been thinking that the only way to change things is for Barbara to conceive."

"Maybe," the doctor answered, "or you could be opening up a can of worms if Barbara's not ready to be a mother."

"I think she is, but she doesn't know it. Floyd wants grandchildren; he hints at it occasionally. Cleta would love it if we had a houseful of kids, but only if we were living at the B&B."

Slapping his hand on his knee, Dr. Marc smiled. "So— you want to get to the bottom of this mystery and see if you're causing the problem?"

The tips of Russell's ears turned bright red. "I'm not much on going to doctors—"

"Not many relish the thought, but I think you're over-due. I know I haven't seen you since last year when you got that bad case of sun poisoning. And I haven't ever seen Barbara."

Russell nodded. "Doctors scare her."

"Well, I promise my examinations are painless. Can you stop by the office Monday afternoon?"

Russell swallowed. "That soon?"

"The sooner the better, wouldn't you say?"

Russell nodded slowly.

Leaning closer, Doc whispered, "I give all my patients cherry lollipops."

Russell grinned. "Just do what you have to do. I'll skip the candy."

Chuckling, the doctor stood up, hoisting Tallulah back into the air. She whined nervously as the two men stretched across the water to shake hands.

Tallulah wriggled again, hoping the doctor would let her slip away, but as the ferry pulled up to the dock, he carried her up the hill, toward home and a low-calorie breakfast of kibble and diet bits.

≈

"Yidl mitn fidl, Arye mitn bas . . ."

Buddy made a face as Yakov's tenor warbling came through the thin wall that divided his living quarters from the storage room beyond. Saturday morning, and a guy couldn't sleep late in his own apartment.

"Hey," he called, kicking the wall at the foot of his bed. "Can you keep it down in there?"

A moment later Yakov's swarthy face peered through one of the metal air vents Mike had placed in the thin wall. "Am I disturbing you, Buddy?"

"A little." Buddy pulled his blanket higher on his shoulder, then dropped his head to his pillow. "Wouldn't be so bad if you'd sing something that made sense."

"You don't know 'Yidl Mitn Fidl'?" A note of astonishment rang in the helper's voice. "Why, everyone in Holland—"

Buddy lifted his head. "You were in Holland?"

A betraying blush darkened the other man's face. "Many years ago. It was . . . during a bad time. I was there to help the Father's chosen people."

Buddy propped his head on his hand and stared. How much did Mike and Dana know about this Yakov guy, anyway? Nothing he said made any sense. Here he was, talking about Holland many years ago, when from the look of his face Yakov couldn't be much older than Mike. And what had he been doing in Holland, and who was this mysterious father he referred to all the time? This Yakov was probably involved with some weird cult, yet naive Dana and Mike had welcomed him into their home.

He frowned toward the air vents. "Hey, dude—did you grow up in Holland?"

"Um . . . no." The flash of a smile shone through the metal flanges. "I am sorry about the song. I could sing something else."

"Whatever." Buddy scratched his chin. "Do you know 'Three Times a Lady?'"

Yakov's dark brows slanted downward. "No. Do you like 'Gut Morgan, A Gut Yor?'"

Buddy clamped down his rising irritation. "What language is that, Japanese?"

"Yiddish." Yakov bowed his head slightly. "A fun language. 'Yidl mitn fidl' means 'Yidl with his fiddle,' and 'Arye mitn bas' is 'Aryeh with his bass—'"

"I don't care what it means! I want to sleep!"

Yakov retreated as if he'd been slapped. "I am sorry," he whispered, then he closed the vent—a silly thing to do, really, because Buddy had the woodstove and the only source of heat in the carriage house.

At least it was quiet now.

Irritated and restless, Buddy pounded his pillow, then buried his face in its softness. He hadn't meant to lose his temper. He hardly ever yelled, but something about Yakov seemed to bring out the worst in him. The man was always happy and smiling, always singing those stupid songs in that crazy language . . .

While he, Buddy, just wanted to be left alone.

A gentle tapping at the front door grated across his nerves. "What?"

He heard the squeak of the hinge as the door opened. Yakov stood there, his face composed and his eyes shining with friendliness. "Buddy, it is not good for a man to be alone. Would you like to help me package a few art prints?"

Buddy stared at him. What was the guy doing, trying to get out of work?

"You're alone," Buddy snapped. "And you don't seem to mind it."

"I am not a man," Yakov replied easily. He hesitated, then pressed. "So—you do not want to help?"

"No!"

Buddy kicked at the footboard for emphasis, but a full minute passed before the hinge creaked again and Yakov withdrew. Lying very still, Buddy clenched his eyes shut and fought against the tide of emotion rising within him.

Not a man? Of course he wasn't, the fellow was a certifiable fruitcake! Dana and Mike were living with a lunatic, but they had been too charmed by his goofy smile and funny language to notice Yakov was 100 percent crazy.

And the townspeople thought *he* was nuts.

∾

"Cleeeeeta! We're going to miss the·ferry!"

Cleta checked her watch. Twelve-forty-five, so they had plenty of time before Captain Stroble would shove off, but Vernie was downstairs in the foyer hollering like a stevedore.

"Coming, coming. Hold your britches." Cleta clunked down the stairs while trying unsuccessfully to stick a pin in her hat. "Goodness, you'd think we were going to a fire instead of the library."

Vernie regarded her with an accusing expression, as if she were dawdling on purpose. "You know this weather isn't going to last. Any moment now it's going to turn on us and Stroble won't be operating the ferry. I'm out of things to read, so hurry up."

"Ayuh, like you'd die if you didn't have Danielle Steele to keep you company."

Vernie stiffened. "I read other things."

"Like what?"

"Like . . . Hunt and Copeland. You know—stuff." She changed the subject. "Barbara going with us?"

"No." Cleta paused in front of the hall mirror, talking around the pin in her mouth. Barbara was the reason she wasn't ready; Cleta had spent the last half-hour trying to talk the girl into coming out for a bit of fresh air.

She met Vernie's gaze in the mirror. "Doodles says she wants to stay home today."

Vernie's brows lifted a notch. "Really?"

Cleta secured the pin, and then stepped back to adjust her earrings. "The child's not acting normal. She stays in her room most of the time and watches those soaps. Can't be good for her."

"Must be the winter blues. Everyone gets them."

"In this kind of weather? Nonsense." Cleta picked up her purse. "Well, let's go. Aren't you the one yakkin' about being late?"

The two women left the house and hurried toward the dock where the ferry bobbed on the waters. Caleb was out back shaking rugs when they passed the de Cuvier house. Cleta and Vernie waved.

The old butler lowered his rug. "You ladies off for the afternoon?"

"Going to the library, Caleb," Cleta called. "You need anything?"

"Nothing, thank you! Enjoy the weather!"

The women stepped aboard the ferry, gave the captain their tickets, and settled onto the bench seats in the cozy cabin as the motors revved. Cleta leaned out the window to wave at Crazy Odell Butcher as he pulled up to the dock.

"Wonder what Crazy Odell is up to today?" Cleta asked, leaning back against the seat.

Vernie snorted. "Probably no good—that's why they call him crazy."

Cleta leaned back, enjoying the feel of the warm sun on her face. Soon they were skimming across the water under a clear blue sky that looked far more like April than January.

~

Certain that her mother had gone, Barbara crept down the stairs, leaning over the railing to see if her dad was in the house. The front room was empty. No television sounds blared from the parlor. The path was clear.

Taking the last few stairs in a rush, she scooted across the foyer and ran out the door, pulling on a light sweater as she sprinted toward the dock.

True to his promise, Crazy Odell Butcher was waiting for her, his wooden-hulled boat bobbing on the waves.

"There you are," he called as she walked up. "Thought you might have changed your mind."

"Nope. Are you ready?"

"Ready as I'm likely to get at my age. You got my fare?"

"Twenty bucks, right?"

"Only ten on a nice day like today. Each way." He grinned, revealing a gap between his front teeth. "Got to make some mitten money."

"Okay, but I'm only going one way. My husband will bring me home."

Barbara slipped a ten-dollar bill from her purse and handed it over, and then sank onto a cracked vinyl seat. The old man took the wheel and the engines roared to life. The wooden-hulled boat pushed through the water like an army tank, taking twice as long as the ferry, but the ninety-two-year-old sea captain didn't have Cleta aboard. When they reached Perkins Cove, Odell tied up his boat at a distance from Captain Stroble's spot. Barbara scanned the area for any sign of her mother, saw nothing, then disembarked and waved. "Thanks, Odell!"

Barbara called a cab from a pay phone, and then got out in the center of town. She had a lot to accomplish in three hours, but with a little help she'd make it. Shivers raced up her spine when she thought of what she was about to do.

It was all for Russell, she reminded herself.

For them.

After another quick look around, she ducked into a nearby building.

~

Cleta and Vernie each emerged from the library carrying a sack of books. The selection was sparse this time of year, being that people were stockpiling for winter weather. Everything new had been checked out, but the librarian and Vernie managed to find enough classics to satisfy Cleta.

Feeling satisfied with their book expedition, Cleta and Vernie decided to stop off at Hamilton's Family Restaurant for a sandwich and coffee. The town was dead in the winter, with few stores open for shopping, but the ferry wouldn't head back to Heavenly Daze until six o'clock, well after dark.

The women settled into their favorite booth and placed their order. The booth was next to the front window and offered a great view of Shore Road—not that anything much was happening in the quiet town.

Cleta took out one of her library books and thumbed through it, eyes alight. "There's nothing like a good read."

"Ayuh," Vernie agreed. "Nothing like it."

~

Barbara came out of the Snip and Clip, then hurried toward the ice-cream store where she'd promised to meet Russell. The store was closed, of course, but it offered a sheltering awning where she could stand without being blown away by the wind . . .

Her heart thudded when she spotted her tall husband coming down the sidewalk. She tugged at the ends of her hair. What would he think?

She smiled as their eyes met. His long legs covered the ground quickly, then he lifted her in his arms and twirled her on the sidewalk. Pulling away for a better look, he grinned. "I like it."

"You do? Honest?"

He pretended to rethink his opinion, looking her over closely. "No. I was wrong."

Her heart sank.

"I *really* like it."

She threw her arms around him and hugged tightly. "Thank you."

"No, thank *you*. I feel like I have a new wife."

"You weren't happy with the old one?"

"I adored the old one. But even a beautiful boat can benefit from a sprucin' up every now and then."

She was tempted to playfully slug him, then thought the better of it. They had other, more important things to consider.

"Come on," she said. "We have one more stop."

"No, two," he corrected.

Her eyes widened. "Two?"

"Don't ask; it's a surprise. Let's do your stop first."

～

Cleta and Vernie cackled so loudly the waitress threatened to evict them. They'd been telling stories of days gone by and lost track of time. It was nearing five o'clock when they gathered their books and purses and asked for the check.

Feeling better than she had in days, Cleta looked across the table at her old friend. "Veronica, you're a nut."

"It takes one to know one, girl." They broke into snickers again.

"Land, I'm so full of coffee I'll slosh when I walk," Vernie complained as she pushed herself out of the booth.

That set Cleta off in another round of giggles. After paying their bill, they were about to step outside when Vernie grabbed Cleta by the arm and pulled her back into the restaurant.

"What's wrong? Need a bathroom?"

"Unless my eyes deceive me, Barbara and Russell just walked into that house across the street."

"What?" Cleta shoved her aside. "You're imagining things. Barbara is home, probably in bed."

"I don't think so, Cleta."

The women stared at the house, their gazes focusing on a prominent FOR RENT sign hanging over the front porch.

Cleta worried her lower lip. "Barbara wouldn't look at a house without telling me first."

Vernie shook her head. "Maybe I'm wrong, but if that wasn't Barbara and Russell, it was their clones."

The two women sank onto the bench in front of the restaurant and waited, their eyes trained on the large two-story house across the street. Cleta drank it in—why, that house would be a terror to heat, and it was so old the electricity probably wasn't up to code. The front porch looked rickety from here, and those colors! How could a body sleep at night with such colors blaring through the walls?

"Barbara wouldn't do such a thing without telling me first," she repeated. "We share everything."

"Maybe I made a mistake." Vernie threw out a lifeline. "My eyes are getting bad, you know that. And it was dark. The sun goes down so early these days, and these street lights aren't the best."

They sat, waiting.

After ten minutes, Cleta grabbed Vernie's arm. "What are they doing in there?"

"Well, if they're house hunting I imagine they're looking the place over."

"Barbara wouldn't house hunt without me!"

"Then maybe . . ." Vernie's words drifted away as the sound of voices filled the early evening air. A porch light had come on across the street; a young couple emerged from the house. Cleta blinked as her eyes focused. For a moment she felt like melting in relief, for the woman's hair was all wrong, then her heart pounded when she saw that the man was definitely Russell. And that was Barbara, but she was so different!

Vernie waved her hand helplessly. "Maybe Russell was in there cutting her hair."

"Ohmigoodness!" Cleta gripped Vernie's arm. "What has she done?"

"It doesn't matter," Vernie answered. "But we'd better get out of here before they catch us spying."

Too dumbfounded to protest, Cleta bolted from the bench and ducked around the corner of the restaurant. Peering through the thickening darkness, she watched as her daughter walked down the street and laughed up into Russell's face. Her long, beautiful hair was now styled in a short spiked do. She looked like one of those punk rockers.

How long had her daughter been living a secret life?

Bursting into tears, Cleta pressed her hands to her face.

"Hush now," Vernie handed over a tissue. "For heaven's sake, Cleta, it's a haircut. It will grow back."

Sniffing, Cleta accepted the tissue. "You don't understand, Vernie. You never will because you don't have kids of your own."

Vernie flinched.

"That was thoughtless of me," Cleta apologized. "Don't mind me, I'm so confused I can barely think straight. What is going on? Barbara looking at houses, getting her hair cut without asking me—"

"She's almost twenty-three years old, Cleta. She doesn't have to ask you if she can get her hair cut."

"You just don't understand!" Cleta whirled around and started down the darkened street. "I'm going to find out exactly what that girl's up to and why she would do me this way."

"I wouldn't start anything," Vernie advised, following. "You'll only alienate her and then where will you be?"

"I'll be her mother, like I've always been! I have a right

to know what she's doing, especially since she's doing it under my roof. And just now Doodles wasn't wearing her glasses—how many times have I told her she has to wear her glasses, she's blind as MaGoo the cat without them."

By the time they reached the landing at Perkins Cove, Barbara and Russell were nowhere to be seen. As the wind blew cold and frosty across the dark parking lot, Cleta scanned the area lit by a single streetlight. "Where could they be? The ferry hasn't left yet."

"Maybe we were both seeing things—you know, it was dark. Maybe it wasn't Barbara and Russell at all. Maybe we're both kooks."

Cleta turned to give Vernie a blistering look. "Are you saying I don't know my own daughter?"

Vernie shrugged. "I didn't say that."

Cleta sat down on the bench outside the ferry office.

Vernie took a step toward the waiting ferry, then turned and placed a hand on her hip. "What are you doing?"

"Waiting. They have to be around here somewhere. They'll show up soon."

"You're going to sit out here when we could be inside the boat where it's warm?"

Cleta crossed her arms.

Vernie stamped her foot. "Good grief, woman! It's twenty minutes until the ferry leaves. If you stay out here all that time, the wind will chap you like shoe leather."

"I don't care."

"You're a stubborn old goat, Cleta Lansdown."

"I'm a mother. Mothers are allowed to be resolute."

Shaking her head, Vernie stalked over the ferry gangplank with her stack of books on her hip. Cleta watched her go, then shifted her gaze to the road leading to the cove.

Vernie would never understand. Nobody whose only dependent was an old fat cat could ever empathize with a mother worried about her own flesh and blood.

~

Back at the bed-and-breakfast, Floyd closed his mechanical engineering book, wiped his thick glasses, then glanced at the kitchen clock. Six-fifty-five, the sky as black as tire rubber outside, and no sign of Cleta. Pacing between the sink and the refrigerator, he asked, "What in blue blazes is keeping your mama?"

Barbara set a bowl of stew on the table and blinked back tears. She had a wad of tissues in her dress pocket fat enough to smother a moose.

Russell dug into the stew, took a big bite, and grinned up at her. "This is great, hon. I always knew you could cook."

Smiling timidly, she wiped her eyes.

Russell picked up a piece of hot cornbread and reached for the butter. "Pop Lansdown, what do you think of Barbara's hair?"

Floyd turned from the window, his eyes focusing on Barbara's hair for the first time. Frown lines appeared between his brows. "What'd you do to it?"

Barbara tugged on the fringe of hair at her neck. "I cut it, Dad."

"Oh." He turned to consult the clock again. "What's keeping your mother? If she caught the last ferry, she should have been home half an hour ago."

Blinking, Barbara took her place at the table. She dabbed again at the stream of tears.

Russell reached out and squeezed her hand. "You doin' okay, hon?"

She smiled at her husband. "I'm fine." She hesitated. "In fact, I'm great."

Floyd pulled out a chair and sat down. He had just filled his bowl when Cleta burst through the back door. Riding a cold wind into the cozy kitchen, she stopped in the middle of the kitchen and pointed a reddened finger at Russell and Barbara. "Where have you two been?"

Barbara felt a familiar guilt rise in her chest. Her mother had looked at her in that same way the time she came home an hour late from the Wells football game six years ago . . .

Russell sprang to his feet, knocking his chair over in the process. "Uh . . ." He swallowed a mouthful of cornbread. "We've been right here, Mom Lansdown. Why?"

"Don't lie to me!" Reaching back, she slammed the door, fluttering the kitchen curtains. "I sat outside the ferry landing until the boat left, and you weren't on it. How did you get here?"

Barbara blinked, tears streaming down her cheeks. "Why'd you do that?"

"I have a boat," Russell said, calmly settling back into his chair. "I took my wife home on the *Barbara Jean.*"

Barbara felt a thrill rise within her. Russell was a rock, so strong and sure in the face of her mother's frenzy. Why couldn't she be more like him?

Floyd dropped his spoon into his bowl. "How'd you get home, Cleta?"

She gave him a look of pure exasperation. "Crazy Odell. That rascal had the nerve to charge me double for the ride, 'cause it was after dark. I stink like fish! He made me ride on the livewell."

Barbara thought a bit of sympathy might be in order. "That's awful, Mama," she said, dabbing at her damp cheeks.

Cleta looked at her, then her narrowed eyes widened. "What's wrong, baby? Why are you crying—never mind, I can see the reason myself. I'd cry, too, if someone did that to me. Great balls of fire, who cut it? A goat shearer?"

Barbara's hand flew to her hair. "No! Nadine Lott cut it—she's been to beauty school in Boston, Mama. She's really good."

"She's butchered you!"

"Oh, Mom." Barbara sank in her chair and felt her shoulders slump. The balloon of happiness that had sustained her through the afternoon was deflating now, her joy escaping in a slow leak . . .

"Too late to cry about it now. We can get you a wig."

From beneath the table, Russell tugged on Barbara's jeans. She shot him a resolute look, then took a deep breath and turned to face her mother. "I'm not crying about my hair, Mom. I happen to love it. I'm not crying at all. My eyes are watering because of the contacts."

"Contacts?" Clutching at her chest like Fred Sanford having "the big one," Cleta staggered backwards. Quick as a rabbit, Floyd slid a chair beneath her backside just as her knees collapsed. "What has gotten into you, Barbara Jean Lansdown?"

"Higgs," Russell quietly corrected. "Her name is Barbara Jean Higgs."

Cleta threw him a stay-out-of-this glare.

Stiffening her spine, Barbara turned to face her mother. "I got contacts this afternoon, Mom. I detest glasses; I wanted contacts. I love them. And the doctor said my eyes would stop watering as soon as I got used to them." She sniffed, defiantly taking another swipe at the moisture dribbling down her cheeks.

For once Cleta was speechless. "Well," she finally said, looking from Barbara to Russell and then to Floyd. "I don't know if it's a full moon or solar flares causin' the trouble, but something is definitely wrong with the world when the child who wouldn't get a drink of water without asking will put glass in her eyes and run her hair through a weed whacker without so much as asking my opinion."

Aware of her husband's encouraging eyes upon her, Barbara returned to her stew and ate a huge mouthful, pretending that her mother's words hadn't hurt. Beneath the table, though, her knees trembled and her stomach had shriveled to the point where she doubted she could eat more than three bites.

~

At 10 PM, Dana Klackenbush teakittled up her kitchen, then climbed the stairs to join her husband in bed. Bringing her knees up under the comforter, she adjusted the angle of her magazine so the bedside lamp didn't reflect on the glossy pages. Beside her, Mike snored softly while a basketball game thumped softly from the small television on the bureau. She ignored the TV—Mike fell asleep to the

muted sounds of crowd noise, and if she changed the channel or turned the set off, he'd wake in a heartbeat. Only
after he'd been dozing a half-hour or more would he be in
a deep enough sleep for her to snap off the set.

Sighing, she flipped through the glossy pages of
Northeastern Living. The expensive monthly periodical featured pictures of the most stately homes in the Boston area.
Though she couldn't afford the decorator treatments she
saw in those estates, she took quiet pride in knowing that
her house was at least as historic as many of those in the
magazine. By all accounts, the Klackenbush home had
been built in 1798 when Jacques de Cuvier founded the
town, so though it was patched and clothed in homemade
curtains, her home was every bit as significant as some of
those places on Boston's Snob Hill . . .

She paused as a picture of a particularly elegant brick
house caught her eye, then she dropped her jaw when she
saw a photograph of the owner—a handsome man with
dark eyes, a tidy silver beard, and a mane of coiffed hair.
"Dr. Basil Caldwell," the caption read, "poet laureate at
Boston College, lives in Hobbleton Hall, a lovingly restored
home built in 1799."

She thumped her elbow against her husband's back.
"Mike, look at this!" Rising up on her knees, she bent over
him with the magazine. "Basil Caldwell! He went to Wells
High School with me!"

Mike grunted.

"Hey!" Leaning over, Dana shook her husband to
wakefulness, then held the magazine before his bleary eyes.
"Look at this guy. I know somebody famous. Isn't that
something?"

"Dana!" Mike closed his eyes. "I'm sleeping."

"No, you're not." Pulling the magazine away, Dana settled back onto her side of the bed and held the page closer to the lamplight. "I remember him. He was older than me—class of '90, I think, 'cause I was '92 and Buddy was '93. I was a sophomore when he was a senior—"

She halted when she realized Mike was snoring again. Blowing a hank of hair off her forehead, she pulled the blankets up to her waist and leaned toward the lamp as her fingertip traced the line of Basil Caldwell's strong jaw. Buddy probably wouldn't remember him, but he wouldn't have noticed Basil the way she did. When she was an underclassman, the senior boys were like tall, broad-shouldered, and supremely confident princes. Basil had been the crown prince of Wells High—smart, handsome, and athletic, an unheard-of combination. President of the student body and quarterback; member of the National Honor Society and homecoming king. Not many boys had all the finer qualities wrapped up in one package, but Basil Caldwell certainly did.

She read the article about his house, then smiled slowly when she noticed the writer did not mention a Mrs. Caldwell. So . . . either the hunk of Wells High hadn't found what he was looking for, or he hadn't been able to make a go of his marriage. Yet one thing was certain—if he lived in a home lovely enough to grace the pages of *Northeastern Living*, he was prospering. And if he'd earned the title of poet laureate for Boston College (whatever that meant), he'd obviously managed to maintain his unique blend of success and sensitivity.

Sighing, she settled into the mound of pillows at her

back. She loved her husband, but a girl never forgot her first crush, and Basil Caldwell had been hers. He had waltzed into her biology class one afternoon, all neck and shoulders and charm, and made an announcement about the senior class carnation sale. And then, while all the sophomore girls were about to melt onto the floor, he had leaned forward and tweaked Dana's nose. "So if any of you want to send me a carnation, make sure it's red," he'd said, flashing a blinding assortment of perfect teeth. "Because red is the color of true love."

Dana glanced at Mike, who had never sent her a red carnation in his life. Daisies, occasionally, in the summer, and roses on their anniversary because he thought that's what men were supposed to do. But on that day back in 1990, Dana would have given her entire Whitney Houston album collection if Basil Caldwell had sent her even a fringed petal from a red carnation . . .

Blowing out her cheeks, she turned the page. In a shaded sidebar, a bold headline announced the Basil Caldwell Poetry Contest for unpublished poets. Interested contestants were to send any unpublished poems to Mr. Caldwell in care of the magazine, and the winner would be treated to lunch with Mr. Caldwell, receive a free critique of any works in progress, and a valuable prize.

Dana spent a full moment searching her brain for any wisp of a poem that might be lingering in the crevices, then shook her head, resigned to the fact that she had not inherited even a trace of her father's gift for rhyme. She flipped the page.

Better to remember Basil as she had once adored him than to torture herself with things that could never be.

Chapter Five

On Monday morning, Buddy got up, dressed in his most comfortable overalls and jacket, then moseyed down to the mercantile with Butchie in search of something to do. Outside the air was still cold but not frigid, the temperature probably in the low forties.

He gave the bulldog a slow smile. "The old-timers would call this mortifyin' weather," he said. "Like when a sudden thaw catches everybody with their long-handled underwear still on."

The dog barked in agreement, then trotted off toward Frenchman's Fairest, probably in search of Tallulah. Buddy shrugged and crossed Ferry Road, then entered the wide double doors of the mercantile.

Shuffling down the first aisle, he ignored Vernie's sharp glance and browsed the candy counter.

"Elezar!" Vernie shouted. "Did we get my order placed?"

"Ayuh, Vernie." The patient clerk shot Buddy a wink when their gazes met. "You faxed it in Saturday afternoon."

"All right, then. You seen MaGoo?"

"He's here, under my feet. If you want him, just crinkle the cellophane on that new cat food he likes."

A moment later Buddy heard crinkling, then a black-and-white blur raced past his feet.

"Bet you haven't seen many cats like my MaGoo," Vernie called, a note of pride in her robust voice.

Buddy shrugged. "Whatever." Truth was, he couldn't

care less about a fat old cat. MaGoo did nothing but lie around, eat, and take up space . . . which is probably what most of the townspeople thought he did all day. But at least MaGoo had Vernie and Elezar, who doted on him, and Vernie and Elezar had each other. Vernie even had her straying husband, Stanley, who'd been living in a guest room while trying to smooth things over with his missis.

Buddy caught himself watching Vernie feed her cat, then lowered his gaze and reminded himself that he didn't care about any of these people. He didn't care about Vernie, or about Birdie and Bea, the sisters who lived next door to the mercantile, or about flighty Babette Graham and her family. The pastor was a vain and foolish old fuddy-duddy, and his wife a simpering Pollyanna. The only person on the island who'd earned an ounce of Buddy's respect was Salt Gribbon, who until recently had appeared to be a pillar of strength, living alone in the lighthouse without needing anyone or anything other than the barest necessities . . .

But at Christmas, the entire town saw Salt's softer side, and they learned the old curmudgeon had been hiding his two grandkids in the lighthouse to protect them from his alcoholic and possibly abusive son. Now Salt was allowing the entire town to pitch in and help with those kids, so the old sea captain wasn't nearly as self-reliant as he pretended to be.

Maybe Salt was cracking up . . . or maybe being alone wasn't such a good thing.

Buddy sniffed, then wiped his dripping nose on his coat sleeve. The other day Weird Yakov had been muttering something about how it wasn't good for men to be alone, but Yakov had his craziness and the other loony Smith guys to keep him company. And whether he grew up in Holland, Timbuktu, or on the moon, it was a sure bet Yakov hadn't been a skinny kid going to a school populated by thick-necked, big-handed farm boys who could lift girls as easily as they flipped two-hundred-pound opposing fullbacks over their shoulders. They grew tough kids in the State of Maine, the locals said, resilient kids, kids who could take care of themselves.

So Buddy, who had barely weighed one hundred pounds in his boots, parka, clothes, and long-handled underwear, had somehow been born in the wrong state. Growing up in Maine had been easy for Dana, because people expected girls to be thin and sensitive and melancholy, but Buddy had felt like a gormy misfit ever since middle school. He'd thought he'd finally feel like part of a team when he joined the Navy, but even there he'd been the odd man out. Developing an incurable case of seasickness hadn't helped matters, either.

Now he had never felt so alone . . . and like such a malcontent.

Oh, the townspeople tried to help him fit in. They greeted him with a smile every time they met, and made him feel welcome at every church function Dana prodded him to attend. But sometimes their smiles seemed a little frayed, and more than once he caught the older biddies whispering as he walked by. He knew he was welcome solely on Dana's behalf, only because Heavenly Daze had embraced her and Mike. Sometimes he caught certain conversational currents that implied the townsfolk fully expected him to leave . . . and he would, if he only could think of some place to go.

Obeying the urge to move on, he shuffled past the candy counter and paused at the magazine rack. Vernie hadn't put out any new Superman comic books since his last visit—or, if she had, she was hiding them behind the counter. He'd heard rumors about Babette complaining that Buddy read them without paying, then left them all fluffed and wrinkled for Georgie to buy.

He froze as a new magazine caught his eye: *Exotic Wild Life*. For a moment he stared at the title, then shifted his gaze to the stern woman behind the counter. Had Vernie lost her mind? What would the preacher say if he knew the mistress of the mercantile had placed a naughty men's magazine on the newsstand for even the island youngsters to ogle?

Turning so that his back blocked Vernie's view of the magazine rack, Buddy gingerly lifted the glossy periodical from its slot. The cover featured a lovely lass with flowing blond hair, a fetching smile on her painted lips, and some sort of fur draped over her palm. Then his eyes fell to the headline in the lower corner: Aussie's Foxy Loxies All the Rage in America's Heartland.

Not quite sure what a foxy loxy was (he'd certainly never heard the term in the Navy, and in the Navy a man heard about everything), Buddy leaned against the wall and flipped to the article. On the facing page, the blonde appeared again, but in this picture Buddy could see that the fur on her palm was an animal of sorts, a squirrel-like creature with a pointed face painted a bit like a raccoon's.

This wasn't a men's magazine at all.

"Buddy, are you going to buy something or stand here reading all day?"

Lowering the magazine, Buddy gulped as Vernie's

broad face came into view. She stood twelve inches in front of him, and by the look in her eye, he'd better buy the magazine or come up with an awfully good excuse about why he needed to read this article . . .

His hand reached into his pocket, fumbling for change. No sense in even trying to think of a retort; he'd never been quick-witted.

"Um, put it on Dana's tab," he said, finding nothing in his pocket but lint. He folded the magazine and took a quick half-step back. "I'll read it at home."

Vernie's eyes narrowed. "Your sister know you're down here running up a tab?"

"She won't care." Buddy took another step back, sending his elbow into a tower of spice canisters. Red and white jars of spices flew in every direction as he back stepped out of the mess.

Flushing, he caught Elezar's eye. "Sorry," he said, feeling heat at the back of his neck.

"Buddy, you're an accident waiting to happen," Vernie scolded as she bent to help her clerk replace the spices.

Buddy sidled away, momentarily wondering why the mercantile needed a tower of spice canisters to supply a town with a population of less than thirty, then he turned and pushed his way through the front door.

Might as well get away before he had a chance to do more damage.

~

Vernie's head snapped up when she heard the jangling bell over the Mooseleuk Mercantile's door ring again. She'd been filling the de Cuvier order, trying to figure out what

Olympia was going to do with five cans of black olives. Was she having a party?

She hadn't mentioned a word about it to Vernie or Cleta.

What kind of party did anyone have in January? And was Olympia not going to invite her? If not, why, that was a lousy way to show her gratitude for all they'd done. Since Edmund's passing at Thanksgiving, everyone on the island had been so concerned with keeping Olympia occupied they'd let their own work go, but now Olympia must be forging on past her grief, if she was ready to throw parties and the like . . .

Barbara Higgs entered the store, closing the door behind her.

Vernie nodded in the young woman's direction. "Mornin', Barbara."

"Morning, Vernie." Barbara paused to pet MaGoo, scratching behind the feline's ears. The lazy cat purred without moving a muscle.

Elezar chuckled as he stacked bags of potato chips in a wire bin. "That cat's so lazy he has to hire somebody to scratch him."

Barbara giggled and agreed with Elezar's affectionate assessment. MaGoo stared at her beneath shuttered lids, his tail lackadaisically sweeping the floor.

Straightening, Barbara moved on to the small corner that served as the infant section. Vernie scratched her head. Everything in that corner needed dusting; she didn't think Elezar had put out any new baby stock since August. There were no babies on the island this winter; and none were expected . . . yet.

She narrowed her gaze at Barbara. The younger woman was examining the cans of baby formula, bottles, and teething rings. She picked up a can of Similac and read the label.

Vernie's gaze shifted back to Elezar, who raised his shoulders in a "Who knows?" shrug.

She lifted her voice. "Just browsing this morning, Barbara, or did you need something particular?"

"Just browsing, thanks." The young woman continued to peruse the baby formula ingredients as if the can might contain toxic waste.

"Nice haircut, by the way," Vernie called. "Very modern looking."

Barbara flashed her a smile of honest appreciation. "Thanks, Vernie."

"There's something else different about you, too." Vernie pressed her fingers to her lips, thinking.

"It's the contacts." Barbara gave her a timid smile. "No more glasses."

Vernie nodded. "Maybe that is it. Nice to see your whole face for a change."

She kept an eye on the girl as Barbara looked over the baby shelves, then reached out to finger the soft bunting material of the infant sleepers.

The mercantile owner paused, studying Cleta and Floyd's only child from beneath lowered lashes. She didn't make a habit of ogling her customers, but Barbara was acting strange this morning.

Vernie let out a long, low whistle. Could Barbara finally be in the family way? Cleta hadn't breathed a word . . . but Cleta must not know. If Cleta knew her

Doodles was pregnant, she'd have rented a skywriter by now.

What a child Barbara and Russell would produce! Maybe a little boy with Russell's dark eyes and full black lashes coupled with Barbara's heavy brows. Vernie would do a little tweezing here and there if they were her brows, and if she were Barbara she might have some of that collagen shot into her lips . . .

She nodded in approval as Barbara left the infant section and moved toward the cosmetics. The girl studied labels, opened a few tubes of lip gloss to examine their colors, and then set the lipsticks back in the holder. Browsing a minute more, she finally applied a dark color, Raisin Rum, with a disposable applicator Vernie kept handy for that purpose. Stepping back, Barbara pressed her lips together and peered at her image in the vanity mirror. Her brows lifted up and down while her lips pursed and slackened. She turned to catch a glimpse of herself from a side angle. Then she straightened again.

"That's a nice shade on you," Vernie called. "How's Russell today?"

Barbara came forward and dropped the applicator into the trash bin. "Russell's fine. Mom's making chili for supper and she's out of tomatoes."

"Got plenty of canned tomatoes." Vernie stepped to the shelves to get the requested item, then turned and lifted her hand. "You know, you ought to run by Olympia's and get a sack of fresh ones." She chuckled. "Annie's tomatoes are actually ripening. Caleb stopped by earlier and said they planned to have bacon-and-tomato sandwiches tonight. I haven't had any, but they sure look good on the vine."

Barbara smiled wanly, and Vernie had to admit the girl looked a little streaky. Quite possibly pregnant. Saturday they'd been out looking at houses to rent.

She smiled in satisfaction. Barbara had to be pregnant. Now that a baby was on the way maybe Russell would put his foot down and they would get a place of their own. A change of scenery would be good for Barbara, and ought to erase the bored look off her features.

"Let me have two cans of tomatoes, please," Barbara said, gesturing toward the shelf, "just in case Olympia doesn't have enough for Mom's chili."

"Fine, honey. You get whatever you want. If you get a craving for something, it's best to satisfy it."

Barbara paid for the tomatoes, then glanced back at the cosmetics display.

"Raisin Rum is a pretty color for winter," Vernie said, trying to be helpful. "And it looks real good on you—brings out the sparkle in your eyes."

Barbara shrugged. "I don't wear lipstick much anymore."

"You don't?" Vernie sacked two cans of tomatoes, and then slid the bag over the counter. "That's a shame. You used to fancy up more."

Barbara took the package. "I have to be going now. I promised Bea I would help with the angel mail."

Angel mail—letters resulting from a crazy e-mail that had been zipping through the Internet—had been pouring into Bea's tiny post office since November. According to the rumor, angels actually resided on Heavenly Daze and could work miracles for those who took the time to write. The islanders took turns responding to the letters and praying for the various needs. Though Vernie had sent out dozens of e-mails to rebut the rumor, requests for heavenly intervention just kept coming.

Vernie gave her best friend's daughter a fond smile. "Have a good time with Bea, hon. And you take care of yourself."

Grinning at the thought of a baby in Heavenly Daze, she returned to Olympia's order. Caleb would be by in a few minutes to pick it up, and she didn't like to keep her customers waiting. Behind her, the bells over the door jangled.

"Just a minute, Caleb," she called, not turning around. "I've almost got everything together, but you're gonna have to tell me why Olympia wants five cans of olives—"

She jumped as a pair of arms slipped around her waist. Instinctively she reached for the hammer she kept next to the register, then she heard Stanley's soft rebuke. "Don't pound me! I've just dropped in to say hi, Sweetums."

Her cheeks burned. Dropping the hammer, she spun out of the embrace. Stanley stood before her, with a smile the size of Texas and . . . wet hair?

"You scared a year's life out of me, Stanley Bidderman," she snapped, straightening the bib of her apron. "You keep your mitts to yourself!"

Stanley backed off, holding his arms up in mock surrender. "Just wanted to bring you something."

"You keep running around with a wet head, and you're liable to end up in the hospital."

His grinned deepened. "Couldn't be helped."

She glared, aware her heart was beating like a trip

hammer and not from fright. He was starting to make a habit of bringing gifts every day—trying to butter her up, no doubt. "What is it this time?"

Stooping, he picked up a large vase of red roses he must have set on the floor before attacking her. Her eyes widened, then narrowed. What was this? Another peace offering?

He took her hands and wrapped them around the cool vase. His touch was oddly soothing. "Happy Birthday, Veronica."

She stared at the beautiful flowers and blinked away a sudden rush of tears. Stan had brought her roses every year for her birthday . . . before he skipped town, that is. Roses and the largest Whitman's Sampler he could find.

She glanced up, half-hoping to spy a box of chocolates in his hand, then frowned at her own foolishness.

She quickly shoved the vase back at him. "It isn't my birthday."

Ever so gently he wrapped her trembling fingers back around the vase. "I know. But I missed a few while I was gone, and a woman like you should never have been without flowers on her special day." Then he reached inside his coat and withdrew a large box of Whitman's chocolates. Tucking them in the crook of her arm, he kissed her cheek and whispered, "Get used to it, Vernie. I have twenty years to atone for."

She cleared the frog from her throat. "Don't you have somewhere to be, Stan? If you keep getting under my feet, I'm going to send you back to the Lansdowns'—"

"I do have a job. I'm helping the pastor with his bathroom."

With a wink and a grin, Stanley left the store as quietly as he had entered.

Stunned, Vernie tiptoed to the front window. Stan was walking toward Ferry Road with definite energy in his step.

"The old fool," Vernie murmured, bending to inhale the sweet fragrance of the roses. She swiped a tear away. If Stanley thought he was going to win her back with chocolates and roses, he . . . well, he was on the right track.

Burying her face in the bouquet, she giggled.

≈

At noon, Vernie called for Elezar to mind the store, then pulled on her jacket. Her curiosity had been stirring ever since Barbara's visit, and she had to know if—and what— Cleta knew about her daughter's condition.

Stepping out into cool air that smelled of brine, seaweed, and fish, Vernie shoved her hands in her pockets and set out across the street, then stopped in her tracks as Russell Higgs crossed the front porch of the B&B and started down the paved pathway. He caught Vernie's eye and waved, then strode confidently toward Dr. Marc's cottage behind Frenchman's Fairest.

Vernie cocked her head and stared at him. Unusual enough to see Russell out and about in daylight hours, but to see him in jeans and a sweater instead of orange waders, coat, hat and knee-high gum rubber boots . . .

Russell wasn't working, he was going to visit the doctor.

Vernie's hand flew up to cover her mouth. Russell was ailing, and now, with a baby coming? Was it serious? Why, the boy looked the picture of health.

A moment later she jogged up the steps of the B&B and burst through the front door. "Cleeeeeta!"

"Up here!"

Vernie followed Cleta's voice up the stairway to the second floor landing. She peeked in the open doors at empty bedrooms.

"Where are you?"

"Keep comin'!"

Propelled by curiosity, Vernie took the attic steps two at a time. She found Cleta in the attic room that Stanley had occupied before Christmas. "Cleta!"

About to shake out a clean sheet over the bed, Cleta jumped as if she'd been shot. She sank onto the side of the bed and pressed her hand to her chest, eying Vernie with a sour look. "Why are you screamin' at me?"

Struggling to catch her breath, Vernie sank into the chair by the door. "No special reason. Just thought I'd drop by and see what you were doing."

Cleta gave her a doubtful look.

Vernie crossed her legs in an effort to be casual. "What's going on over here this morning?"

Standing, Cleta shook out the sheet and let it settle on the bed. "Not much. Of course, you've seen Doodles's hair, and I suppose you know about the contacts."

"Barbara told me about them this morning. I saw her in the store."

Cleta sighed wearily. "She hasn't said a word about the house she and Russell were lookin' at, and I haven't dared broach the subject. It was nothin', I'm sure. Just some silly little something to pass the time."

"Maybe." Vernie uncrossed her right leg, then crossed her left.

"So." She propped her elbow on the arm of the chair, then dropped her head to her hand. "How is Barbara today?"

Cleta made a face as she tucked in the sheets. "Fine—didn't you just say you saw her? I worry about you, Vernie."

"I'm worried about Barbara—she was looking a mite streaked today."

"Well, she's delicate." Cleta plumped a pillow. "Always has been." She moved toward the doorway, then lifted a brow in Vernie's direction. "I'm done in here, unless you want to sit a spell."

"No, I'll follow you."

Vernie trailed Cleta down to the second-floor landing, then followed her into Barbara and Russell's room. Cleta yanked back the bedspread and proceeded to pull the sheets from the mattress.

"I want to get to Ogunquit again soon," she said, dropping the sheets to the floor. "Saw the prettiest pink ruffled spread and curtains in a window there. I think I'll surprise Barbara."

Vernie frowned. "I thought Barbara and Russell picked out this spread and curtains."

"Oh, they did, but just look at these colors." Cleta tssked. "Russell has no taste in fabrics—who could live with these colors? I'm going to buy a new spread. Pink will look better in here, and the kids will love it once they get used to the change."

"You think Russell will be happy sleeping in a sea of pink ruffles?"

"Why not? Men these days aren't so persnickety about protecting their he-man image."

Vernie bet she knew a certain lobsterman who wouldn't agree. She looked around. "Where is Barbara?"

"In the basement, I think. Looking for something."

Vernie leaned closer to her friend. "You interfere too much, Cleta."

Cleta laughed. "Barbara loves my little indulgences."

"But you shouldn't be meddling. If those kids picked out this spread and drapes, they like this. Not pink."

"Oh, fizzle. How could they like anything like that?" She pointed to the dark green and navy blue plaid drapes. "What person in their right mind wouldn't be grateful to get something new and not have to pay for it?"

Realizing Cleta was blind to the obvious, Vernie changed the subject. "Guess who I saw a minute ago?"

Cleta carried the dirty linens to the hallway, then dropped them on the floor. "Beats me. Who?"

"Russell."

"Really? I thought he took the boat out today." Without missing a beat, Cleta moved to the nightstand and picked up the fabric-bound journal beside the lamp. Sitting on the edge of the bare bed, she flipped through the pages.

Vernie blinked. "Cleta."

She looked up.

"Isn't that private?"

Cleta shook her head. "Barbara doesn't have any secrets from me."

"Still, it is her room. And a journal is supposed to be a person's private thoughts."

Cleta hooted. "Private? Listen to this: Had dinner with Mom and Dad. Watched *On Golden Pond* with them and Russell. R was very sweet and attentive and we are blessed to be living with Mom and Dad." Cleta looked up, a smug smile on her face. "What's so private about that?" She closed the book and carefully laid it back in the same spot. "Now, what were you saying about Russell?"

Vernie braced herself against the wall. "He was going to see Dr. Marc." Vernie lifted a brow, waiting for Cleta's reaction. The pieces of the puzzle were beginning to fall into place, for wouldn't it be logical for a young father to visit the doctor after he'd discovered his wife was pregnant? The poor boy probably needed assurance or something, and right this minute Dr. Marc was telling him that everything was going to be all right with the mother and wee one . . .

Lifting the lamp, Cleta dusted under it.

Vernie stared in stupefaction. "Did you hear me?"

Cleta shrugged. "Russell went to see Dr. Marc."

"Well?" She hesitated, giving Cleta time to absorb the facts. "Is he sick?"

Cleta paused long enough to look at her. "Why, no, he's not sick. What makes you think that?"

Vernie gave her friend the look she'd have given a very slow child. "Because he went to see Dr. Marc. He's over there right now. So . . . if he's not sick, what do you suppose he's doing?"

Cleta's smug smile reappeared. "I imagine he's there because Dr. Marc asked him to take a look at a leaky faucet.

Russell's good with those things—you remember when he fixed your outside connection when it was dripping? He put in new seals."

Vernie deflated. "Ayuh. I'd forgotten all about that."

"Vernie Bidderman, sometimes I do think you gossip too much." Cleta gave the nightstand a final swipe with her dust cloth, then stood. "What sort of conclusions were you jumpin' to? That Russell had some kind of disease? That he was dyin' or somethin'?"

Vernie bit back a growl. "Nothing like that, Cleta." She pulled herself off the wall. "Guess I should be getting back to the store." She hesitated, biting her lower lip. "You're sure he isn't sick—cold? Flu? Maybe a stomach ailment?"

Cleta shook her head. "He's healthy as a horse. And has an appetite to match."

Vernie's face fell. "Oh. OK. I'll be running along, then."

Cleta paused, dust cloth in hand. "You can't stay for a cup of coffee?"

"No, got work to do. Talk to you later."

Vernie was halfway down the front stairs when she heard Cleta call, "You need a vacation, Vernie Bidderman! A good long one!"

She let herself out, then nearly bumped into Edith Wickam on the front porch. Edith's eyes were wide, her curls bounding. "Vernie! Thank goodness. You've got to help me."

"Why, Edith, whatever is the matter?"

"It's the bathroom!"

Vernie had never seen Edith in such a state. "What's wrong with the bathroom?"

Edith paused to catch her breath. "Winslow tried to put up the border without removing the old paper—and it just fell off. Stanley tried to help him string up the border, but it dropped onto his head and I spent hours sponging the paste out of his hair. To make matters worse, whoever painted the bathroom before the wallpaper didn't put sizing on the walls. Now Stanley and Win have got the border up, but it's a mess. Half of it is falling off, while the other half is stuck tighter than a tick. The part they tried to pull off took the old wallpaper with it, and in a couple of places they stripped the plaster! My wall looks like it's filled with moon craters! We've got to do something!"

Vernie closed her eyes, imagining Stanley's role in the disaster. "Oh, my. I can just imagine—"

"If you don't have a can of that stuff that loosens wallpaper, Win will have to go to Ogunquit and rent a steamer. This could take all night. I don't think I can sleep in the house with that room looking the way it does."

Vernie slipped her arm about Edith's shoulders and led her off the porch. "I can see you're upset. Let's go to the store and see if we have a can of stripper. I'm sure we can find something."

The women crossed the street and entered the mercantile. Vernie poured Edith a vanilla Coke—"Guaranteed to make you feel better," she promised—then she called out to her clerk. "Elezar?"

"Back here."

"Do we have wallpaper stripper? Remember maybe a year ago when the Klackenbushes had to take old paper off in the schoolroom? I'm sure we had at least a quart left over somewhere."

"I don't remember seeing it, but I could be wrong. I'll look in the hardware section."

Vernie patted Edith's shoulder. "Don't you worry. If we have it, we'll find it. You just calm yourself."

Edith took another sip of her Coke, then sniffed. "Oh, Vernie, you wouldn't believe what they've done to my pretty little house. It will take hours to get it cleaned up. I wish I'd never started this. It was all right the way it was."

Vernie handed her a tissue; Edith blew her nose.

"Hang in there, honey. Things will work out."

"What a catastrophe," Edith groaned. "Now that border's hanging in strips, torn and mutilated. I can't believe what a mess they've made."

Elezar came out from one of the aisles, wiping his hands on a small towel. "I don't believe we have any of that stripper." He gave the minister's wife a sympathetic look. "I've checked in the back as well."

"We must have some," Vernie insisted. "Look again."

While Elezar went down to the basement, Vernie searched under the counter to make sure no can of stripper had inadvertently been overlooked.

Ten minutes later, both Vernie and Elezar had come up empty-handed. Edith appeared to be minutes away from a genuine crying jag.

"I'll call Mike," Vernie said. "He might just have some stripper left over."

She dialed the Klackenbushes and waited, then spoke to Dana.

Thirty minutes later Vernie had called every house on the island. "No one has any stripper," Vernie told Edith. "I'm sorry."

Edith slumped on the stool.

Both Vernie and Edith turned when the bells above the mercantile door jangled. In came Stanley and Winslow, both men somber and subdued.

Edith pressed her lips together. "Don't tell me there's more trouble."

Stanley hung back, staring at the floor. Winslow's face flushed. "Not exactly," he said.

"What, then? I can tell it's something. What have you two done now?"

Winslow cleared his throat. "The stool, um, had to be taken up so we could paper behind it. You know how difficult it is to—"

Edith covered her ears. "I don't want to hear how difficult it was, I want to know what you've done now."

Winslow swallowed. "Well, taking up the stool was harder than we anticipated. It's been there a long time, you know, and the seal—"

"Yes?" Edith prompted.

"Well . . . we had a little accident."

"Little accident?"

Vernie listened with growing concern. She'd rarely seen Edith in such a mood. Why, her eyes were flashing!

Stanley, to his credit, stood up for his share of the blame. "We knocked a little hole in the wall while we were getting the stool up," he said. "It's not a big hole—"

"A hole? In the wall?" Edith's eyes went round as cannonballs, and looked about as dangerous. "Any hole is too big, Stanley! I can't believe this! Alst I wanted was a new border. Is that too much to ask?"

She whirled, imploring Vernie.

"It's not too much, hon," Vernie answered. "I'd be upset too."

Winslow stepped forward and patted Edith's shoulder as gently as if she were a bomb about to explode. "I'm sorry, dear. I didn't intend for this to happen. My little project just grew into a big mess." He glanced at Stanley. "But we'll fix it. It'll be good as new by evening."

"By evening?" Edith thrust her hand into her hair. "Winslow, what do you expect us to use for a bathroom if you've pulled up the toilet? We live in a one-bathroom house."

Vernie moved toward the phone. "Cleta has more toilets than she knows what to do with. I'll call her, and I'm sure she'll let you use one of her bathrooms."

Winslow gave his wife a relieved smile. "See there? Stanley and I will catch the one o'clock ferry over, rent a steamer, and get Mr. Butcher to bring us back straightaway. We'll have that bathroom set to rights before you know it."

Leaving his wife whimpering by the counter, Winslow motioned for Stanley, and the two men left the mercantile.

Vernie frowned into the phone, watching her husband follow the minister toward the ferry landing. Why did some men have such a knack for messing things up?

❧

Renting a steamer proved more difficult than Winslow anticipated. He and Stanley finally located an old but usable model at an Ogunquit hardware store. The clerk apologized for the machine's condition and gave them a 10-percent discount.

Before going back to Perkins Cove, where they hoped

to catch a ride with Crazy Odell, Winslow's stomach reminded him it had been some time since breakfast. "I'm for getting something to eat before we go back."

Stanley frowned. "I don't know. Maybe we'd better get on back and get the job done. Your wife seemed awfully upset."

Winslow waved his concerns away. "She gets that way every once in a while. The slightest thing makes her weepy. She won't mind if we eat something first. A man can't work on an empty stomach."

They found an open café and quickly downed a Po' Boy sandwich, complete with onions, green peppers, kraut, and pastrami (which Win was sure would come back to haunt him), then caught a cab back to Perkins Cove. Riding in the back of the cab with the heavy steamer sprawled across their laps, Winslow looked at Stanley. "You know anything about operating a wallpaper steamer?"

Stanley shook his head. "Never even seen one before today."

"Great," Win said with a sigh.

~

Curled up in his apartment behind the Kid Kare Center, Buddy Franklin whiled the afternoon away flipping through his magazine. The term *foxy loxies,* he learned while reading *Exotic Wild Life,* was nothing but a cute nickname for sugar gliders, Australian marsupials fast becoming popular pets in the United States. According to the article, sugar gliders were intelligent, playful, inquisitive, and irresistibly cute. They didn't carry fleas or odor, and were relatively inexpensive to maintain.

Buddy turned the page and stared at a life-size picture of one of the little critters. The animal reminded him of a squirrel, but with more interesting markings on the head. The little guy's expressive dark eyes tugged at his heart.

"Like the American possum, sugar gliders are marsupials and carry their young in pouches," the caption read. "Their name comes from their affinity for sweet things like the sap that leaks from wounds in trees. In the wild, their diet consists of sap, nectar, insects, and baby birds. They are nocturnal, so as pets they're most active in the evening."

Buddy grunted. A nighttime pet would be good company for him because he often had trouble falling asleep. According to the article, sugar gliders grew to about eleven inches in length, with over half of that length taken up by the tail. So the compact little critters could easily be trained to ride around in their owners' pockets. "In fact," the article assured Buddy, "the best way to train your glider is to make a cloth pouch with a drawstring long enough to go around your neck. Hang this pouch in the cage so your glider will use it for a nest, then, while it is sleeping in the pouch, take it out and wear it around your neck. The glider will become used to your voice, smell, and movements, and soon your pet will love going everywhere with you!"

Buddy leaned back on his bed and dropped the magazine onto his chest. A constant companion! An adorable little animal that would go everywhere with him and, when appropriate, would pop out and charm anyone they met! A sugar glider would also be small enough to hide, so the pastor couldn't complain if he took it to church. If anyone objected to the glider's presence, why, he'd just slip the pouch into his jacket. The little guy would sleep most of the day and only come out to play at night, when Buddy was usually sitting alone in his room, bored and desperate for something to do. A sugar glider would be the perfect pet!

Inspired, he raced through to the end of the article, then jabbed his finger at a blue box on the side of the page. The sidebar listed a number of sugar glider breeders, and each one had an e-mail address. With a little luck . . .

Tucking the magazine inside his back jeans pocket, Buddy stepped outside and marched up to the house. If Mike didn't mind, Buddy would use his computer and write a couple of breeders. With a little good fortune, his lonely nights would soon be a thing of the past.

> To whomever has the sugar gliders:
>   My name is Buddy, and I would love to have one of these animals for a pet. I would take very good care of it, feed it whatever it needs, and wear it around my neck. I live alone, and think one of these little critters would be perfect company.
>   Please e-mail me back right away. Thanks!
>   mail to: BuddyFranklin@excite.com
>   Buddy

Buddy leaned back in his chair and studied the note. He had learned all about computers in the Navy, and he knew he could hear back from someone within minutes of sending the e-mail. The thought made him shiver with anticipation.

In the address box he typed in the e-mail addresses of

three sugar glider breeders, double-checked the spelling, then clicked "send." A moment later his message vanished.

Rising from his chair at the dining-room table, he stretched and yawned, then realized he'd better make a few preparations. If one of these folks responded, they'd probably send the little creature by Federal Express, and that meant his pet could arrive by the end of the week.

Stepping out into the hallway, he scratched at the tuft of hair on his neck and called, "Dana!"

"What?" Her voice, coming from the kitchen, held a note of impatience.

"You don't still have a parakeet, do you?"

She stepped into the kitchen doorway, her arms holding a mixing bowl. A wrinkle of exasperation marked her forehead. "Buddy, that bird died two years ago. It drowned in the goldfish bowl when you left the cage door open."

Buddy scratched again. "Oh."

"Why? You wanting a bird?"

Buddy squinted at his sister. The look on her face was anything but pleasant. "Did I say I wanted a bird?"

"No, but if you're thinking of getting an animal, you can just forget it. I have my hands full keeping the three of you men fed, and I'm not going to add one more thing to my list of responsibilities. No birds, Buddy. Besides, it's too cold up here. When we had that bird I had to keep the heat cranked up to seventy-six even when we went out of town, and I can't afford that kind of extravagance in winter."

Sighing, Buddy dropped his hand. "I don't want no bird. I wanted the cage." He tilted his head. "You still got that?"

Dana's eyes narrowed, but she nodded. "It's out in the

workroom somewhere, probably under some boxes. It's sure to be a mess."

"That's okay."

Her blue eyes were now openly suspicious. "What are you up to, Buddy?"

"Making somethin', that's all. Don't worry, you won't have to do a thing with it."

"I'd better not." She moved away as the timer on the stove buzzed. "Take whatever you need from the carriage house, just don't ask me to help. I don't have the time."

Buddy shrugged and turned, about to shut down the computer, but then he heard the tiny chime of an electronic mailbox. Checking his excite.com inbox, he discovered a single note:

> Hi, Buddy!
>   My name is Rozella Jones, I live in Florida, and I breed sugar gliders. I have a group of joeys ready to find new homes right now. If you're seriously interested, write me back, and we'll discuss details. I prefer to sell them in pairs, if at all possible, because they tend to get lonely when their owners go to work.
>   They are wonderful pets. I know you will fall in love with one of these little guys.
>   Rozella

His long fingers flying, Buddy tapped out a response:

> Dear Ms. Jones:
>   You wouldn't have to worry about one of them being lonely with me. I don't have a job, you see,

and even if I did, I'd take the little guy with me. I am
trying to open my own restaurant, but it is a long
process and I don't know how long it will take. So I
have plenty of time to train and take care of a new
pet.

Yes, I am seriously interested. Write back
soon, please.

Buddy

An instant after clicking send, he looked up to see Dana
watching him from the doorway. "Dinner's almost ready,"
she said, her eyes abstracted as she stared at the computer
screen. "So you can get cleaned up now."

"OK." He pushed back his chair, ready to stand, but
Dana came forward and pressed her hand to his shoulder.

"Who were you writing? An old Navy buddy?"

He shook his head. "A lady in Florida. I just met her."

"You met someone on the Internet? Like in a chat
room?" A warning light filled Dana's eyes. "You should be
careful, I hear some really weird people hang out in those
places—"

"It weren't no chat room, and you don't have to worry
about me." Irritated, Buddy wriggled out of Dana's grasp.
"You don't have to play big sister anymore. I'm a grown
man, you know."

Dana drew her hand back, and now her eyes were
swimming. "Sorry, kiddo. I'm only trying to look out for
you."

"I don't need protecting."

The chime of incoming e-mail broke into their conversation, and Dana's gaze drifted toward the screen.

"If you don't mind," he pulled himself closer to the keyboard, "I would like to answer my new friend before dinner. I'll be out in a minute."

Dana nodded without a word, then left the dining room. Buddy felt a twinge of guilt as her footsteps echoed down the hallway, but he forgot all about that unpleasant emotion as he opened Rozella's latest note.

Dear Buddy:

Okay! Here's how it will work. If you will send me $100 (you can send it through one of those Internet money-transferring services), I will send out one of my sweetest babies to you. She'll be coming by overnight Fed Ex (shipping will cost you another $45), and you must be able to guarantee you will be on hand to sign for delivery. Sugar gliders are desert animals, and they can't handle the cold, so we can't have this package sitting on a chilly doorstep. You gotta keep your glider warm. Okay?

In addition to the animal, you may purchase a six-month supply of special sugar glider feed (an additional $100), a sugar glider bonding pouch ($15), and a book that will tell you everything you need to know about the care and feeding of sugar gliders ($5).

Thank you very much! As soon as I've received your payment and shipping address (no P.O. boxes, please), I will send an adorable sugar glider straight to you!

Rozella

Buddy added the numbers, then consulted his mental bank balance. Out of his two thousand trust fund dollars per month, he had to spend $400 on a car payment (for an uninsured car that was stolen), $250 on health insurance, and $850 to pay down the balance of a credit card he no longer used—well, actually he was no longer allowed to use it. When he had first come to Heavenly Daze, Dana forced him to sit down and figure out all his liabilities and assets . . . and if there had been more assets, he was fairly certain she would have suggested that he pay her a monthly rent. But when she saw his lists of debts, she demanded his credit card, snipped it in half with a pair of scissors, and tossed the two pieces back to him.

"Your monthly expenditures are fifteen hundred a month, and your income only two thousand," she said, her smile drooping. "By the time you tithe and keep a little for personal expenses, you won't have much left."

"I'd be happy to sign my trust-fund check over to you," Buddy offered, more than willing to rid himself of the hassle of paying bills. "Then I can just ask you for whatever I need—"

Dana threw up her hand. "Oh, no. You keep your money, you take care of your own expenses, and you can live in the carriage house. I'll feed you, too, but I ask this one thing—you have to come to church with us. The church is the heart of this community, and if you want to fit in, you're going to have to become a part of it."

He had agreed, reluctantly, and he had managed to pull himself out of bed on enough Sunday mornings to keep Dana off the warpath. And now he was grateful he'd kept a hold of his own purse strings, because there was no way in this world Dana was going to shell out $265 for a sugar glider . . .

He did a quick search for an Internet electronic money-transfer site, found a good one, then signed up for an account. After typing in his bank account numbers, he clicked on the button that said "Send money. "

"Bud-deeeee!" Dana's exasperated voice rang out from the kitchen. "Your dinner's getting cold!"

"Just a minute!" he snapped, momentarily feeling ten years old again. While Dana clattered dishes in the kitchen, accompanied by Yakov's baritone rumble, Buddy e-mailed a payment of $265 to Ms. Rozella Jones, then followed up with a confirmation message containing his address.

"Thank you so much," he concluded the note. "I look forward to many happy days with my new pet."

"Maxwell Buddy Franklin! I'm not calling you again!"

Sighing, Buddy clicked his way out of the e-mail program and returned to the desktop. He wouldn't mention a thing to Mike, Dana, or Yakov about his new pet. He'd hang out on Main Street until the Fed Ex delivery arrived on the ferry, then he'd squirrel his little pet away.

What Dana didn't know couldn't hurt her.

≈

While the last ferry docked at Heavenly Daze, Russell Higgs whistled a jaunty tune and strode over the gangplank carrying a Flower Tree bouquet in a crystal vase. The bouquet of pink minicarnations, pompons, alstroemeria stat-ice, and monte cassino waved under the bright streetlight. He had protectively cradled the bouquet in his arms on the windy ride.

"Barbara's gonna love 'em," Captain Stroble had said as he guided the boat across the dark waters. "I need to bring my Mazie flowers more often. These days you can have flowers in the dead of winter; they fly 'em in from all over the world."

"I'm glad they do," Russell had answered, meaning every word. Barbara deserved flowers tonight. He would have rented a car and driven to Boston if he hadn't been able to find some in Ogunquit.

When he reached the B&B, Russell quietly eased the front door open, his eyes darting toward the empty parlor. Seizing the moment, he stepped inside the foyer, closed the door, then made a beeline for the stairway.

He didn't get far, for Cleta's Doppler radar was on full sweep. From the kitchen, she yelled, "That you, Russell?"

"It's me, Mom Lansdown." His mood sank. A few minutes alone with his wife—was that too much to ask?

Cleta kept the bulletins coming. "Supper's nearly on the table—we have cod tonight!"

Cod was his least favorite anything.

Russell took the stairs two at a time, dimly aware that water was sloshing out of the vase and dampening his sleeve.

Cleta poked her head around the kitchen doorway, catching him on the landing. "You feeling all right today?"

"Fine, Mom Lansdown. Just fine."

"Flowers!" Cleta smiled. "How nice. You should bring 'em down here, though, let me put them in some fresh water."

"They're fine!" he called, tamping his rising irritation.

As the carnations gyrated wildly, he hurried down the hallway, then thrust the bouquet behind his back and flung open the door to his bedroom. Barbara sat straight up from the bed, her eyes wide. The theme from *Gilligan's Island* played from the little television on the bookshelf.

Closing the door with his foot, he walked to the bed, grinning foolishly.

"Hi, honey." Barbara—and boy, did she look good with that haircut—gave him a sweet smile. "You scared me coming into the room that way." She laid her journal aside.

"Sorry." He sat down on the side of the bed, still trying to conceal the flowers. Barbara leaned in for a long kiss. The embrace lasted longer than he expected, so Russell had to pull away because his hand cramped from holding the heavy vase. Barbara didn't seem to notice.

His eyes focused on the black book. "Writing in your journal again?"

"Ayuh."

"Yours or the one your mom reads?"

She wrapped her arms around her knees. "Mine."

He grinned. "Don't you think it's deceitful to keep two journals?"

Barbara laughed. "Not at all! One's private, the other's for the grapevine. Mom's happy thinking she knows everything going on in my life, and I get to keep my thoughts to myself. It's a great compromise."

Barbara's beautiful eyes focused on his arm. "Is it sleeting outside? Your sleeve is wet."

"No, not sleeting." He brought the vase forward, smiling when his wife squealed with delight.

"For me?"

"For the most beautiful girl in the world."

She threw her arms around his neck and showered him with kisses while he laughed and held the flowers out of the melee. When she finally settled down, he set the flowers on the bedside table, then he stretched out on the blue and green bedspread.

"Pink," Barbara said, sniffing at the carnations. "My favorite color. Why, Russell, these must have cost you a fortune!"

"Not really, but what if they did? You're worth every penny."

Teasingly, she stretched out beside him and brushed her lips against his ear, whispering, "What have you done?"

"Nothing."

"Then what have I done to deserve flowers?" She pulled back, her gaze meeting his. "You're the one about to celebrate another birthday."

"Not for four days."

"Thank you, sweetheart." Barbara gave him a long, thorough kiss, then pulled away and lowered her gaze. "I needed these—lately I've been wondering how you could still love me . . ."

The vulnerability in her voice tore at him. After setting the vase on the bedside table, he gathered her snugly into his arms. "Babs, why in the world would you question my love? Don't I pay enough attention to you? I try, but with my job—"

"Don't blame yourself, honey." She patted his back. "It isn't you, it's me. I can't seem to give you a baby."

Squeezing her tightly, he whispered. "That reminds me. Guess who I saw today?"

She smiled. "Who?"

"Dr. Marc."

She pulled back, her eyes assessing him through unshed tears. "You went to the doctor?"

He caught her fingers, then slowly and deliberately kissed each one. "Ayuh," he said, his lips against her thumb. "And guess what? I'm fine—in fact, I'm better than fine." He murmured these words against her index finger. "I'm healthy, got the cholesterol of a four-year-old." He kissed her pinkie. "And Doc said he can't see any reason I shouldn't be able to father a child."

Barbara sat back, her palm smothering a giggle.

Grinning, Russell waggled his brows. "Great news, huh?"

She nodded, her hand dropping back to her side. "Sure. Great news."

He kissed her again, then propped his head on his palm. Her look of happiness had faded, and a shadow now lurked behind her eyes. "Why the worried look? Aren't you happy?"

"Of course I'm happy." She shrugged, reaching out to twirl a lock of his dark hair around her finger. "It's just that—"

He sat up straighter. "What?"

"I am happy—but I didn't know you were thinking about going to the doctor."

"I wasn't. Dr. Marc stopped by the boat Saturday morning to ask me about a leaky faucet he wants fixed, and the subject got around to kids. He asked if I'd had a physical lately and I hadn't. So I went."

"You hate doctors."

"I don't hate doctors, as a group, they're all right. But

this is different. If I was holding us back, I wanted to be sure I could get something done about it."

Barbara's eyes darkened further. "But if it isn't you, it's me."

"Ah, hon, there's nothing to the physical. It's over before you know it, and Doc said it's probably something very minor. Lots of women need to have a little fine-tuning. Doc said infertility could be caused by all sorts of things—maybe the ovary isn't working right, or the Philippian tubes are damaged."

Barbara smiled. "I think that's *fallopian* tubes, honey."

"Right. But there are a lot of things that could be stopping you from conceiving. And most are fixable."

Dropping her head to her arm, Barbara closed her eyes, leaving Russell to guess at her thoughts. Was she afraid to have a baby? He couldn't blame her if she were, with all of Cleta's offhand remarks about the agonies of childbirth and how she considered labor the equivalent of passing a head of cabbage through the eye of a needle. That kind of talk would scare the daylights out of anybody.

Barbara opened her eyes and playfully pinched him. "Fine-tuning, huh? You're confusing me with your boat engine."

He drew her back into his arms and held her. They lay still for a moment, each digesting his news. He knew she was hesitant about motherhood; for all her maturity, she was still a child in Cleta's house. Cleta deliberately kept her close, refusing to let Barbara meet life on its own terms. She had Barbara convinced motherhood was akin to sainthood, and not many deserved the honor.

"I'll be with you all the way," he murmured. "Through

the labor, childbirth—I'll even go to the doctor with you."

"I'm capable of going to the doctor by myself, Russell." Abruptly she sat up, reached for the remote, and switched the television to the evening news.

"Then why not go?" he persisted. "I'll make the appointment and we'll get it over with. If it turns out we can't have children, then we'll think about adoption. That takes time, and we need to get our name on a waiting list."

"I don't know . . ."

He reached out and turned her face toward his. "You got your hair cut; you got contacts, and your mom lived through it. She'll live through you going to see Dr. Marc. If you're scared—"

"I'm not afraid. I'm delicate." She rolled off the bed and walked to the window, then stood staring out at the darkness, her arms crossed. She shifted from one bare foot to the other. "You said the examination didn't hurt?"

"Didn't hurt at all."

"Nothing like passing a cabbage?"

"No, Dr. Marc is very gentle, and very . . . understanding. I thought I'd be embarrassed, but he made it all seem matter-of-fact. He was great."

"And we can afford it?"

"We can afford a dozen doctors. I have good insurance, so you can have the nicest room in the hospital if you want."

"Or have the baby on the side of the road like that poor woman the women were talking about at quilting circle."

"Good grief, Babs. That hardly ever happens. Childbirth today is quick and painless—"

"I don't know about that. I've seen movies where women are screaming and fussing and hanging on the bed-post—some of them even die!"

He shook his head. "That's only in the movies—and maybe in a few rare cases where the women weren't in good health to begin with. Giving birth is a natural process."

"Men can say that. Mom says if a man and woman took turns giving birth, there'd be only two children per family."

Standing, he pulled her to him. "If I could have our child, I would."

"Even if it felt like passing a cabbage?"

"Even then." He held up his palm. "Honest."

"Liar."

He grinned.

"Well." Barbara bit her lower lip, then shifted and sighed. "OK. I'll go to see the doctor, but you have to let me do this in my own time and my own way. Doctors scare me, but if the problem is serious, we ought to start thinking about getting our name on an adoption list."

He smiled down at her. "While you're there, ask him about that cabbage thing. I'm sure he'll have a different viewpoint."

Her cheeks flamed crimson. "Russell Higgs! I couldn't!"

Scooping her off her feet, Russell swung her around until she was breathless and giggling. Gently dropping her to the bed, Russell whispered, "Why don't we give serious thought to that house we looked at the other day?"

"I loved it," she admitted. "But it was kind of run-down. Could we look around a little more?"

"We can look to your heart's content, but there isn't

that much available in Ogunquit, not in our price range."
His fingers walked along her rib cage, then began to tickle
her. She squealed, thumping her heels on the floor as she
laughed.

A sharp rap from beneath the floorboards brought
their fun to an abrupt halt.

"Sorry," Barbara said, frowning at the floor. They both
knew the rap had come from the end of Cleta's broom in
the kitchen below. "I suppose she'll be rapping again before
long, telling us that dinner is getting cold."

"Right now," Russell said, breathing a kiss onto her
neck, "I'm not hungry for dinner."

Collapsing in a heap on the bed, the two lovers kissed,
giggling between breaths as Cleta's voice rose like a foghorn
over the staircase. "What's all that thumping! What are you
two doing up there, moving furniture? You leave that furniture where it is! I paid a fortune to have that chair
cleaned—don't you be roughhousing and dirty it up."
Then, gruffly, "Supper in five minutes!"

Barbara and Russell sobered, their eyes caught in a
lover's moment. Barbara broke the silence first. "Whatever
we do, we do it alone. We don't tell Mom about the doctor's appointment or the house. Not yet. Deal?"

He frowned. "That's up to you, but having your mom
involved might make it a little easier for you."

"That's the problem. If Dr. Marc finds anything wrong
with me, she'll worry herself to death, and she'll hate any
house we look at no matter what. She'll imagine everything
from termites to aliens in the attic. I know Mom. No, I'll
make the doctor's appointment and I'll go by myself. And
we'll go house hunting again Saturday. It's better that way."

Better for all concerned, Russell agreed, but by then his mind was centered on his pretty wife and the five minutes remaining before supper.

"Hey," he whispered.

She laced her fingers through his. "Hey, what?"

"Will you fix that Mexican casserole for my birthday?"

Her eyes shone with warmth. "The one that gave you indigestion for a week?"

"It was great." He squeezed her hand. "Great because you made it. You're turning into a good cook."

"Thank you, sir."

"You're welcome, miss."

And for the next four minutes and thirty seconds, Russell and Barbara brushed the worries of the day aside.

≈

Next door at the Kid Kare Center, Dana stared at her kitchen table and fought back tears. Three sets of dirty plates stared at her, but the fourth set, nearly arranged at her right hand, sat unused. Yakov had come promptly when she called, Buddy had finally come out of the dining room to eat, but Mike, her own loving husband, had sent word with Yakov that he'd come "in a minute."

An hour had come and gone since that message, but Mike was still out in the carriage house workroom, sorting a new shipment of art prints from the wholesaler.

Resisting the tears that stung her eyes, she stood and began to clear the table. She knew she ought to be glad her husband had found work he enjoyed, but ever since getting that computer she scarcely saw more than the side of his head. Each morning he woke with the sun, ran to the dining room to check his ongoing auctions, and then he grabbed a quick cup of coffee and a sausage biscuit, which he ate while sitting at his computer.

After answering the e-mailed questions from bidders that had arrived during the night, he went out to the carriage house to select new prints to list for auction. She often overhead him and Yakov discussing the psychology of Internet auctions—if they listed more than two Van Gogh *Harvest Landscapes* in a single auction, weren't they competing with themselves? Surely it was better to space out the *Harvest Landscapes* so they offered no more than one per week, but was it better to feature Van Gogh in one week and Monet in the next? Mike also tried to keep running charts on how much certain pictures sold for other dealers, so he could set a competitive starting bid price . . . the angles went on and on.

He'd been an eBay seller for only a couple of weeks, but Dana was already heartily sick of the entire process. Mike spent fifteen hours of every day either in the carriage house or at his computer, and she missed his company. He kept telling her that soon he'd grow his business enough to hire people to help share the burden, but Dana wasn't sure that day would ever come. After all, he had Yakov's help now, and he could probably have Buddy's help if he needed it (and dared risk it), yet he was still working one hundred hours a week. Shoot, most people were only awake one hundred twelve hours a week—she'd done the math.

She slid a load of dishes onto the counter and plugged the sink, then ran the water, holding her fingers beneath the stream to test its heat. She ought to let Mike have it with both barrels when he finally came in. They rarely argued, so they were overdue for a heated discussion. She would tell him that she didn't marry him just to clean his house; she'd remind him that due to her trust-fund income they didn't need a ton of additional money. He didn't need a career, but she needed a husband. She needed his attention; she wanted to see his face a few times a day; she wanted him to look at her when she talked. She wanted him to eat the lunches and dinners she cooked while they were still hot; she wanted him to lie in bed with her and watch TV until they were both so sleepy they couldn't hold their eyes open . . .

Her thoughts trailed away as she realized how selfish she would sound if she said those things. *She* needed? Mike needed things, too; surely he did. Men needed to feel useful, they needed to know they were contributing to the support of a household. Buddy might fashion a career of doing nothing, but Buddy was an anomaly. Mike had turned their ramshackle old house into a lovely home and school, but now that work was finished. The Kennebunk Kid Kare Center wasn't his thing—everyone knew the school was really Dana's occupation. She supervised the kids, she put up the bulletin boards, she served sandwiches and took the kids out for walks on the beach on sunny days. Mike had single-handedly renovated that little bathroom off the classroom, but men didn't get extra credit for those kinds of things. Everyone just took that kind of work for granted.

She dropped a handful of silverware into the soapy water and watched it glisten through the suds like the silver lining at the base of a cloud bank. Yes, Mike had needs, too, and maybe she was approaching this problem from the wrong perspective. Her mother had always told her a girl could catch more flies with honey than vinegar . . .

She paused a moment, her hands in the dishwater, then smiled as an idea bloomed in her brain. Why not surprise Mike with something unexpected? He would probably stay out in the carriage house for another hour or so, then he might come in and return to the computer. But he'd eventually come upstairs, and if she had put everything away in the kitchen he wouldn't stop to eat. So if she planned a little surprise picnic . . .

Grinning, she began to scrub with renewed purpose.

～

Cleta scrubbed a baking dish and laid it in the drainer. Barbara hadn't eaten much tonight, and when he wasn't looking at his wife, Russell had mostly kept his eyes on the food. Barbara seemed preoccupied; now, what could that be about? The two lovebirds had made eyes at each other all during the meal, occasionally snickering, and Cleta wondered if they weren't playing footsies under the table. She hadn't seen a thing humorous about their behavior. All through dinner, Floyd talked about the Wickam's bathroom and giggled at the thought of the pastor's discomfiture. Edith, though, must find the bathroom situation anything but funny. From what Cleta'd heard, the room looked like a demolition zone.

She heard a knock at the front door, then the creak of Floyd's TV chair. A moment later Caleb's and Abner's voices drifted to the kitchen. Olympia's butler and Birdie's baker were out for their nightly stroll.

Before Cleta could dry her hands and make herself presentable, Winslow and Stanley knocked on the kitchen door to say they had the steamer—an awkward, burdensome relic that look as if it might take a couple of men to operate.

"Sorry to bother you," Winslow said, stepping into the warmth of her house. "But I need to ask a favor. I don't know if you've heard about our bathroom situation at the parsonage—"

Cleta lifted a hand. "Oh, we've heard."

Floyd giggled. "Vernie's been over."

Pastor Wickam pressed his lips together. "I see. Well, if you don't mind, Edith and I are in a bit of an embarrassing situation. While we were in the midst of wallpapering—"

"Their toilet is sitting in their tub," Stanley interrupted. "And not very useful at the moment, if you know what I mean."

"Vernie already told me she'd volunteered my bathrooms," Cleta said, grateful for an opportunity to show hospitality to someone who would appreciate it. "You and Edith can pop in any time. We'll leave the back door unlocked for you."

Floyd pointed to the stainless-steel monstrosity Stanley had dragged in. "What is that, part of an artificial lung?"

Stanley looked offended. "It happens to be the only wallpaper steamer in Ogunquit."

"It looks," Floyd said, his gaze sweeping over the machine, "like it could use some new rubber. Those tires are nearly as bad as our fire truck's—"

"If you don't mind," Winslow interrupted, nodding toward the coffeepot. "Stanley and I would love a cup of coffee before we drag this contraption all the way down to the parsonage. We about froze on the ferry."

Cleta wiped her hands on a dishtowel. "I thought you two were supposed to steam the walls this afternoon."

"We tried," Winslow said. "But Odell Butcher was nowhere to be found. So we had to wait for the last ferry."

Cleta nodded. The ferry ran to Heavenly Daze only three times daily in the off-season—at seven, noon, and six. More than once she'd been stranded in Ogunquit for an entire afternoon.

Placing her hand on her hips, she surveyed the decrepit machine. "Looks like an older model."

"Ayuh," Floyd agreed, drawing on his pipe. "Looks like it could have come over on the Mayflower."

"It was all they had, and we were right glad to get it," Winslow said. He covered his mouth with his hand and belched, apologizing. "Sorry—the sandwich I had for lunch is backin' up on me."

"You too?" Stanley popped an antacid into his mouth.

"Let me get your coffee." Cleta moved to the coffeepot, then smiled at Caleb and Abner as they came through the swinging kitchen door. "Welcome, gentlemen. Looks like you're just in time to help Stanley and the preacher drag this monstrosity down to the parsonage." She frowned as she surveyed Caleb, the butler. Though she had no idea how old the man was, he looked every day of eighty years old. Maybe he shouldn't be out in the evening chill.

"I can't stay but a moment." Caleb smiled, handing Cleta a small brown bag. "Olympia was feeling a little poorly when I left, so I told her I'd be back as soon as possible. But she thought you might enjoy a couple of fresh tomatoes."

Cleta peered inside the bag, then pulled out two plump red jewels. "Why, have you ever? Tomatoes in January. Who'd have thought it possible? Annie must be thrilled with her experiment."

Caleb nodded. "Ayuh. These beauties should put her in the textbooks, and they're some good. Nice and meaty, with few seeds. Olympia enjoyed a couple of slices with her dinner this evening."

"My." Stanley's eyes widened at the sight of the red beauties. "They're really edible? They look perfect enough to be plastic."

"Of course they're edible. I'll show you." Cleta walked to the counter and pulled out a knife, then sliced one of the largest tomatoes. After adding a dash of salt and pepper, she spread the slices on a plate and grabbed a handful of forks.

Holding the plate over the kitchen table where the men were gathered, she offered the utensils and nodded. "Go ahead, taste one."

Stanley and Winslow cautiously cut a bite, then bit into the flavorful fruit. "Yum," Winslow said. "Delicious."

Stanley wiped his mouth on a napkin. "Looks like Annie's a genius."

Caleb laughed. "I think so—but then I have always believed in her."

Floyd grinned. "Even the time she blew up the shed trying to make soda pop?"

"Even then," Caleb admitted. "She's always been exceptionally bright . . . and curious."

Floyd had to get in on the tasting, and soon the three men had finished off the whole tomato.

"I'm saving the other one," Floyd remarked. "For tomorrow."

"Delicious," Stanley said. "Never ate one any tastier."

"Well, Abner and I must be going," Caleb announced. "We still have to walk a mile before we can go home."

Abner frowned. "Caleb is a hard taskmaster."

Caleb patted his friend's extended belly. "Ah, but exercise is good for mortal bodies."

Winslow buttoned his coat. "Edith will be steamin' herself by the time we get there. I promised her we'd get the job done tonight, which means we'll have to strip the paper off the bathroom wall before we can go to bed. And we promised to have the steamer back in twenty-four hours."

Floyd, his thumbs hitched in his suspenders, rocked on his heels and pulled on his pipe. "If you need any help, just holler. I'm studyin' mechanics, you know."

"Ayuh, will do."

Cleta closed the door behind the departing men and gave Floyd a reproachful look. "If they need any help? Of course they need help. They're incompetent!"

"Ayuh, and I plan to go over first thing in the morning and clean up their mess. Winslow's bathroom is small, so I'd only be underfoot if I were to go over tonight." He chuckled. "Sometimes you've got to let a man learn that he can't do a thing before he's willing to step aside and let somebody else have a go at it."

Cleta shook her head, but realized Floyd was probably right. Pastor Wickam seemed a lot better suited to preaching than wallpapering, but he'd made his wife a promise, and he had every right to honor it . . . if he could.

"I'll leave the light on," she said, carrying the empty tomato plate to the sink, "so Edith and Winslow can find their way if they have to use our bathroom during the night."

꙳

By 11 PM, Dana Klackenbush had spread her antique double bed with a red and white checked tablecloth. A basket in the center of the cloth held a warm crock filled with Boston baked beans, while another basket held fragrant roast-beef sandwiches served on croissants, Mike's favorite bread. A pair of tall scented candles gleamed from her nightstand, while soft music played from the radio on her husband's.

When she heard the slam of the downstairs door, she slipped out of her bulky chenille robe, then curled on the bed beside her heaped pillows, arranging her hair so that it flowed over one shoulder. She wore a charming ruffled nightgown of white cotton, sleeveless and thin . . . altogether impractical, considering the temperature outside, but this was a special occasion.

She heard the groan of the stairs, then the squeak of the bedroom doorknob. Dana clicked off the television remote, then gave her husband her best come-hither smile. "Hi ya, honey." She kept her voice low and husky. "Hungry?"

Mike winced as he entered, pressing one hand to the

side of his neck. "I think I got a crick or something from staring at the computer screen." Without even looking at her, he moved toward the bathroom. "Man, it hurts! Do we have aspirin in the medicine chest?"

Dana rose up on one elbow. "You want aspirin?"

"We have any in here, or is it in the kitchen?"

She glanced at the basket, the candles, the sandwiches, the bean pot. She didn't see how he could have missed such a spread, but perhaps the pain in his neck had distracted him.

"Honey," she raised her voice so it would carry into the bathroom, "aren't you hungry? You missed dinner."

"I couldn't eat if I tried." She heard the creak of the medicine cabinet, then the sound of water in the sink. "I'm bushed. I'm going to brush my teeth and go to bed."

She straightened as he thrust his head out of the bathroom doorway. "The aspirin's not in here, hon. Would you mind running down to the kitchen and bringing it up?"

She gave him a frosty glare. "Is that all you want?"

"Ayuh, thanks." His eyes wandered to the checked tablecloth. "Having a midnight snack? Hope you didn't get crumbs in the sheets. But I'm so tired I think I could sleep in an ant bed."

As he disappeared back into the bathroom, Dana took one last look at her festive picnic, then blew out the candles. Gathering the tablecloth by its four corners, she jerked the entire thing straight upward, then swung it over her shoulder. Heedless of the mess, she carried the entire setup downstairs to the kitchen, then dropped her burden onto the kitchen table.

"You want aspirin?" she muttered between clenched teeth. "You come down here and get it yourself."

Unfolding the tablecloth, she pulled out the basket, then tossed the gourmet sandwiches into Butch's bowl. The dog, who'd been watching her from his bed by the back door, sprang to attention, then trotted toward the bowl, grunting in appreciation.

"Your neck hurt?" she growled, pulling the bean crock from the mess. She lifted the lid, then dumped the steaming beans down the garbage disposal. "Your neck's gonna hurt worse if you end up sleeping on the couch for a week, husband o' mine."

The beans had spilled in her unconventional cleanup, so she grabbed a fork from the pile of utensils and scraped the sticky mess from the tablecloth linen, then slung bean goop into the sink.

Making far more noise than was strictly necessary, she tossed dirty dishes into the dish drainer, the silverware into the sink, the tablecloth into the laundry hamper. Then she sat at the kitchen table and crossed her arms, her toe tapping in a quick rhythm as she waited for Mike to come down and see why she was taking so long with his aspirin.

Five minutes passed. Ten. Twenty. Finally, fearing that she was wasting a good pout, Dana crept up the stairs and discovered her husband asleep in bed, the side of his face pressed into the pillow and one hand brushing the wooden floor.

The adrenaline that had fired her drained away, leaving her feeling empty. Too weary to work up another good temper, Dana crawled beneath the covers and curled into a ball, shivering as tears streamed from the corners of her eyes and into her hair.

~

On his bed, working by the dim light of a forty-watt bulb, Buddy Franklin lay on his stomach and peered at the legal pad propped against his pillow. He had an inclination to write something, but the words hadn't yet caught up with the urge . . .

After dinner he'd gone into the workroom half of the carriage house and found Dana's big birdcage beneath a stack of cardboard boxes; now it stood in one corner of his small room, next to the woodstove on one wall and his chest of drawers on another. The ornate freestanding cage seemed at home in the room, and by tomorrow night it would be home to the cutest critter in Heavenly Daze. Let Dana and Mike fawn over Butch, and let fussy Olympia de Cuvier dote on that Tallulah mutt—he was going to have the most unique, most clever pet on the island. Little Georgie Graham was going to go nuts when he saw it, so Buddy would probably have to avoid the kid for a while, just to give his sugar glider time to get adjusted. As a matter of fact, he should avoid everyone for a while, lest someone slip and tell Dana about the new pet. She'd come around eventually, but she had seemed awful determined the other day about not wanting any more animals in the house.

But Buddy's apartment wasn't really her house. And the sugar glider wouldn't be her responsibility. He would belong to Buddy alone.

His heart brimmed with euphoria too rich for words, yet words bubbled up and pushed at him, straining for release. He'd had this experience before—once, in second grade, when a teacher told him he was a sensitive child, and in tenth grade when Jennie McGrady passed him a note that said, "I like you." The feeling was like a beachball he tried to hold beneath the sea, but just when he thought he had it safely tucked away, it got away from him and popped up in some unexpected outburst. Earlier tonight, when he'd been in the workroom scrounging for the birdcage, he had burst into a rousing chorus of "Zip-A-Dee-Doo-Dah," startling Mike and Yakov so badly that they lost their place in their inventory count.

Now the feeling was about to burst out again, but this time he was prepared. Gripping a pencil between his thumb and index finger, he pressed down so intently he nearly broke the pencil point.

"My joy," he wrote. And with the launch of those two words, a stream followed:

My joy cannot be contained in words or song or
    expression—
Letters, juxtaposed puzzles, are rife with discretion,
But boundless joy, the rarest fruit of my heart,
Is far more an elixir of life than mere art.
Two black velvet eyes, a tip-tilted gaze
Have launched me round this sphere in a daze.
My heart doth pound in rapturous beat
Anticipating the warmth of your breath so sweet—

He scratched through the last line, knowing it didn't fit. But what did? Sweet little feet? That rhymed, but didn't seem lofty enough. Tiny little treat? No, nothing little. The love he would feel for his new companion would be anything but small. It would be huge, expansive—

"Ah!" He pressed the pencil to the paper again. "My heart doth pound in rapturous beat, because your love makes my poor life complete."

There. Satisfied with his poem, he read it aloud three times, then ripped the page off the legal pad, crumpled it into a ball, and tossed it toward the garbage can. He had memorized it, and tomorrow night, when his little pet snuggled safely in its pouch against his chest, he would whisper it through the night.

～

Snatching the sleeping mask off her eyes, Cleta bolted upright up in bed. The fluorescent hands of the bedside clock stood at one o'clock. She tensed, listening to a rumble and creaking that could only be someone rushing up her stairs at ninety miles to nothing.

Beside her, Floyd stirred. "Eh? What's going on?"

"Shush, I don't know—go back to sleep. Must be Winslow using the bathroom. But you'd think a body would try to be a little quieter when using someone else's toilet in the middle of the night."

"Sounds like a herd of buffalo." Floyd rolled over, and a minute later a snore rolled from his mouth.

Land almighty. Sinking back to her pillow, Cleta snapped her eye mask back into place.

An hour and a half later, Cleta met Barbara at the kitchen window, blinking heavy eyes as they watched a weakened Winslow shuffle away across the graveled church parking lot, the ties of his bathrobe flapping, his hairy legs stuffed in corduroy house shoes as he shuffled toward the parsonage. Meanwhile, upstairs, the pipes sang as a toilet flushed in another part of the house—her own bedroom, Cleta guessed, from the sound of it. If so, this was the fourth time Floyd had made an urgent trip to the necessary room.

"What is going on?" Barbara asked. "Who keeps slamming the doors?"

"Land, I don't know. Something must have upset their stomachs. Just go back to bed, hon."

Cleta tried to follow her own advice, but at three-thirty, Floyd reared out of bed and lunged toward the bathroom, nearly tripping in flight. The door slammed, jarring the old house.

Cleta sat up. "Floyd?"

A few minutes later he emerged, one hand pressed to his abdomen. "Stomach feels a little queasy—" He dropped off to sleep before he finished the complaint.

The man could sleep through the Second Coming.

Cleta was awakened—well, the whole household was awakened—four more times before she gave up and got dressed just before dawn. Out of curiosity, she peered out a western window toward the mercantile, and through the darkness saw a light burning on the third floor.

So—either Stanley had taken to sleeping with a light on, or he'd been up and down all night, too.

She staggered into the kitchen and flipped on the light, feeling as if she'd been caught in a wringer. She'd never spent a more miserable night. She plugged in the coffeemaker, then padded through the foyer. When she opened the front door, a whiff of chilly air slapped her in the face.

Colder than yesterday, a mite. The unexpected thaw couldn't last much longer.

Winslow Wickam was lucky. If he had ruined his bathroom a week or two later, he'd be running around in the dark in weather cold enough to freeze two dry rags together.

She bent down to pick up the paper. The dedicated newspaper boat servicing all the Maine islands ran in all weather but a full gale, and Cleta marveled that anybody could function in full dark. Must be a special kind of person to thrive before 5 AM; she had never gotten the hang of it.

Her hand closed around the morning news, then she went back into the house, letting the door close behind her.

Chapter Six

$\mathcal{A}$ little after sunup, Micah rounded the corner of the B&B and found Stanley Bidderman hunched in the porch swing and swathed in blankets. The man looked as pale as parchment.

Concerned, the gardener climbed the steps, eying the sick man. "Stanley?"

"A . . . yuh." He stuttered the greeting over chattering teeth.

"Goodness, man, why are you sitting out here at this time of the morning?"

Stanley hung his head. "Vernie said I was keeping her up, so I left. I . . . I can't afford to have her mad at me, not now."

"Are you ill?"

The man nodded. "Must have been something I ate— that Po' Boy sandwich or something." He shuddered. "I can still taste the kraut."

"Come over to my place. I'll fix you some coffee and you can get warm."

Micah helped Stanley up from the swing and steered him across the porch and down the steps. A few moments later they were sitting at the gardener's kitchen table watching the sun gild the morning sky.

Micah poured hot water into a cup and added a spoonful of honey and a tea bag. While the drink steeped, the two men talked. Stanley told the gardener about Vernie and all the years they'd been apart. He said he'd been foolish to leave. He'd gone searching for a rose when he had an orchid in his own backyard.

Micah listened, slowly stirring his tea as Stanley poured out his heart. "I'm afraid too much time has passed," Stanley finished. "I realized my mistake too late."

"You fear she will never forgive you?"

He nodded. "She says she forgives me, but forgetting is another matter altogether. My failure will always be in her mind, and I can't do anything to erase it. She's made a life for herself, a good life, and she doesn't need me in it." He looked away, and Micah studied his profile. Stanley's features were pasty and drawn in the early morning light.

Stanley whispered, as though he were speaking more to himself than to Micah. "Vernie's rough on the exterior, but she has a heart of gold. I was a fool. I didn't appreciate her before."

"Everyone makes mistakes."

Stanley closed his eyes. "I've made more than my share."

Micah set his spoon on the table. "Do you believe in God, Stanley?"

Stanley tilted his head. "I suppose so. As a child I believed in lots of things, including God, but faith became harder when I grew up. Sometimes I wonder if it's all a myth. One thing I know for sure—God has no reason to believe in me."

Micah lifted a brow. "His grace is not sufficient to cover all your mistakes?"

Stanley shook his head. "I sound like an atheist, don't I? I know we're not to rely on feelings, but sometimes emotions are alst I have left. I feel so bad about my mistakes that I can't believe God would have me."

Micah rested his hand on the man's shoulder. "We are given free will, Stanley, so it's not surprising that men make wrong choices. Every man, woman, and child makes mistakes. Only through grace are humans restored to fellowship with God." His gaze met Stanley's and held it captive. "Grace is a marvelous thing."

"Say again?"

"If men were to rely only on their own efforts to reach heaven, they really would be in a pickle, wouldn't they?"

The mention of food seemed to make Stanley grow paler. He clutched at the edge of the table, then leaned forward, his face twisted in an expression of pained concentration. "May I?"

The angel pointed. "It's that way."

Lurching from his chair, Stanley disappeared down the hall, then slammed the bathroom door.

Micah chuckled in quiet sympathy, then leaned back in his chair, sipped his coffee, and lifted his gaze to the window. The day outside was glorious, another testament to the Father's grace and mercy. The citizens of Heavenly Daze ought to have been buried in snow and ice by now, yet few of them had stopped to consider that God had allowed them a respite. Fewer still had thought to wonder why. The good weather was a gift, pure and simple. Just like grace.

Micah smiled as his thoughts returned to Stanley Bidderman. God's grace was more than sufficient to cover sin, but a mortal man's mistakes often rose up to haunt him. Stanley and Vernie had wasted many years, and they would waste even more if they continued to look back instead of moving forward. Cleta was also looking back—longing for the days when her daughter had been truly dependent. That sincere woman needed to cut the strings that bound her to the past and seek God's will for her future.

What was it about humankind that made them yearn for the opposite of God's good plan for them? God had given them two weeks of splendid weather; they muttered about the snow and ice to come. They complained about loneliness, then spent their time in activities that corrupted the soul and proved insatiably addictive. Two years ago Cleta had become hooked on soap operas, and that addiction had nearly cost her the friendship of every woman on the island. And though she knew the danger of daytime drama addiction, still she allowed her daughter to watch the silly shows, knowing that the habit kept Barbara close to home.

Humans squandered things of eternal value and hoarded worthless, temporary baubles. They wept buckets over silly fictional movies, and found it difficult to sustain a dull ache for the terrible tragedies of real people's lives. They found ten minutes of prayer tedious, yet wasted hours surfing the World Wide Web and watching television.

They yearned for God, but the God they sought was a safe, grandfatherly deity who would send them good weather and keep them safe as they went about their daily business. Few of them realized that the God they cajoled in prayer wasn't grandfatherly at all, and he was certainly not safe. The sovereign God of heaven and earth was a consuming fire, and his overriding purpose for men and women was not safety or comfort, but holiness . . .

Micah's heart softened as he prayed for Barbara and

Russell, two dear children who struggled to find and follow the Lord's will. God had promised to provide and care for them, but presently they were choosing to live a safe life rather than an obedient one. Barbara had allowed fear to blind and bind her, and that same fear would prevent her from discovering all the blessings God had allotted for her.

Micah shook his head.

His dear charges, the occupants of the Baskahegan Bed and Breakfast, had much to learn about walking in faith and light.

⟜

Trying to appear as though he hadn't a care in the world, Buddy Franklin whistled as he stepped into the mercantile, then checked his watch. High noon, and no sign yet of the ferry or a Federal Express package. Fortunately, the temperature was above freezing, so his sweet little sugar glider wouldn't freeze his stripes off if he were stuck in a truck somewhere in Ogunquit.

"Can I help you, Buddy?" This from Elezar, who stepped out from behind the counter.

"Um, ayuh. Whatever." Buddy looked around for Vernie, then sighed in relief when he didn't see her. Seemed like that woman knew everything that went on in Heavenly Daze, and Buddy didn't want word of his special pet getting out—at least not yet. He'd have to judge Dana's mood before he could let her know about his new addition, and he knew he'd have to get through at least a couple of months with her not knowing before he'd be able to prove he could have a pet without bothering her in the least.

Elezar craned his neck to look around Buddy. "Butchie didn't come with you this morning?"

"Naw. Butchie stayed home." Buddy stepped closer to the store clerk and lowered his voice. "I need something, you see, and I don't want Vernie knowing about it. My sister, either."

Elezar's eyes crinkled at the corners. "I can keep a secret, Buddy."

"Good." Buddy edged closer. "I'm looking for a little bottle, the kind of thing you'd hang in a hamster's cage."

Elezar nodded. "I think you're in luck. We have a few pet supplies in a drawer in the back, and seems to me we got in a few hamster-type things back when Georgie Graham was talking about gerbils."

He turned and walked toward the rear of the store. "You thinking about getting a hamster, Buddy?"

Buddy followed the clerk. "No."

"Well, then." Stooping, Elezar bent before a dusty shelf and pulled out a box. "Here we have an assortment of small rodent toys—a little ceramic dish for food, a wheel, and—ayuh, here's a water bottle."

Eyeing the toys, Buddy said, "If I get some of those things, you promise you won't say anything to Vernie?"

Elezar shook his head. "She won't even know they're gone until someone else comes in here looking for them. The odds of that are pretty slim."

"OK." Buddy pointed to the box. "I'll take the little dish, the bottle, and . . . well, ayuh, give me the wheel too. I don't know if I'll need it, but you never know."

Elezar lifted a dark brow. "Not a hamster, huh? Thinking of getting a gerbil?"

"Um, no."

"A mouse?"

"No."

Elezar made a face. "Don't tell me you're getting a rat!"

Buddy managed a grin. "No."

Elezar's smile faded. "Don't tell me you've already caught a rat."

Buddy shook his head. "No, and I gotta go, OK?"

Elezar stood. "Shall I put this on Dana's tab?"

Buddy was about to nod, then realized that certainly wouldn't work. Dana examined her receipts with an eagle eye. "No, I'll pay cash."

Elezar's eyes widened to the point that Buddy feared they'd fall out of his head, then he grinned and led the way to the counter. Buddy forked over the money quickly, lest Vernie come down the stairs and catch him in a cash transaction, then he stuffed his purchases inside his coat and left the mercantile, whistling as casually as he could.

~

Still cloaked in a residual fog of Bad Mood, Dana knocked on the door to Buddy's apartment, then grunted in relief when he didn't answer. Pushing the door open with her hip, she stepped into the room, then blinked in amazement when she saw her birdcage, nicely cleaned, standing in the corner.

Coming closer, she peered into the empty depths of the huge cage. "What in the world?" She glanced around the apartment, but saw nothing out of order. Buddy's bed was an unmade mess, as usual, and the fire in the woodstove had been banked to a low glow through the tempered glass. His bureau stood as cluttered as always, with half the drawers cockeyed, and decorated with a pair of underwear and two socks hanging over the rim of an open drawer.

Why in the world would Buddy want to put her bird-cage in his room? Was he missing her parakeet? He'd never paid it much attention, except, of course, for the time she asked him to clean the cage and he left the door open. Two hours later the bird had vanished, and then they found him, the victim of an attempted dive into the goldfish bowl . . .

Surely Buddy wasn't feeling guilty about that. The parakeet was ancient history, so what was he thinking about now?

Her mind drifted back to an arts-and-crafts show she and Buddy had visited in the fall. A dealer from Wells had specialized in old birdcages filled with arrangements of silk flowers and driftwood. So maybe Buddy was feeling artis-tic . . . maybe even noodling on the idea of making some-thing for her. The idea brought a small niggling of pleasure, but it still seemed incredible. If he'd wanted to make some-thing, he could have kept it in the workroom . . . unless he didn't want to get in Mike's and Yakov's way.

She scratched her head, then shrugged and reached outside the door to bring in her utility-sized garbage bag. Buddy was an enigma, and even though the same blood flowed in their veins, she had never been able to figure him out. She had never understood why he joined the Navy when he got seasick in the bathtub, nor had she been able to comprehend why he'd found it necessary to tattoo him-self. No one else in their family had a tattoo, yet Buddy sported three of them, two on his right arm and one on his left. Dana knew the preacher cringed every time Buddy helped pass the offering plate in short sleeves. All those tattoos somehow seemed out of place in church.

She dumped Buddy's trash can into the garbage bag, then bent to pick up a crumpled sheet of paper that had obviously missed the mark. She held it for a moment, thinking of the birdcage, then sat on the bed and smoothed out the wrinkles. In Buddy's distinctive blocky handwriting she read:

> My joy cannot be contained in words or song or
>   expression—
> Letters, juxtaposed puzzles, are rife with discretion,
> But boundless joy, the rarest fruit of my heart,
> Is far more an elixir of life than mere art.
> Two black velvet eyes, a tip-tilted gaze
> Have launched me round this sphere in a daze.
> My heart doth pound in rapturous beat,
> Because your love makes my poor life complete.

She lowered the page, her thoughts racing in a thousand different directions. Buddy . . . was in love! But with whom? He couldn't be in love with anyone on the island; everyone here was married, too old for him, or distinctly not interested. And this wasn't the poem of a man suffering from unrequited love . . . this man had hope! That could only mean he had written this for someone he'd met recently.

She pressed her hand to her lips, trying to remember if any eligible single women had visited the island in the last few weeks. Annie Cuvier had come for Christmas, but she'd been fixated on the doctor's son throughout her visit. Besides, Annie was too brainy for Buddy—he had depths to his personality, but few people took the time to explore them. Most people assumed he was as dull as he was slow to speak, but Buddy had always had a gift for the written word, like their father, so if he'd been writing someone . . .

She snapped her fingers as a memory surfaced. Last night Buddy had been writing some woman on the computer! He'd been pretty intense about it, too, and at least a couple of messages had zipped back and forth in the short time Dana was calling Buddy to dinner.

She pressed both hands to her face, then laughed aloud. Buddy had found a girl through the Internet!

Mike would be glad to hear it—unless, of course, Buddy decided to marry and bring his wife to live in the cramped carriage house. But that wasn't likely to happen. No self-respecting woman would agree to that; she'd want Buddy to live in her town and be married in her church . . .

Dana smoothed the page and read the words again. Not a bad poem, actually, though apparently Buddy hadn't liked it enough to keep it. He must have written another one to e-mail his female friend . . . so he wouldn't mind if Dana used this one.

Her thoughts skittered back to the photograph of Basil Caldwell and the announcement of his poetry contest. Why not enter this poem? It wouldn't win, not with all the wannabe Robert Frosts in the Maine woods, but it'd give her an excuse to paper clip a little note to Basil on the entry form. She'd write something cheery—"Saw your picture, you look good, stay in touch!" If she sent in a poem, he'd have to acknowledge her entry, wouldn't he? So he just might drop her a little note in return, and from his message she'd be able to tell if he remembered her at all.

Humming in anticipation, Dana folded Buddy's poem, slipped it into her jeans pocket, and then dragged the trash bag back outside.

⟡

With a bag filled with mailing tubes slung over his shoulder, Mike approached the ferry landing shortly after noon, then stared when he saw his brother-in-law seated on the bench.

"Hey, Buddy," he called, dropping the heavy bag to the dock. "You going to Ogunquit?"

Buddy glanced at Mike for a moment, then returned his gaze to the watery horizon. "No."

Mike quirked a brow, but apparently Buddy didn't want to embroider his response. That was his way. He rarely said more than twenty words at a time to anyone but Dana.

Sinking to the opposite end of the bench, Mike slipped his hands into his pockets and turned his face toward the sun. "Can't believe this weather we're having. Feels more like October than January."

Silence from Buddy, then, "Whatever."

Mike pressed on. "Yakov and I had a dozen auctions close yesterday. Someone paid eighty-five dollars for a sixteen-by-twenty canvas print of Van Gogh's *Starry Night*."

One of Buddy's shoulders rose in a shrug.

"And I sold thirty-five of those eight-by-ten canvases, each for at least twenty bucks. Can you believe it? I think they cost me about a dollar each. Of course they cost the

printer about fifty cents, so it's not like we're ripping anybody off—"

"What about Van Gogh?"

"Huh?"

"Aren't you ripping him off?"

Mike blinked at the unexpected question. "Well . . .
he's dead, Buddy. Been gone a long time, so I don't expect
he cares much about royalties."

They lifted their heads in unison as the gleaming ferryboat appeared on the horizon. Captain Stroble's ship
came forward steadily, her bow slashing through the
wind-whipped waves. Mike felt his pulse quicken as it
always did when the ferryboat drew near. A body never
knew what surprises it would bring, for Captain Stroble
brought the mail, packages from various shipping compa-
nies, and visitors, of course, though off-islanders were rare
in January.

Grabbing the strap of his canvas bag, Mike stood and
waved at the ferry. Five minutes later, the boat pulled up to
the dock. Captain Stroble's deck hand threw out a bowline
as thick as Mike's wrist. Catching it, he slipped the end of
it around a mooring cleat, then walked down the dock and
grinned at the captain.

"Good afternoon to you, sir! I've got a bag of mail for
you."

Captain Stroble, his tanned face flushed, thrust his
head out of the cabin and grinned at Mike over his beard.
"How be you, Mike? I'll be happy to take your mail, as
long as it has Miss Bea's stamp of approval."

"Miss Bea's already put postage on all these." Mike
swung the canvas bag over the narrow space between the

boat and the dock. "I thought I'd spare her the trouble of hauling all my mail down here."

"And that's right thoughtful of you." Stroble caught the bag, then nodded toward Buddy, still sitting on the bench. "What's your brother-in-law up to?"

Mike gave the captain a one-sided smile. "I have no idea. But if he's got to do nothing, I suppose this is as good a place as any to do it."

Stroble lowered his voice. "I hate to say it, Mike, but he looks a little squamish."

Mike leaned closer. "He's not sick; Dana thinks he's in love. She says he met a girl on the Internet."

One of the captain's bushy white brows shot up. "Really? I wouldn't know much about such things. I have a computer, but I try to stay out of those chat rooms."

"You have a computer?" Mike tilted his head. "I never would have thought you were the computer type."

"Ayuh." Stroble stepped into the cabin and came out with a tray of mail, which he handed to Mike. "I love my machine. I use it to e-mail all the grandkids, and they send me pictures taken with one of those new digitized cameras. Plus, Mazie and I used the Web to find the perfect hotel for our Florida vacation." He winked. "We leave the first week of February."

Mike set the tray on the dock, then turned to accept another load of whatever the captain had to offer. "I'm selling quite a bit in my eBay business."

"That's obvious. I've never seen so much mail from you folks."

"But it's so frustrating sometimes! We have to use a phone connection, and I'm always getting bumped off.

Either Dana will pick up the extension and mess things up, or sometimes I get bumped off for no reason at all—at least, no reason I can figure. And it takes forever to upload the digital pictures of my art prints."

"I used to think pictures took a long time too." Stroble handed Mike another mail tray, this one only half-full. "But then Mazie signed us up to get one of those cable modems. It's amazing. In two minutes I can download stuff that used to take two hours on the phone line."

Mike nearly dropped the mail into the drink.

"Careful there," Stroble admonished. "People tend to get a little upset when their mail is waterlogged."

"A cable modem? Ogunquit has cable modems?"

Stroble nodded. "Came in about three months ago, I guess. Anyone with television cable can get them."

Mike felt his heart sink. While Heavenly Daze had been able to get quite a few modern conveniences, the island still had no cars, no fast-food restaurants, and no cable. The Lansdowns had a satellite dish, but he and Dana didn't have that luxury.

"Man," he moaned. "I'd give anything for a cable connection. Dana's always griping that the computer takes up too much of my time, but if I had cable, I could cut my online time in half."

Stroble paused. "Hmm . . . I hate to suggest this. Might be taken as a bit presumptuous."

"Go ahead."

"Well, my granddaughter just moved into the old Miller place on Shore Road. She's got a cable connection. And she's having a little trouble making ends meet, having just bought the house and all, so she might be willing to sorta rent her computer if you wanted to use it for a couple of hours each morning while she's at work."

"Really?" Mike grinned. "Why, that'd be perfect! Can I call her?"

"Sure. Gimme a second."

Stroble stepped into the cabin for a minute, then returned with a name and number written on a slip of paper. "Give her a call tonight, after five. She's a nurse, so she sometimes keeps odd hours, but keep calling until you get her. And if she wants to know who you are, just tell her that her grandpa recommended you."

Mike slipped the paper into his pocket. "Thanks, Captain." As he reached for the last box the captain had pulled from the cabin, Buddy suddenly sprang to life.

"That one's mine," he called, leaping over mail trays as he sprinted toward the boat. "It's got my name on it, right?"

Tilting his head, Stroble read the label. "Mr. Buddy Franklin, Main Street, Heavenly Daze."

Mike frowned as he studied the blue and white Federal Express package. Did this have something to do with Buddy's loan? Probably not—the bank had said it'd take at least six weeks to process his application.

"You be careful with that," the captain called as Buddy grabbed the box and turned toward home. "I had to sign for it at the dock, so if whatever you ordered is dead—"

Mike made a face. "Dead?"

The captain looked at him. "Ayuh. The box had one of those live-animal stickers on it."

Mike scratched his head. "Live animals?"

Stroble chuckled. "Who in Florida would be sending your brother-in-law a live animal?"

Mike shrugged. "Beats me."

Unless Buddy had ordered some kind of nonlocal lobster to use in a cooking experiment, he couldn't imagine what the fellow was up to.

≈

Inside his room, Buddy gently peeled away the tape on the package, then lifted the cardboard flaps. Inside he found a smaller ventilated box. The sound of soft scratchings made Buddy's heart rate increase.

He lifted out the inner box and held it up to the light. Through a mesh screen he saw his sugar glider—a smallish creature about the size of a squirrel, but with a thinner tail, a boldly painted face, and huge dark eyes.

"Hi, guy," Buddy whispered. "Welcome home."

And then . . . the animal barked. Buddy gaped in astonishment, then grinned. Carefully lowering the box to his bed, he rummaged among the torn paper and found a bag of food, a book, and a note.

Hi, Buddy:

I have sent you a female joey, twelve weeks old and ready for training. I think you and this little girl will get along very well.

The Ziploc bag in this box contains food for your joey—she will need a diet of at least 25 percent protein, and this food is a perfectly balanced mixture. If you like, you can catch grasshoppers and other bugs for your glider; bugs are high in protein, as are mealworms, crickets, and eggs. Your joey will also have a sweet tooth, but that doesn't mean you can give her candy! You can give her sugar cubes, pecans, and a tiny dish of apple-sauce occasionally. They also like monkey biscuits; I feed my gliders a monkey biscuit every night.

Have fun with your glider! Do not be alarmed by the sounds they make. Gliders make many different sounds, but when they bark they are looking for another glider. Come when she barks, and your pet will soon learn to bark for your attention.

Thank you! E-mail me if you have any questions!

Rozella Jones

Running his hand through the remaining shredded paper, Buddy found the soft pouch Rozella had promised to send. He set it on his bed next to the animal in the box, then piled all the shredded paper on the floor of the birdcage. With the bedding in place, he inserted the wheel he'd bought at the mercantile and hung the water bottle. Then he filled the little glass dish with a small handful of the food and set it on the floor of the cage. He hung the pouch on a bent wire on the wall of the cage, leaving the mouth open so the animal could curl inside. Finally he took the venti-lated box, opened one end, and held it next to the door of the birdcage. By tilting the box and calling in a solicitous tone, Buddy managed to slide his little glider into her new home.

The joey landed amid a pile of torn newspaper, and

then blinked and stared at Buddy with wide eyes. She made another sound—an indescribable noise that reminded Buddy of an electric pencil sharpener—and then hustled to the ceramic bowl, where she proceeded to eat her dinner with dainty paws.

Buddy sat in his only chair and leaned forward, entranced. Propping his elbows on his knees, he rested his chin on his hand and whispered to his new pet. "You need a name, don't you? I've been trying to think of one all day, but I wanted to see you first. Now I think I'll call you Roxy."

Roxy made no reply, but kept nibbling at the little bits of dried fruit and something that looked like cereal. Buddy looked through the box again, hoping Rozella had tossed in one of those monkey biscuits, but there was nothing else. He'd have to ask Elezar if the mercantile could order a box.

Settling down again, Buddy watched the little animal eat and drink and eat some more. He would have been happy to sit there all day, if the door to his apartment hadn't rattled . . .

He sprang to his feet, alarm bells clanging in his brain, then rushed to block the door with his body. Peeking through the opening, he saw Dana on the porch, a bewildered look on her face.

"Whatddya want?" he asked.

"Can I come in? I'd like to ask you about something."

He stepped out into the cold, pulling the door closed behind him. "Let's talk outside. I've got a fire going and don't want to let the heat out."

"That's why you should invite me in."

"Naw—my room's a mess."

"Like that's something unusual." The corner of Dana's mouth drooped, but she wasn't the type to waste words. "Buddy," she lowered her gaze, "you remember how Dad was always writing poems?"

He nodded, wondering where this conversation was headed. Their father had died when they were teenagers, so she was digging up ancient history. "Ayuh. I guess I remember."

"Well, I'm no good with words, no good at all. And it seems a shame to waste Dad's talent, don't you think?"

Buddy nodded again, then leaned against the door frame, just in case she decided to make a dash for the door.

"Buddy," she pulled a crumpled sheet of yellow paper from the pocket of her jeans, "I found this while I was emptying your trash."

His racing thoughts came to a dead halt. She held his poem, the one he'd written while thinking about Roxy.

"I think it's a good poem, Buddy, and it shouldn't be wasted. So I was thinking maybe I could send it to this guy I knew in high school. He's having a poetry contest, and while I can't promise you'll win, I'm sure he'd enjoy seeing it. So . . . can I send it? Please?" She looked up at him, her lashes fluttering.

For a moment the question didn't register. Buddy was still mentally reciting the poem, making sure nothing in the verse would give his secret away, and Dana was asking him—what? To let her send the piece into some stick-in-the-mud poetry guy?

"I don't care what you do with it." He waved her away. "It's nothing."

She beamed. "Thanks, Buddy."

"And sis?"

"Ayuh?"

"Don't empty my trash anymore. I'll do it myself. You shouldn't have to come in here at all."

For a moment surprise blossomed on her face, then she sent him a smile of pure sunshine. "I always knew you'd grow up and start taking responsibility." She reached out to pat his cheek. "Alst I can say is, may God bless her."

His heart skipped in a double beat. "Her who?"

"Don't worry—your secret is safe with me." Again with the cheek patting. "As long as you treat this young lady with respect, you'll get no complaints from me."

As Buddy's thoughts roiled in confusion, Dana leaned closer. "By the way, where does she live?"

"She?"

"Don't be coy with me, Buddy. I know you were e-mailing a girl the other night."

Understanding dawned. "Oh, Rozella. She lives in Florida."

Dana nodded. "Nice place. Maybe you'll get lucky and she'll invite you down for a visit soon. Florida sunshine sounds a boatload better than the State of Maine in February, doesn't it?"

While Buddy mutely agreed, Dana turned and took three steps, then spun on the ball of her tennis-shoed foot. "By the way, are you going to let me cook that lobster?"

He stared. "What lobster?"

"The one you got from Fed Ex today. Mike said he thought you must have ordered a Florida lobster or something, maybe to experiment a little for the restaurant?"

"Oh . . . no." He lifted his hand and waved it toward the sea. "You can't cook it. It's gone."

"Buddy Franklin, you old softie." She spoke in a tone of great disappointment, but still she smiled. "What, was it too small for you? Well, I hope it enjoys its freedom before Russell catches it in one of his traps."

Leaving Buddy alone and bewildered, Dana turned and walked back into the house, his poem fluttering in her hand.

From the path on the other side of the carriage house, Yakov halted when he heard voices. Leaning against the building, he closed his eyes and listened to the conversation between Dana and Buddy. When he heard the crunch of Dana's retreating footsteps, he slid down the wall and folded his hands in meditation.

Change was afoot in the Klackenbush household, bringing the inevitable tension, and he hadn't yet been able to put his finger on the source of the trouble. Since Christmas Dana had often seemed moody and depressed, and Mike was far too wrapped up in his Internet business to notice. Yakov tried to help with the business as much as he could, but the more they accomplished, the more Mike wanted to expand. And Buddy . . . Yakov didn't know if Buddy was capable of feeling tension, but lately the young man had definitely been more alert than usual.

Ayuh, something was stirring in the Klackenbush home, and he wanted to be prepared to minister through it.

He made a mental note to ask Gavriel for advice at the next angel meeting.

⤺

Dana leaned against the door frame of the dining room, where Mike's business papers and computer now occupied most of the table. "Mike," she said, noticing the way the monitor gently lit his handsome face, "the weather's beautiful. You want to go over to Ogunquit and take in a movie? If there's nothing good playing there we could go over to the Cineplex in Wells, spend the night in one of those little inns, and come back in the morning . . ."

Mike didn't even look up. "Sorry, hon, but I've got thirty e-mails to answer before I can think about relaxing."

Dana lingered a moment more, then back stepped away from the door. Mike didn't seem to want to do anything these days, and it was all the Internet's fault! Whoever invented the thing ought to be chained to a chair and flogged with computer cords.

Moving to the kitchen, she poured herself a cup of coffee, then pulled out the copy of Buddy's poem. After gathering an envelope, paper, and a pen from her bill-paying drawer, she settled at the table and began to recopy the poem in her own handwriting. As Basil's magazine photograph watched approvingly, she tasted the words on her tongue and found that she liked the verse better each time she read it.

When she had finished copying the poem, she pulled out a sheet of her finest stationery and wrote "Dear Basil" in the most casual script she could manage with a pounding pulse.

Hello! I don't know if you'll remember me, but we went to Wells High School together. I'm now owner/manager of the Kennebunk Kid Kare Center on Heavenly Daze. I enjoy my work very much.

It was good to see your picture in *Northeastern Living* magazine. I've enclosed a poem for your contest—not because I think it will win, but because I just wanted to share it.

Hope you're doing well!

Best,

Dana (Franklin) Klackenbush

Dana paused before folding the pages. She hadn't mentioned anything about Mike, but did she have to mention her husband in every single conversation? Of course not! She wasn't trying to start something with Basil Caldwell; she only wanted to say hello. And that's all she had said, nothing more and nothing less.

"It's only a friendly letter and a poem," she muttered, folding the two pages together. "If Basil likes it, maybe I can encourage Buddy to pursue poetry instead of that ridiculous Lobsters R Us idea. Besides, if he's going to get serious about this girl in Florida, he'll have to get serious about making a living, too."

She addressed the letter, affixed a stamp, then propped it against the salt and pepper shakers in the center of the table. Tomorrow she'd walk it down to Bea's post office and then . . . probably nothing would happen.

Nothing at all.

Yakov came in from the workroom and stomped his boots on the doormat as she finished cleaning her kitchen. "All done out there?" she asked, pouring the rest of the coffee into the sink.

"A full day's work, no doubt," Yakov answered, rubbing his hands in the warmth of the room. Dana felt a twinge of guilt at the sight—the only heat in the workroom came through the vents in the particleboard wall separating the workspace from Buddy's apartment. He had a freestanding woodstove, but he rarely lit a fire during the day. No wonder Yakov's cheeks were red with cold.

"You want some hot cocoa?" she offered, moving to the cupboard. "I could fix some in a jiffy. You look a little frozen."

"I am fine," Yakov answered, walking toward the stairs. "But many thanks for the kind offer."

Dana felt a twinge of envy as she watched him take the back stairs up to his room. Why could some people be content living simple lives while others had to constantly be and do? Though he was close to the other Smith men on the island, Yakov apparently had no family. And while he was an invaluable help to her and Mike, he never seemed to need anything. She fed him and housed him, yet she had the distinct feeling that if she ever forgot to give him his breakfast or lunch, he'd keep right on working, never asking or reminding her of what he lacked.

Did his heart ever yearn for something more, some . . . connectedness? She used to feel connected to Mike, but now the computer had come between them. As a child, she had been close to Buddy, but now he seemed a million miles away.

Feeling irritable and listless, Dana wiped her hands on a dishtowel, and then carried her thoughts upstairs to bed.

Chapter Seven

"The first thing you need to know about gliders," Buddy read aloud the next morning, "is that they are susceptible to chills, which may lead to pneumonia, so you must keep them warm. The ideal temperature for young joeys is around ninety degrees Fahrenheit. At night, you may wish to put a heating pad into the cage, but keep it set on low. Make sure it doesn't cover the entire floor, so your glider can escape the heat if the temperature gets too high. You don't want to cook your new pet!"

Buddy glanced over at the cage. Just as Rozella had predicted, Roxy had crawled into the hanging pouch. Was she warm enough? He didn't have a heating pad, and on Heavenly Daze it would be hard to heat any room to ninety degrees in January.

Dropping the book, Buddy glanced over at his woodstove. The remaining stumps of last night's logs glowed softly through the tempered glass window, and he usually left the fire alone in the daytime. But if he was going to keep Roxy warm, he'd have to keep it blazing constantly. A constant fire would require more wood from the woodpile, and Dana would be sure to notice if he took much more than usual. She had bought two cords of wood back in October, figuring that amount would see them through the winter. She and Mike had a furnace in the big house, of course, but she liked to build a fire at night when they relaxed in their bedroom. The carriage house woodstove, however, was

Buddy's only source of heat . . . and now it was Roxy's, as well.

Buddy chewed on the inside of his lip, thinking. He'd have to slip out and collect some driftwood to augment his stores. A log here and there would help, and maybe Dana wouldn't notice that her firewood was disappearing at twice the usual rate. He'd look for bugs, too, but the cold weather of December had probably cleared the island of any creepy-crawlies a glider would enjoy.

"Hey, Roxy." Leaning forward, he tapped the wire of the cage. "You awake in there?"

A soft chattering sound answered his call, and Buddy sat back in his chair, pleased. The little critter had learned to recognize his voice, and though she'd kept him awake half the night with her barking and chittering, they were bonding.

"I'm gonna go get some wood," he said, pushing himself up. "You sleep tight in there, and I'll soon have this room nice and toasty."

The little pouch swung gently, and though he couldn't see through the soft material, Buddy could almost imagine that Roxy had lifted a delicate paw and waved him out the door.

≈

Dana dropped her copy of the morning newspaper as Mike entered the kitchen dressed in dark jeans, a flannel shirt, and his nicest down jacket. The outfit was some different from the tattered sweatshirt and sweatpants he usually wore to work at the computer.

She lifted a brow. "Going somewhere?"

Mike moved to the coffeepot without looking at her. "Thought I'd go over to Ogunquit—Russell said he'd drop me over there when he heads out this morning."

Dana glanced at the clock—nine o'clock. With the ferry's restricted winter schedule, if Mike didn't return on the noon ferry she wouldn't see him until six-thirty, well past dark.

She swallowed the sudden rise of anxiety in her throat. "Will you be back for lunch?"

"Should be. Do you need anything from town?"

Dana shook her head.

"OK, then." Mike brought his steaming coffee mug to the table, dropped in two teaspoonfuls of sugar, then paused to kiss the top of her head. "Catch you later. If I don't make the noon ferry, I'll try to hitch a ride with another boat."

She gulped as he left the kitchen, then she leaned sideways to peer around the wall and watch him in the hallway. He paused at the door, picked up a bulging manila folder, then stepped out into the cold.

Groaning, Dana straightened in her chair and lifted her coffee mug. Some bit of mischief was afoot, had to be, and folks said the wife was always the last to know. Last night she'd come downstairs and paused outside the dining room while Mike was supposed to be working on his auctions, but he wasn't on the computer. He was on the phone, speaking in low tones, and employing that self-conscious, hyperpolite voice he always used when he talked to a woman. He had laughed softly, and she'd caught the words, "I'm Mike," and "tomorrow morning?"

Then he had murmured several things she didn't catch before he closed with, "Thanks so much. Can't wait till tomorrow."

Now the pieces settled into place with an almost-audible click. Like Buddy, Mike had met someone on the Internet. Except Mike's someone lived nearby, maybe even in Ogunquit, and he was on his way to meet her.

Pushing back from the table, Dana ran to the front door and threw it open, then stepped out onto the porch. Mike was already at the dock, greeting Russell Higgs as his dory bobbed next to the dock. The *Barbara Jean* was anchored at a distance, out of the ferry's way.

"Mike!" she called, but the rising wind snatched her words and carried them in the opposite direction. She thought about running to the dock after him, but what would that do, besides give her neighbors something to gossip about? If he wanted to go meet some woman in Ogunquit . . .

She took a deep breath and forced herself to calm down. Maybe this was innocent, harmless. After all, she knew her husband, and Mike was as constant and faithful as a flowing river . . . but sometimes rivers dried up.

Closing her eyes to trap the sudden rush of tears, Dana turned and walked back into the house. Yakov was standing in the kitchen when she returned, so she moved woodenly past him toward the laundry room, not wanting him to see her quivering chin.

"Shalom aleichem," he called cheerily.

Unable to speak, Dana waved at him over her shoulder, then closed the laundry-room door. Pulling a load of dirty clothes from the hamper, she dropped them at her feet, then reached for one of Mike's dark T-shirts and used it to blow her nose.

Served him right.

She stuffed the shirt into the washer, then picked up his jeans. "What's wrong with me?" she whispered, bewildered by the currents of jealousy and fear raging through her. Mike had been working too hard, true, but he'd never given her any reason to think he was interested in another woman. How could he have time for an affair? He scarcely made time for his wife!

Then, searching for stray change, she thrust her hand into his jeans pocket and pulled out a slip of paper bearing a name and number: Jodi Standish, 555-4983, 321 Shore Road.

Shore Road was in Ogunquit. Jodi, spelled with an *i,* was a woman's name.

Weeping in earnest now, Dana sank into the pile of dirty laundry and watered it with her tears.

～

In the mercantile, Vernie rose from a crouch, her knees protesting. She turned to Elezar. "It's driving me nuts. Why in the world did Olympia need five cans of black olives? Is she having a party? She hasn't said anything, and I haven't gotten an invitation—"

"Vernie," Elezar said, his voice patient and calm. "Caleb hasn't mentioned a party, and I'm sure he would have if that were the case."

"Then why in the world would an older woman need five cans of black olives? They're not rich in hormones, for heaven's sake."

Elezar shook his head. "Maybe she just doesn't want to run out of black olives. If I may remind you, you ran out of nutmeg last month. Perhaps Olympia has learned the value of stockpiling."

Vernie made a face. "Is there an olive shortage?"

At that moment the bell above the door jangled. Vernie shifted her attention to her new customer, and grinned as Floyd approached.

"Floyd, you know anything about black olives?"

"Naw, can't say I do. They give me heartburn." He shucked off his gloves and dropped them on the counter. "Been over to the parsonage, even though I'm feelin' a mite queasy. That place looks like a bomb hit it."

Vernie leaned forward. "Do tell!"

Floyd chuckled. "Well, the bathroom's destroyed, but you knew that. And it seems that the boys tried to replaster the hole in the wall, and they tracked plaster dust all through Edith's parlor and dining room. Then they dripped wet plaster—they got the mix a little too runny, to my way of thinkin'—and it ran down into the baseboards. Then one of those geniuses poured the runny mix into the sink, thinkin' Edith wouldn't notice, and it done set up and blocked all their pipes. Now they don't even have sink water. Edith is fit to be tied; she's sleepin' in the guest bedroom. And those baseboards are stuck to the wall tighter than a tongue to a frozen pump handle, and those guys are still feeling sick, to boot! They run in there just long enough to mess something up worse, then they have to trot over to our place for an emergency bathroom run—"

"Sounds like you could use some prayer," Elezar offered.

"Ayuh, 'cause it'll take a gall-durned miracle to get that place back in operation. Cleta says I should just take over, but—" he winked at Vernie, "it's been too much fun watching 'em tear things up."

"Floyd," Vernie scolded. "That's not very Christian. Those people are hurtin'."

Floyd giggled. "Ain't it the truth?"

All three heads turned as the doorbells jangled again. Buddy Franklin came through the doorway and stood, staring at all three of them with an open mouth.

The silence lengthened.

"Mornin', Buddy," Vernie said. "Something I can do for you?"

Buddy cleared his throat. "I'll just browse for a minute."

Vernie rolled her eyes. Under her breath, she muttered, "Watch him—he's going to go back there and read all those Superman comics before Georgie gets a shot at 'em."

Elezar jerked his head toward the back of the room. "I'll go see if I can help him."

Vernie and Floyd chatted about the amazing weather for a minute, then Elezar reappeared with Buddy in tow.

"Um," the corner of Elezar's mouth twitched, a sure sign he was trying not to laugh. "Buddy has an unusual request. He asked me to order them, but I told him you placed all the orders."

Vernie looked straight at Buddy. "What can I do ya for, Buddy?"

The lanky young man scratched at his neck. "Um, I need a box."

"A box of what?"

"Biscuits."

"Biscuits? They come in a can. Unless you want Bisquick, which comes in a box—"

His face brightened. "Do monkeys eat it?"

Vernie looked at Floyd. "Well, that's a matter of opinion. But I'm guessin' they don't." She turned back to Buddy. "You have a monkey?"

"Nope. But I want monkey biscuits. A box of 'em."

Vernie looked at Elezar. "Smell his breath, please."

Elezar grinned. "He's sober, Vernie."

"I want monkey biscuits." The boy's eyes flashed with the most fire she'd ever seen in them.

"Why," she choked, "do you want monkey biscuits?"

He paused. "I like 'em."

"Do tell!" She gaped at Elezar. "Are you sure they *make* monkey biscuits?"

"I know they do," Buddy replied, pulling himself to his full six feet and something inches. "And I want you to order a box for me. Please."

With that, he turned and walked out of the mercantile, his head held high. Vernie, Floyd, and Elezar stared after him, waiting a full thirty seconds before breaking into hysterical gales of laughter.

Wiping her eyes, Vernie said, "That's the funniest thing I've ever heard."

Elezar caught her wrist. "You are going to order them, aren't you?"

"Why should I?"

"Because it's a legitimate request."

She coughed out another laugh, then nodded. "Ayuh.

All right, gentlemen. If you'll excuse me, I'm going to go try and find a monkey bakery."

~

After lunch, Buddy stacked the last of his gathered driftwood against the wall, and then shoved another log into the firebox. The driftwood, bleached dry by the sun and wind, burned hot and bright, and heat poured from the woodstove. Roxy had awakened from her nap, and now her chocolate-brown eyes peered above the rim of the pouch, watching him.

"Good afternoon," Buddy called, shrugging out of his flannel shirt as perspiration beaded on his forehead. "Did you have a nice nap?"

The little animal rose up further, then propped her dainty hands on the edge of her pouch, delighting Buddy. Moving slowly so he wouldn't frighten her, Buddy reached into the cage and unhooked the string, then lifted it out. Roxy retreated into the bag as it swung through the air, but she didn't protest when he slipped the long string around his neck and let the pouch dangle before his chest.

Wearing the pouch like a necklace, he moved to the mirror propped on his dresser. "Look there," he said, pointing to the mirror. "You and me, Roxy. What a team we make."

And lo and behold if the little creature didn't pop up to look, and seem fascinated by its reflection. Roxy's catlike ears twitched toward the mirror, and her black eyes widened in what looked like surprise. Buddy watched, grinning, until the animal looked away, then he gingerly walked to his bed and stretched out, letting the small bag settle against his chest.

For the next hour, as Roxy gained the courage to venture out of her fabric nest and pad around on his undershirt-clad chest, Buddy folded his hands behind his head and sang all the sea songs he could recall from his childhood and Navy days.

~

Back in the house, Dana went about her housekeeping and vacillated between hope and despair. Ayuh, Mike was seeing another woman; no, there had to be a good reason for his odd visit to Ogunquit.

Then an idea struck her.

Moving into the computer room, she picked up the telephone extension on the dining room table. She'd never been tempted to spy on her husband, but Babette Graham had once taught her a little trick that might come in handy now. By punching in a certain code, Babette had said, you could make your phone redial the last number that had been dialed on that particular extension.

Dana picked up the slim receiver and stared at it. Never before had a phone felt like an instrument of betrayal. After all, she didn't know that Mike had called this Jodi person. Maybe he hadn't. Maybe that slip of paper with her number was left over from some old job or something. Maybe Jodi Standish was a little old lady who needed her house painted. Dana didn't know that he'd been talking to Jodi last night while he was whispering in this room, but there was one way to know for certain . . .

She punched in the three-digit code, then held the

receiver to her ear. The phone rang once, twice, three times, and no one picked up. Then an answering machine came on the line: "Hi, this is Jodi, and I can't come to the phone." She giggled. "You know what to do. Beep, you're on."

Dana hung up before the phone could beep.

Mike had called this Jodi person, who didn't sound at all like a grandmother. She didn't even sound married. She sounded young and beautiful and flirtatious.

No wonder Mike had been whispering.

~

A long, cold twilight with frost in its breath had begun to envelop the island before Yakov's curiosity got the best of him. He'd been packaging art prints in the workroom for several hours, and through the thin wall and heating vents he'd heard Buddy giggling, singing, and crooning in a low voice.

Yakov feared for the man's sanity.

After slapping on the last mailing label, he pulled on his coat, stepped out of the workroom, and walked around to the door of Buddy's apartment. He knocked, then heard a muffled, "Just a minute." A full three minutes later, Buddy stepped out onto the stoop and closed the door behind him.

Yakov dropped his jaw. The thermometer on the back porch read twenty degrees, but Dana's brother wore cutoff denim shorts, a sweaty tank top, and absolutely nothing else. Yakov's gaze fell. Buddy Franklin had hairy legs, as hairy as Esau's. Who'd have guessed?

He blinked. Angels weren't often surprised by the sons of men, but this—

He lifted his gaze to meet Buddy's. "It is twenty degrees."

"Ayuh." Buddy wiped a film of sweat from his brow, then jerked his thumb toward the door. "It's about ninety in there."

"Why?" Yakov tried to peer into the apartment, but Buddy blocked the window with his lanky body.

Buddy shivered suddenly. "I, um, did it for you, man. Dana said you were freezing in the workroom, since there's no heat. Well—you were warm today, weren't you?"

Yakov nodded. He had been warmer than usual, but he'd been so distracted by the sounds coming from Buddy's apartment he barely noticed.

"So . . . that's all right, huh?" Buddy grinned, then ran his hands over his noodlelike arms. "Gotta go. It's cold out here with nothin' on."

Yakov lifted his hand to protest, but Buddy opened the door. He would have slipped back into his apartment without another word, but Yakov planted one of his boots in the opening. Sometimes a guardian angel had to exercise a little force on behalf of his charge . . .

"Buddy, you do not have to roast yourself on my account," he said, insinuating his shoulder into the narrow space. "When it is cold outside, the prudent thing to do is put clothes on. That's why I dress warmly for the workroom."

"Now you won't have to wear so many clothes," Buddy said, maintaining a steady pressure on the door. "Don't see how you can paste labels wearing gloves, anyhow."

Yakov didn't budge. "Buddy," he insisted, squeezing

his face into the crack between the wall and the door, "I have been concerned about you all day—"

That's when the bed moved. Not the bed exactly, Yakov saw when he focused his gaze, but a small brown pouch on the bed. It looked like the sort of bag a boy carried marbles in, but this pouch was writhing as if it contained something alive—

"Oy!" With the barest touch of supernatural strength, Yakov shoved the door away, then stepped into the room and slid into a squat beside the bed. He fingered his chin and stared at the squirming fabric bag. "Buddy, what have you got there?"

Suddenly belligerent, Buddy slammed the door. "I got a pet," he said, crossing his arms. "But don't tell Dana, 'cause she said I couldn't have one. But that's not fair, because she has that mangy bulldog."

Yakov tilted his head. "You think I should tell Dana about a thing like this . . . thing?" He rubbed his hand over his stubbled chin, then pointed to the bed. "What is that, anyway?"

Buddy relaxed, his arms drooping to his side. "You promise you won't tell?"

"It is not my place to tell about such a thing. You are a grown man, and responsible for your own actions."

"That's what I keep saying."

"If you want to tell Dana, that would be a good thing, but it will have to be your choice."

"I don't know if it's a good thing, but ayuh, it's my decision. I'll tell when and if I'm good and ready."

"So." Yakov stared at the pouch. "Are you going to tell me, or shall we play twenty questions?"

"It's Roxy."

Yakov shook his head. "In all of creation, I've never heard of a roxy."

"That's her name. She's a sugar glider."

Yakov frowned. "The little marsupial native to Australia?"

"You've heard of them?"

"I am familiar with all the Lord's creations. But a sugar glider—here? In winter?"

"I know." Buddy's face fell. "The lady who sold her to me didn't know I live in an igloo."

"This is not exactly an igloo." Yakov spread his hands, indicating the space around them. "But you will have to keep the fire blazing. I do not think your Roxy will handle the cold very well."

"She's young, too—only twelve weeks."

"Then it is doubly important that she be kept warm." Yakov glanced at the pile of driftwood against the wall. "You are planning to clear the beaches?"

"I can't use too much of Mike and Dana's firewood. They'd know something was up."

"Better not let Dana catch you in your cabana wear, then." Yakov stood, and as he did the animal thrust her pointy face out of the pouch. In spite of his misgivings, he smiled. "She is cute, Buddy. One of the Lord's most adorable creations."

"You promise you won't tell Dana or Mike?"

"I will leave that for you, Buddy . . . when you find the chutzpa." He placed his hand on the doorknob, then turned and winked at his young charge. "And tomorrow, I will wear something sleeveless to work."

Chapter Eight

$\mathcal{A}$fter nearly twenty-four hours of intermittent weeping, Dana pulled herself off her bed, washed her face, and steeled herself for a confrontation with her husband. She'd been too distraught to accuse him yesterday, and he hadn't given her a chance. After coming back from Ogunquit on the late ferry (and not keeping his promise about coming home for lunch), he'd gone straight out to the workroom to check on his shipments, then come up to their bedroom, where she lay quietly sniffling beneath the blankets. Mike hadn't noticed her emotional condition or, if he had, he'd chosen to attribute it to PMS. In any case, he'd gone straight to sleep.

This morning he rose before her and headed off to Ogunquit again. But this time when he came home, Dana was determined to ask him what terribly fascinating thing he had discovered in Ogunquit . . . and on Shore Road in particular. If, in fact, Jodi Standish's house was where he'd been headed.

Going downstairs to the kitchen, she pulled a defrosted chicken from the refrigerator and tossed it in her largest pot, then covered it halfway with water. Cooking gave her something to do, and for the moment, at least, she was grateful for something else to think about. She had no appetite, but Buddy and Yakov deserved a good dinner.

Setting the pot on the stove to simmer, she sprinkled salt and pepper over the chicken, then covered the pot with a lid. While the burner ticked as it began to heat, she lowered herself to a chair at the table and rested her head on her palm.

After only twenty-eight short years, her life was over. Her adoring husband no longer loved her. They hadn't even made it to the seven-year itch; they'd barely lasted thirty-six months. But she couldn't deny the proof written on a certain slip of paper, or the unwavering doubt that gnawed at her gut . . .

The phone rang, interrupting her thoughts. Fearing that something had happened to Mike, Dana leaped to answer it. "Hello?"

"Dana? Dana Franklin?"

"Yes?"

"Basil Caldwell here. I received your poem."

Dana clutched at the back of a chair as the kitchen began to spin. "Basil . . . my poem? But I only mailed it yesterday!"

"And I just opened it. It's wonderful, truly. First I was delighted to hear from you, then when I read your exceptional submission—well, I was astounded. I never knew you'd been touched by the muse."

Dana twirled a lock of hair around her finger. "I haven't been, not really—wait, you were delighted to hear from me? You remember me?"

"How could I forget that cute little blonde girl who used to sit on the front row of the bleachers at our basketball games? I'll bet you haven't changed much, either."

Dana laughed. "Oh, I've changed a little, thank goodness."

"I can't wait to see you."

Dana froze, her hand twisted in her hair. Basil

Caldwell wanted to see her? "I'm sorry, we must have a bad connection—it happens sometimes on the island. What did you say?"

"I said I can't wait to see you. I'd like to have lunch, if possible, and discuss the publication of your poem. I'll drive up from Boston, of course, but am I correct in assuming Heavenly Daze is pretty much closed down now?"

She blinked. "It's the off-season."

"Then how about meeting me in Ogunquit . . . say, next Thursday? I was thinking we could have lunch at that nice seafood restaurant down by Perkins Cove. It's the Oarweed, isn't it? I don't want to inconvenience you too much, and I know things are primitive on that God-forsaken island."

Dana cleared her throat. "Um, ayuh, the Oarweed is right across from the landing. I could take the one o'clock ferry and meet you there at half past—"

"Wonderful, let's consider it a date. Of course, I'd like to extend the invitation to a guest, if you'd like to bring someone . . ."

The implication was both tactful and obvious—*if you want to bring your husband or a special friend*—but Dana had never felt less inclined to accept an invitation for her husband. If Mike was going to keep secrets from her, well, she could keep a secret too. Hers was an innocent secret, but Mike deserved to experience a little tit for tat.

"I'm afraid it'll be just me," she said, injecting a false note of regret into her voice. "And I'll look forward to it, Basil."

After hanging up, Dana moved to the stove and lifted the lid on the chicken pot. Guilt bubbled through her conscience as she swirled a wooden spoon through the simmering broth, but she was not going to let guilt stand between her and a pleasant poetic afternoon with Dr. Basil Caldwell.

After all, her trip to Ogunquit would be motivated by love for Buddy. At the Oarweed she'd tell Basil that the brilliant poet he sought was none other than her own introverted brother. It was the only way Buddy would ever be discovered. He would certainly never agree to go meet Basil, but perhaps, with the right amount of persuasion, she could convince Basil to come to Heavenly Daze and encourage Buddy to pursue his gifts. Poetic genius deserved a little special attention.

Blowing out her cheeks, Dana pushed her bangs away from her forehead and lowered the lid on the chicken.

Her confrontation with Mike would have to wait. Like two partners on a seesaw, the addition of her secret had balanced things out. If Mike could teeter in midmarriage with a mystery in his lap, so could she.

≈

Barbara's hand hesitated over the telephone. Should she call Dr. Marc? Maybe her mother would make the call for her. Cleta had always made Barbara's appointments, had always gone with her to the dentist and the pediatrician.

No, she needed to make this call herself. Besides, she had promised Russell.

Barbara quickly dialed Dr. Marc's number. Fortunately, the doctor was in, and said she could come over right away.

She felt her stomach knot as she hung up the phone.

She'd done it, but now what? What if Dr. Marc found something seriously wrong with her? What if the problem couldn't be fixed? How would she tell Russell? How would she tell her mother? Her stomach churned, and for a moment she felt she would be really sick.

Moving like an automaton, she stepped into the shower, then dressed and put gel in her spiky new haircut. After worrying mascara onto her lashes and adding a bit of lipstick for color, she went downstairs. Her mother was in the kitchen, scrubbing a mixing bowl while a pan of oat-meal bread rose on the stove. Cleta turned, her eyes bright and appraising, when Barbara came into the room.

"Are you feeling all right, Doodles?"

"I'm fine, Mom."

"You've spent a lot of time upstairs today." Cleta pressed the backs of her fingers to Barbara's forehead. "You look a little pale."

"I'm fine. I'm going out for a while."

"Going for a walk?" Cleta frowned. "OK, but the weather's breezin' up out there. Be sure and wear your heavy coat. Wait a minute—I'll go with you. I could use some exercise—"

"No, Mom!" Barbara interrupted, then cringed. Gen-tling her tone, she added, "I'll just walk a little way. I need some time to think."

Cleta shot her a pointed glance. "Think about what?"

"Some stuff. You stay here—it looks like your bread is about ready for the oven."

"Hmmm." Cleta turned toward the stove. "I suppose it is."

Barbara breathed a sigh of relief as she escaped the

house. Hoping no one saw her—no one who would report to Cleta, anyway—she cut through the de Cuviers' back-yard and slipped into Dr. Marc's waiting room.

Edmund and Olympia de Cuvier, acting as town benefactors, had donated their carriage house for the establishment of a medical clinic on Heavenly Daze. Dr. Marcus Hayes had come to the island to retire, but kept his medical skills up to par by tending to the town's thirty residents. Barbara had never visited the doctor's office, but she knew Georgie Graham visited the doctor at least once a week.

Now, as she looked around, she was grateful for the small clinic. A large medical center might have intimidated her, but this waiting room was cozy, with a pair of comfortable chairs, a huge silk ficus in the corner, and a pretty painting of the Heavenly Daze lighthouse on the wall.

Despite the pleasant surroundings, fear that the doctor would find something seriously wrong lay like a stone in her stomach. She sat down, glad to be alone in the room . . . and then she heard her father's voice.

"Thanks, Doc. We appreciate you seeing us."

Panicked, Barbara jumped up. Dad couldn't see her here! He'd have all kinds of questions, but they'd be nothing compared to the grilling she'd face if he told Mom about finding her in the doctor's office . . .

Feeling like a frightened child, she hid behind the ficus tree in the corner, hoping the weeping fig's straggly branches would hide her. As she pressed her back against the wall and tried not to breathe, Floyd, Winslow, and Stanley came down a hallway and walked out the door without glancing up. All three of them looked pale and worn.

After the door closed behind Stanley, Barbara squeezed from behind the ficus and slipped into her chair again. A moment later Dr. Marc came out to greet her.

"Barbara! Good to see you. Come on into the office and let's talk a bit."

Dr. Marc's office was all leather and bookshelves, the kind of room where someone could read and think. More silk plants lined the windowsill. Pictures of his son, Alex, and his late wife sat on the corner of his desk, along with an engraved silver pen set. Everything looked perfectly normal and very . . . comfortable.

But she couldn't relax.

"How can I help you, Barbara?"

She twisted the straps of her purse together as a flush of embarrassment heated her cheeks. "I, um . . . Russell and I have been married three years, and we'd like to start a family."

She glanced up and saw that the doctor was sitting with his hands folded beneath his chin, his head tilted to one side as if what she was saying was the most important thing in the world. The knot in her stomach relaxed a little.

Dr. Marc nodded. "Ayuh, Russell and I talked earlier—as I'm sure you know. I imagine you're now concerned there's something physical preventing you from achieving a pregnancy."

Relieved that he knew all the right words, she nodded.

"Well, let's do an exam, then we'll talk again. All right?"

Barbara nodded, more weakly this time.

Dr. Marc stood. "Your first time here, right?"

"Ayuh."

He laughed. "Well, it's nothing fancy, but we get the job done. We only have one exam room, and it's not very imposing. Follow me."

She got up and trailed him back into the hallway, then into another small room with a padded table, sink, mirror, and a chair. Pausing, he lifted a green gown from a shelf and handed it to her. "What a pretty haircut."

"Thank you."

"Put this on, then crack the door when you're ready. I'll be in and we'll see if we can find the problem."

As her hand moved to undo the buttons at her throat, Barbara suddenly wished Cleta were with her. Her mother had always gone with her to the pediatrician, even the time they went to have a splinter removed.

Barbara caught a glimpse of her face in the mirror above the sink. She was as white as the porcelain bowl.

She undressed quickly, wondering if she had done the right thing. Maybe coming here was idiotic. Maybe if she and Russell were patient only a little longer she'd conceive naturally—

No, they had waited long enough. She was doing the right thing.

She slipped on the gown, struggling with the armholes and ties, then modestly pulled the gown closed in front. Holding the edges with one hand, she cracked the door, then perched on the edge of the padded table. She was feeling like a sitting duck when the doctor opened the door again.

"All ready?"

Barbara nodded.

"Okay, let's see what is going on." He smiled as he took Barbara's hand. "Just lean back and relax, everything is going to be fine."

Relax? How could she relax? She was scared of what he might find, and what he might not find. What if there was nothing to be done? What if she couldn't have babies because God didn't want her to have babies? Russell would be so disappointed. But if God didn't want them to have babies, maybe they weren't supposed to have any. Maybe God knew she'd be a terrible mother, so he had done this to spare the kids she might have had if she'd had her own selfish way . . .

From the end of the table, Dr. Marc examined her. In between questions about her health and her cycle, he talked about the weather, Russell's boat, and Tallulah's fondness for sweets. As he worked, he quietly explained what he was doing, then asked about Russell's work. Was it another banner year for lobstermen?

Barbara smiled, understanding. The doctor knew how well the lobster industry was doing. Everyone did. But she appreciated his efforts to put her at ease. His conversation kept her mind off the examination. Somewhat.

He pushed back and snapped off his rubber gloves. "OK, Barbara, we're all finished. After you're dressed, come out to the office and we'll talk a bit."

All of her anxieties came flooding back as she dressed. There was something wrong; she knew it. The doctor would have told her everything was OK if she was fine. He was probably in his office now, looking through medical books for the right word to describe the horrible malformation he'd found inside her.

She closed her eyes, wishing Cleta were with her. Her mother would know the right questions to ask.

Barbara took several deep, cleansing breaths.

No, she didn't need her mother. This was her decision, her life, and she needed to live it. She was acting independently for the second time in her life, and it felt good. At almost twenty-three, it was high time she visited a doctor by herself. Still . . . her mouth went dry at the thought of what Dr. Marc might say.

Though her hands were trembling, she finally managed to get her clothes on straight. Dr. Marc had a file open on his desk when she entered his office.

"Sit down, Barbara."

She sat, her fingers wrapped tightly around her purse. The doctor's gaze focused on her white-knuckle grip, then he smiled. "First, relax. You're in excellent health. Normal blood pressure, your weight is good, and that's a miracle. If I ate Cleta's cooking every day I'd be thirty pounds overweight."

He chuckled, and Barbara tried to smile.

"So—" He clasped his hands. "How do you feel?"

"I feel fine. It's just that—"

"You and Russell want to have children."

"Ayuh."

Dr. Marc leaned forward. "There is a problem."

Barbara's heart stopped. "How—how serious is it?"

"Well, I can't say for sure now. But given your answers to my questions, I suspect you've been suffering from endometriosis, which can cause scarring of the fallopian tubes."

"Is that . . . permanent?" Her voice sounded strange even to her.

"Not necessarily. But I can't make a definitive diagnosis without a laparoscopy, which could be done as an outpatient or in the hospital. I'm going to recommend that we do it in York Hospital. I don't have privileges there, but one of my colleagues, Dr. Phyllis Comeaux, does, and she's a superb surgeon. If endometriosis is confirmed, Dr. Comeaux can go ahead and use microsurgical techniques to remove the adhesions that are blocking your fallopian tubes. After the surgery, you will remain in the hospital four or five days."

Barbara felt her eyes fill with water. "You'll be there with me?

"Every step of the way."

"And after the surgery? Will I have babies?"

His eyes gentled. "I don't want to give you false hope, Barbara. Although you'll feel fine within a few weeks, it may take your pelvic tissues up to a year to become normal enough to produce a pregnancy. If the adhesions are severe, you'll have a 30 percent chance of pregnancy. If they are not severe, your chances will improve."

She looked down as her eyes burned. Thirty percent? The number seemed so small . . .

"Do not despair," he said, with quiet emphasis. "God works miracles every day, and he may work one for you. We may get in there and discover that the scarring is minimal. Given your young age, I suspect we'll find very few adhesions."

The knot of nerves in her stomach loosed and she suddenly felt very weak.

"It's a simple procedure?"

"I promise." He smiled. "It's done every day. And the sooner we do it, the sooner your body will have a chance to heal and prepare for a child."

The idea of surgery, even a simple procedure, scared her spitless. But wasn't knowing something better than worrying about an infinite army of possible problems? And a 30 percent chance was better than 0 percent. Zero percent was what they'd have if she did nothing . . . or chickened out.

She drew a deep breath.

"If you want, I'll schedule the surgery . . . unless you need to talk to Russell first."

Her fright came back in a rush. "Well, OK—no. Maybe I should think about it, talk to Russell. Could I let you know in a few days?"

"Of course. When you feel comfortable with the arrangements, give me a call and I'll schedule the procedure in York."

"All right," she managed to mutter, her tongue feeling oddly detached.

Dr. Marc walked her to the door, then squeezed her shoulder. She barely felt the pressure of his hands, so preoccupied was she with new and whirling thoughts.

≈

An hour later, Barbara paced the dock, walking up and down with her hands behind her back. In the hour since she'd left the doctor's office she had vacillated from wanting to have the surgery to swearing off hospitals forever and urging Russell to think about adoption. After all, what did it matter, really, if a baby came from your own cells? Every baby deserved a happy home, yet thousands of children around the world would never know the love of a mother and father. She and Russell could be parents without having to think about surgery and scars and general anesthesia.

Still . . . the miracle of childbirth was a precious thing. How must it feel to have a life stirring within your womb? To know that the coming child was a combination of you and the man you loved more than life itself . . .

Her heart leaped when the *Barbara Jean* appeared on the horizon. She waited until the boat drew closer, then lifted her hand high over her head and waved, hoping Russell would look out the cabin window and see her. He would be alone now, having dropped his mates at Perkins Cove, and he'd be anxious to hear her report.

Russell steered the boat to the dock, then tossed her a mooring line. She slipped it over a post, then shyly walked forward until he jumped from the deck and wrapped her in his arms.

"Hi, daddy," she whispered in his ear.

He pulled back, his eyes searching her face. "What does that mean?"

"It means," she said, gulping, "that we might be able to have babies if I have surgery. I went to see Dr. Marc."

He hugged her close. "I'm proud of you, honey."

Though he was hugging her so tightly Barbara felt a little strangled, she pressed on. "But something's wrong with me. Endometriosis. That means I'll have to have surgery, and after that it'll take time to recover, and after that there's a possibility we still won't be able to have kids—"

"But there's a chance we will, right?"

She pulled back this time, and looked him evenly in the eye. "Maybe. Maybe not. But it's gonna take time."

He reached out and touched her hair, her cheek. "Babs, we've got time. And we've got love to share. I'll do whatever you want to do about the surgery, but why don't we think about adoption too? Why not raise a family both ways, through adoption and biology?"

Unexpected laughter bubbled up from her throat. "You mean it?"

"Ayuh." His brown eyes caressed her. "I do. I think you'd be a great mom to a dozen kids."

Wordlessly, Barbara reached out and hugged him tight. With a man like this beside her, she could face anything . . . but maybe two or three kids would be more manageable than a dozen.

His hand fell upon her head. "Have you told your mother any of this?"

Barbara shook her head. "I wanted to tell you first."

His smile told her how pleased he was that she'd taken another step toward independence. "Then we'll tell your folks together."

Russell slipped his arm around her shoulder and began to lead her toward the B&B. She matched his stride, step for step. "Mom made meat loaf for dinner."

"Good. Has your dad recovered from his stomach bug?"

"I don't know. He and Pastor Winslow and Stanley

were at Dr. Marc's when I came in. I hope their stomachs have settled down."

Russell laughed, and as they climbed the hill Barbara thought she'd never heard a more beautiful sound.

⌇

Barbara took her seat at the table, then squeezed her husband's hand. Her mother blinked at the sign of tenderness, then her gaze swept the steaming dishes. Apparently convinced all was in order, she took her seat next to Floyd.

"Grace," she reminded him.

Thankfully, Floyd's prayer was short. Cleta looked a little perturbed at her husband's brief blessing, but Barbara sighed in gratitude. The sooner she got this announcement over with, the sooner she could get on with her life.

"How's your stomach, Pop Lansdown?" Russell asked, passing the potatoes.

"Still a mite queasy," Floyd answered. He took a healthy portion of the mashed potatoes, but shook his head when Cleta offered him the meat loaf.

Russell glanced at Barbara, a smile teasing the corners of his mouth. She nervously pleated the napkin in her lap.

Floyd looked at Russell. "How was the catch today?" he asked, gingerly tasting the potatoes.

"All the traps were full. It's been a good week."

"Put some money back against the hard times," Cleta advised, not for the first time.

Russell winked at Barbara. "We are."

Barbara took a deep breath. "Mom, Dad—I went to see Dr. Marc today."

"I knew it! I knew you didn't feel well," Cleta burst out. "You should have told me!"

Barbara lowered her head. "Mom, I went to talk to him about why Russell and I haven't been able to have a baby."

Cleta locked her lower jaw. "Babies will come along in due time."

Taking Barbara's hand, Russell nodded his reassurance. "Tell 'em, honey."

Barbara turned to her mother. "I have a problem."

Cleta paled. "A problem?"

Russell leaped to the rescue. "It can be repaired with surgery. It's nothing dangerous to her health, just to her fertility."

Cleta turned on him, her eyes snapping fire. "And who made you the expert?"

"Nobody. Dr. Marc said so."

She snapped her mouth shut. "Oh."

Floyd set his fork down and looked at Barbara. "You're sure it's nothing dangerous?"

"It's endometriosis, Daddy. A female problem. Dr. Marc said there's a procedure that should take care of it. It's done all the time."

"Surgery? On my baby? And you didn't say a word about it?" Springing up, Cleta grabbed a dishtowel and held it to her face.

Barbara cast a quick glance at Russell, then reached toward her mother. "It's OK, Mom. It's going to be all right. Once I have the surgery, Russell and I will greatly improve our chances of pregnancy. But we've decided we're going to give you a grandchild any way we can. We're going to look into adoption, too."

"Grandchildren would be nice," Floyd said. "Real nice."

Cleta lowered the dishtowel and met Barbara's eyes. "You—you went to see the doctor without me? Something as important as this, and you went alone?"

Barbara lowered her gaze. The hurt and accusation in her mother's eyes cut deeply.

"I felt it was something I needed to do on my own, Mom."

Cleta lifted her chin. "I see. Well. Fine, then."

But it wasn't fine. Barbara could see that in her mother's jerky movements as she stacked her dishes and carried them to the sink.

"Mom, I'm sorry you're upset."

Cleta turned on her with the fury of a wounded tigress. "You're not sorry about anything, Missy. You obviously don't care a whit about my feelings. Alst I've ever done is sacrifice for you, work for you, suffer for you, and yet you cut me out of your life at the time I would most like to be there—"

"I'm sorry, Mom. I guess I can't do anything right." Turning on the ball of her foot, Barbara fled the kitchen and ran upstairs.

≼

Cleta buried her face in her apron and bawled, rattling Floyd's nerves. Black liquid splashed over the side of his coffee cup as he lifted it. After-dinner coffee and dessert just weren't relaxing when one's wife was on a crying jag.

He took a sip from his coffee and lowered his cup, resolved to weather the storm. The fur had finally hit the fan and he didn't know why Cleta was so surprised. He'd seen this coming for months.

Cleta lifted her head, then dabbed at her eyes with the corner of her apron. "Barbara didn't even tell me, Floyd. Me, her mother. She told someone else first!"

"She told her husband, Cleta."

Cleta bawled harder into the cotton fabric, pushing out words between her sobs. "We've always shared everything, the good and the bad. How could she have told Russell before telling me? I knew her first! And running off to see Dr. Marc that way, it's downright indecent." Flapping her apron, she frantically fanned the air. "I should have been with her at the doctor's office. It's a mother's place to be with her daughter at a time like this."

Shoving his half-eaten cobbler aside, Floyd reached for his pipe. Women and their hysterics; it was all a man could do to keep his wits. Russell had had sense enough to flee the kitchen even before Barbara.

He picked up his pipe, then fixed his wife in a steady gaze. "Won't do you any good to get worked up over this, Mama. Barbara has a right to tell her husband anything she chooses without consulting you."

"All those hours—those agonizing hours it took to bring that child into the world, and this is the thanks I get."

"I was there too." Floyd studied his callused right hand. Cleta had squeezed the stuffing right out of him that night.

"Well." She sniffed, reaching for a dry corner of the apron to blot her streaming eyes. "I suppose she was excited—probably didn't stop to consider my feelings, just blurted out the news to the first person she saw, which happened to be Russell."

Floyd drew on the pipe bowl, then fanned out a match. "I don't misdoubt that." He'd learn a long time ago to agree with his wife.

"No, that wasn't what happened. She was gone too long." Her eyes narrowed. "She ran straight from Dr. Marc's to the dock, and waited for Russell to come in, then told him. She could have told me first, but she must have gone to the docks. And did you see the look on his face when they came in? Smug. Like the cat that'd eaten the canary."

Floyd couldn't stop a grin. "Ayuh. Reminded me of how I looked the day we found out you were having Barbara."

They had prayed for seven years before the good Lord granted them a child. Floyd knew he'd never forget the look on Cleta's face moments after the delivery. Why, she'd gazed at that baby like a little piece of heaven had been delivered into her arms.

Sadly, Barbara would be their only child. Later that night Cleta had complications and the doctors whisked her off for emergency surgery. But she took the news well; nothing mattered but that little red-headed ball of life protectively cradled in her arms.

As if she'd been revisiting the same memory, Cleta dropped her head and cried harder.

Floyd rose from the table and carried his dishes to the counter. As he plugged the sink and turned on the hot water tap, his patience evaporated. "Dadburn it, Cleta, you're making a mountain out of a mole hill. It's time for us to step back from the front page of our child's life. Give her some room. Let her breathe, for goodness sake."

"You're taking her side. You don't care if she hurts me."

Floyd shot a stream of Palmolive in the water. Bubbles boiled around his wrists as he turned to face his wife. "You know that's not true!"

She kept boohooing. "You don't love me—I've known it for a long time. You're tired of me and you don't love me anymore."

"I do love you, Cleta. And I love Barbara. But I'm tired of seeing my girls tied up in emotional knots. Barbara is being pulled in two opposite directions, woman. Can't you see that? She wants to be a dutiful daughter and a good wife. You make her feel like a criminal when someone mentions her need to have her own place."

"Why does she need her own place? She doesn't have to lift a finger around here."

"That's the problem. She needs to lift a finger and a mop and skillet once in a while. Maybe she and Russell want their privacy. Maybe they want to run around the house in their skivvies or eat supper at midnight. Stop mollycoddling her. You want her to be self-sufficient, don't you? A productive citizen, give something back to society?"

Cleta sat mute, looking as stubborn as a Maine mule.

"Don't you?"

"She is productive—I don't see a problem."

Floyd drew a deep breath. "Russell does. And Russell is who she needs to be thinking about. Doesn't mean she plans to throw you to the wolves; it just means she's a grown woman with the God-given right to have her own life."

Cleta lifted her chin. "That boy's been perfectly happy here for three years."

"Not perfectly."

"What?"

"I think the boy wants his wife in their own place."

Cleta straightened, blowing her nose on a tissue. Floyd took hope from the sight. Maybe she was coming around.

"Listen to us," she said, dabbing at the end of her nose. "We're sounding like it's the end of the world because Barbara didn't tell us the news first. You know how she is; she doesn't get excited that easy, but Dr. Marc's news must have put her in such a dither she told Russell before she thought."

She pushed back from the table and dried her eyes. "Tomorrow is Russell's birthday. I'll go first thing into Ogunquit and buy that new spread and drapes—no, better, we'll redo the whole room for him. There." She threw Floyd an accusing look. "Is that nice enough for you? Bedroom furniture, a spread, and new drapes. That will make a lovely birthday gift. He'll see how much I appreciate him."

Floyd frowned. "You talking about that pink spread and curtains?"

"It's not pink, Floyd. It's cotton candy, a very neutral color. Then I'll stop by the butcher shop and I'll get some of those nice veal cutlets Barbara loves."

"Russell wants Mexican casserole for his birthday dinner."

"Oh, he isn't particular, and Barbara loves veal cutlets. Now, let's see." Tears dried, Cleta resumed command and reached for her grocery list. "Veal cutlets, string beans, a nice salad, and lemon cake for dessert."

"Russell hates lemon; why don't you make chocolate? Chocolate's a man's cake. Chocolate with black walnuts in the icing."

She gave him an indulgent smile. "Black walnuts give Barbara heartburn." She moved toward the kitchen door, scribbling on her notepad.

"Dadburn it, Cleta!" Floyd called. "It's Russell's birthday!"

"I know, dear! And it's going to be lovely!"

"Ayuh," Fred grumbled. "For everyone but Russell."

She left the kitchen through the swinging door, but returned an instant later, her head jutting through the doorway. She narrowed her eyes. "Are we in a mood this evening?"

"Cleta, you can't buy that boy a pink spread and drapes!"

"Floyd." Her eyes went as sharp as daggers. "Whose side are you on, mine or Russell's?"

"Didn't know there were sides."

"Which one, Floyd?" She stepped through the doorway and crossed both arms.

Floyd turned to face her, soapsuds dripping from his crossed forearms. "Don't you buy that spread and curtains, Cleta."

The tips of her fingers went white as she squeezed her elbows. "Don't you threaten me, Floyd."

"I'm not threatening you, I'm telling you not to humiliate that poor man because you want to bribe Barbara into living here forever."

Fire shot from her pupils. Widening her stance, she assumed battle position. "That's the meanest thing you've ever said to me, Floyd." A glaze covered her eyes. "You don't love me anymore."

"I do love you—I'm trying to keep you from making

the biggest mistake you've ever made. Feeding Russell veal cutlets instead of Mexican casserole, making lemon cake when the boy loves chocolate—how long do you think he'll put up with your slights? You iron Barbara's clothes, but make Russell iron his own. You always put Barbara first."

"She's our child."

"So is Russell—starting the day he married our daughter."

Cleta waved the rebuke aside. "Of course I'm fond of the boy, but I don't see how you can expect a mother to love a son-in-law as much as she loves her own blood."

"*Love* is an action word, Cleta, and you can start loving Russell by acting like you care about him! Make the boy a chocolate cake!"

"You don't love me," she sniffed.

"Oh, good grief." He turned back to the sink, having had more than enough of the conversation. Cleta would do what she would do, and nothing he could say would change her mind now.

Why did life have to be so complicated? Cleta had to see what she was doing before it was too late. For the last three years she'd been blind to her subtle but distinct interference in Barbara's life. A parent should have enough sense to know when a child was ready to go out into the world on her own.

At almost twenty-three, Barbara was overly ripe. In fact, she was spoiled rotten.

Chapter Nine

The following afternoon, on Russell's birthday, Floyd watched workmen carry in a maple headboard, a new king-size orthopedic mattress and box springs, a chest of drawers, two nightstands, and a dresser with a mirror. Micah paused while mulching a flower bed to watch the activity with his jaw agape.

Sheesh. Floyd sank down in the swing and pulled on his pipe, smoke fogging over his head in angry whorls. Cleta was being some generous with his money.

One of the workmen smiled and said hello as he passed the swing carrying a large parcel. Floyd set his jaw when he saw a wisp of pink fabric poking out of the sack.

Dadburn that Cleta. She had sacked herself up a whole bunch of trouble now.

He knew without looking that they'd be having veal cutlets and lemon cake for dinner.

❧

Russell Higgs stepped out of the shower, wrapped a towel around his waist, and waved his hand to clear the fog from the room. He'd taken off from work early, hoping to spend some time on his birthday with his wife, and he half-suspected Barbara had some sort of grand surprise for him. She had been wide-eyed and jumpy when he went into the shower, so there was no telling what she had planned.

He hesitated. Yes, there were definite sounds of movement from behind the closed bathroom door. He felt a grin spreading over his face. What had she done? Gotten him that new lounger he'd been eying at the furniture store? Or maybe she'd splurged on that new wide-screen television he'd been hinting about. Sure, the TV would be awfully crowded in their bedroom, but he was fervently hoping they'd be out of this place within a few months.

He put his hand on the door handle. She was hoping to surprise him . . . why not surprise her?

Gripping the towel firmly in his right hand, he swung the door open . . . and dropped his jaw.

Gone were the bold navy and green plaid curtains at the window. Gone was his favorite bedspread . . . and his comfortable bed. The leather footstool had vanished, and so had the navy blue pillows he liked to lean on while he read the sports section.

He felt his brows lower. A pair of workers in overalls nodded at him, but his eyes sought and found Barbara. His wife was cowering beside his mother-in-law, whose arms were overflowing with pink ruffles.

"Birthday surprise," Cleta sang out, dropping the pile of pink froufrou on the floor. She picked up the empty curtain rods. "New furniture, drapes, and bed ensemble. Aren't you the lucky birthday boy!"

"Barbara," Russell called, his voice hoarse with frustration.

"Honey, you're not decent." She rushed to him, put her arms around his waist and pushed him back into the bathroom. When they were out of Cleta's hearing, she ran her hands up his bare arms. "Honey, I know pink's not your color. But Mom wanted to do this for us, OK? And since this might be the last of your birthdays we'll spend here, just humor her, please?"

Russell exhaled slowly, then looked down into Barbara's beautiful eyes. When she looked at him like that, he couldn't deny her anything.

"OK," he said finally. "I'll put up with it—for a while. But if any one of you Lansdowns tells anyone in town that I'm sleeping in a pink bedroom, I'm moving out on the next ferry."

Chapter Ten

On Saturday morning, a cold fog moved over the island. It roiled at the windows, softly insistent, and Vernie waded through a soup of the stuff as she crossed the street and headed to the bed-and-breakfast.

"Cleeeeta." Vernie called from the foyer. "I found that blueberry cobbler recipe you've been wanting!"

"In the kitchen."

Vernie followed Cleta's voice. As soon as she entered the kitchen she knew something was wrong. Cleta, Floyd, Barbara, and Russell all sat at the table, a virtually untouched plate of pancakes and bacon on the lazy Susan.

What kind of minefield had she wandered into? Cleta wouldn't meet her eyes, so she'd get no help from her friend.

She shifted her gaze to the man of the household. "How be you, Floyd?"

"Nicely, thank you."

"You don't look so good, if you'll pardon my saying so. You look a bit squamish. I hear Pastor Winslow is still a bit under the weather. He and Stanley haven't been able to do a thing toward repairing the damage they've done to poor Edith's bathroom." She looked at Cleta. "Olympia is down with that intestinal bug now."

Vernie paused, noting the solemn, strained expressions on the Higgs's and Lansdowns' faces.

She took another stab at conversation. "Happy birthday, Russell," she said, patting the young man's shoulder.

"I'm sorry I didn't make it over yesterday, but Elezar and I had to turn the place upside down looking for—"

"I know." Russell's voice was flat. "You had to find lemon flavoring. For my birthday cake."

"Ayuh." Vernie looked at Cleta and lifted a brow, sending her a help-me-out-here look.

Accurately interpreting Vernie's expression, Cleta shrugged slightly. "Barbara saw Dr. Marc."

Vernie looked from the stonefaced Cleta to Barbara. "Is anything wrong? You got a touch of the grippe?"

"Barbara took herself to the doctor on her own," Cleta said, verbally underlining the last word.

"Oh." Vernie didn't know what else to say.

Cleta looked like she had swallowed a persimmon. Crossing her arms, she said, "I've always gone with her. Since the day she was born. I've always gone."

Barbara shook her head and sighed. "Mom."

Vernie pulled up a stool and sat down, grateful that she now understood the flow of the conversation. "She's almost twenty-three, Cleta. A grown woman." Vernie smiled at Barbara. "I take it there was nothing seriously wrong?"

"Well, there is a problem. But Dr. Marc assures me a surgical procedure will take care of it."

"That's good news, then."

"Ayuh, but Mother is a little . . . miffed at me."

Cleta's jaw jutted forward. "She went to Dr. Marc on her own, then ran to tell Russell the news almost before his boat docked."

"And there's something wrong in that?" Slipping off

the seat, Vernie poured herself a cup of coffee, then perched on her stool again. She'd thought to do a little neighboring, but this visit might prove highly entertaining. Best of all, the tale might take up the better part of the morning once everybody at the table had a say.

"You don't understand, Vernie." Cleta fixed her daughter in a frosty stare. "It's something that we've always done. I've always gone with her, made sure everything was all right."

Vernie took a sip of her coffee, then lowered her mug. "But she's married now. Russell should be the one to hear good news first." She smiled at the Higgs boy. "And this is good news. You'll be fixing up a nursery soon, right? By the way, Barbara, did you put a deposit on that house you and Russell were studyin' last Saturday?"

Cleta went as pale as death.

"No, Vernie," Russell said, slipping his arm around the back of Barbara's chair. "We only looked at the house. We haven't made any decisions, but when we do, we'll make them on our own and in our own good—"

Before he could finish the sentence, Cleta ran from the room. Barbara held her hands over her ears until her mother's bedroom door slammed.

Vernie stared at the swinging kitchen door. "Well, what on earth?"

Just then the back door burst open and Pastor Winslow rushed through the room, then headed for the back stairs. When they heard the bathroom door slam, Vernie glanced at Barbara.

The younger woman shrugged. "Well, I guess

whatever Dr. Marc prescribed for those fellows hasn't taken hold yet."

⮜

An hour later, Barbara wadded her pillow over her ears and fervently wished she had freedom and privacy enough to scream. She wished she'd never started this doctor business. Life had been much simpler before she'd told her mother about the surgery. Mom was overprotective, but she loved her, and Barbara loved knowing she was loved.

But she had hurt her mother. Badly. Mom felt betrayed somehow. She hadn't come out of her bedroom since breakfast, and she just might pout until she could convince herself the surgery thing would go away. Now, more than ever, Barbara wanted it to go away.

What was the big deal? Was it unreasonable to want to share good news with her husband before her mother? Barbara hadn't thought so, Vernie didn't think so, but Cleta clearly saw it as a significant break in the mother-daughter relationship. Barbara hadn't anticipated such a fuss—or had she? Maybe she had psychologically sabotaged her relationship with her mother. Oprah would think so. Dr. Phil would say so. But how else could a girl cope with being pulled in opposite directions by the two people she loved most in the world?

The ringing of the bedside phone interrupted her thoughts. She let it ring three times, thinking her mother would pick up, then sighed and lifted the receiver. "Baskahegan Bed and Breakfast."

"Barbara, it's Dr. Marc. How be you this fine morning?"

"Nicely, thank you."

"I spoke with Dr. Comeaux yesterday and she said she can do the procedure we discussed on the twenty-eighth of this month, if you're still interested."

Without warning, fear rose in the back of Barbara's throat and threatened to choke her. Surgery. Knives. Anesthetic. What if she went to sleep and never woke up? Some people did that. OK, not most people, but accidents did happen.

She gripped the phone. "I don't think I'm ready."

Silence rolled over the line for a moment. "Oh, I thought you and Russell wanted to get started—"

"I know, but now that I've thought about it, I—I'm not ready."

"There's nothing to worry about, Barbara. If you're feeling a mite spleeny—"

She twisted the phone cord around her fingers, blinking back fresh tears. "I just want to think about it some more."

"I see. You let me know when you're ready and I'll make the appointment." He hesitated. "Are you sure you're feeling all right?"

"I'm fine. Just a little tired."

"Perhaps vitamins are in order. Call or drop by anytime if you want to talk. Understand?"

"Ayuh. I will."

She hung up the phone, wishing she knew what to do. She couldn't bear Cleta's anger and disappointment. They'd always been so close. Now she felt as if a door between them had slammed shut, and she could never open it again unless she surrendered and went back to her old ways. But Russell would be so disappointed if she gave up on their dreams—and angry that she was running from her problems.

She sat up on the bed and hugged her knees. Why, oh why, didn't God write things on the wall for his modern children like he did for that old Babylonian King Dinglefuzzie in the Old Testament?

She spent the afternoon doing laundry. Cleta found other things to occupy her time, clearly striving to keep out of her daughter's way, which only made Barbara feel worse. When Barbara began setting the table for dinner, Cleta came in and dumped spaghetti in boiling water as if Barbara wasn't even in the room. With tears stinging her eyes, Barbara left the table half-set and went upstairs to avoid her mother's cold shoulder.

When Russell came in a half-hour later, he stripped off his jacket, then took her into his arms. "What's the matter, hon? Have you been crying?"

"Allergies."

She turned away and busied herself laying out clean clothes for after Russell's shower.

But he had other things on his mind. Lowering his head to look into her eyes, he asked, "Did you ask Dr. Marc to make an appointment for the surgery?"

Barbara hesitated, holding his fresh shirt up like a shield.

Russell stood in his socks, his flannel shirt hanging out of his bibs, his hair tousled, hands on his hips, the crease of a frown between his brows. "You did speak to him, right?"

"He called me. I, um, told him I wasn't ready to have the surgery yet."

"What?"

"I told him—"

"I heard what you said. Why?"

Barbara floundered before his hot gaze. "I couldn't go through with it. Mother is so upset about this whole thing—"

"What she's upset about is you having the gumption to do something on your own for a change. Grow up, Barbara! If she had her way, you wouldn't blow your nose without her holding the tissue!"

"That's not true! She loves me and wants to protect me."

"And I don't? Listen, Babs—we could have a baby, you and me. We're married. We've been married three years! It's time to start a family of our own. The Bible says married people should leave and cleave, and you've never left your mama! It's not right, Barbara. And it's not fair to me!"

Barbara wanted to drop through the floor and die. She couldn't make anyone happy, not her mother, not her husband. Nothing she did was right. When Russell stalked into the bathroom, slamming the door behind him, she sank onto the edge of the bed and stared at the wall as tears rolled down her cheeks. Two days ago she and Russell had been so happy, then Cleta got hurt and angry. Now everyone in the family but Micah was either angry or miserable or both.

"I want this to go away," she whispered. "Why can't this go away and everything be the way it was?"

Because . . . Russell wasn't happy with the way things were. He wanted a home of his own. He wanted children.

And, if the truth be told, so did she.

She heard the sound of footsteps pounding up the stairs. Pastor Winslow again. Whatever Dr. Marc had given the sick men clearly hadn't worked. Pastor Wickam had dashed into the bed-and-breakfast a dozen times this morning, whipping past Barbara without a glance, his face sweaty and flushed.

She felt the corner of her mouth twitch in a wry smile. Rumor had it that the restoration of Edith's bathroom had come to a complete halt, resumed, and halted again. Between bouts of abdominal spasms, Stanley and Winslow had worked to chisel loose the plastered baseboards, but they accidentally chipped several of Edith's patterned floor tiles. A quick call to the Home Depot in Portland assured them that the tile had been discontinued. So the floor would have to be replaced. Last Barbara heard they were ordering a new light fixture as well as new tile, because Stanley had slammed the broom handle into the overhead light while sweeping away tile and plaster chips. Edith, Vernie had reported, sat in her rocker on the parsonage porch and cried a lot.

Barbara had half a mind to join her. Didn't misery love company?

≈

A north wind whipped Dr. Marc's overcoat as he knocked on the door of Frenchman's Fairest just after sunset. "Come in," Caleb invited. "I was just about to serve Olympia her tea. Would you care for a cup?"

Dr. Marc rubbed his chilled hands together. "That would be nice. It seems to have dropped ten degrees in the last hour out there."

The old butler smiled. "Could be a storm brewing. Let me take your coat. Olympia is in the parlor if you'd care to go on in. I'll bring the tea shortly."

After giving Caleb his coat, the doctor found Olympia reading a book by the fireplace. The widow put on a good front, but Dr. Marc knew she was grieving deeply for Edmund, who had passed on in November. The genteel woman extended her slender hand as he approached.

"Dr. Marc. Come, sit. You didn't need to stop by—I seemed to be doing . . . well, no worse." She smiled. "Tell, me, how is Alex? I haven't heard you speak of him recently."

"Alex is fine. Says he's too busy to visit this month, but I venture to say he'll make time if Annie plans to come—and a storm doesn't blow in."

She lowered her magazine to her lap. "What's this about a storm?"

"Well, I don't know if it's a storm or just our regular January climate. But I have a feeling our spell of mortifyin' weather is about to pass."

"Ah, here's Caleb. Let's have our tea."

Marc sat silently as the old butler poured from the antique silver tea service, then gratefully accepted a cup of the fragrant liquid. He sipped and smiled as its warmth chased away the chill.

"What brings you over this evening, Doctor?"

Resting the cup and saucer on his knee, Marc met Olympia's direct gaze. "It's about your tests this morning."

Olympia arched a brow. "Is something wrong?"

"I don't think so," he assured her. "But I've become convinced that your stomach distress is neither viral nor bacterial. You, Floyd, Stanley, and Winslow are all experiencing the same symptoms. Stanley and Winslow tried to blame some sandwiches they ate in Ogunquit, but Floyd never ate those sandwiches."

"Nor did I." She shuddered slightly. "Those sandwiches are so . . . messy."

"Then it occurred to me to wonder what the five of you may have eaten, and I came up with one common denominator." He looked up and caught Caleb's eye. "And one exception."

The old butler flushed as silence settled over the room.

"I can't imagine," Olympia murmured, her brow furrowed in thought.

Caleb cleared his throat. "I think I know what you're going to say."

Dr. Marc looked up. "Tell me, Caleb. Tell me why everyone who ate Annie's tomatoes got sick—except you?"

The butler put one hand on the mantle, and shrugged, obviously casting about for words. Finally he looked at Olympia and said, "I have a supernaturally strong constitution?"

"Maybe," Dr. Marc answered. "But four out of five is enough to prove my theory. I stopped by to get Annie's phone number. As much as it breaks my heart to do this, I've got to call and tell her those tomatoes are unfit for human consumption."

❧

The phone rang in Annie's Portland apartment just as she was letting herself in. Dumping her purse and briefcase on the sofa, she lunged for the receiver, praying the caller was A. J. Hayes.

"Hello?"

"Annie! Dr. Marc here. How are things in Portland?"

"Cold," she said, trying to hide her disappointment. Well, if she couldn't talk to A. J., talking to his father was a nice compromise. "How are things in Heavenly Daze?"

"About to get worse, I fear. We've had lovely weather but a bad spell's on the way. Say, about your tomatoes— what results other than growth in inhospitable weather have you recorded?"

Annie pulled her gloves off with her teeth as she considered the doctor's question. "I can't say that there have been any other results to document. Why do you ask?"

There was silence on the other end of the line.

"Dr. Marc?"

"No one in your research group has eaten them?"

"No. When I last visited Heavenly Daze, none of the fruits were ripe enough to eat."

"Oh." The doctor paused again, letting the silence stretch.

"Dr. Marc, is something wrong with my tomatoes?"

"Perhaps. I've been treating Floyd, Stanley, and Pastor Wickam for an intestinal disorder that seems particularly stubborn. Now Olympia has—"

"Aunt Olympia's sick?"

"Nothing serious, dear."

"What does this have to do with my plants?"

"Well, this, um, disorder appeared after they'd eaten some of the tomatoes. Oh, they were lovely tomatoes, and everyone agreed the taste and texture were absolutely wonderful. It's the digestive effect that concerns me."

Annie gasped. "You think my tomatoes gave them—"

"Ayuh, the tomato version of Montezuma's Revenge."

Annie sank to the nearest chair. "Oh my goodness."

"There's nothing else that the four ate that could have produced these disastrous results. To make matters worse, they kept eating the tomatoes during treatment, negating the effects of the medicine I prescribed. Poor Floyd can hardly lift his head. Winslow has lost ten pounds, which he needed to lose, but not this way. Olympia has fared best, but she's still a bit uncomfortable. Stanley has been suffering the same complaint. In fact, the only person who ate your tomatoes and didn't get sick was Caleb."

Annie laughed weakly. "Of course not. Caleb never gets sick."

"Really?"

"Not since I've known him—and I've known him forever."

Annie lowered her head into her hand, trying to absorb this startling information. She had manipulated the tomato's genetic makeup in order to create a hybrid that would grow in winter weather, but she'd never even considered that such manipulation might render the fruit indigestible.

Shoot. To have this happen just when the experiment looked so promising! Her plants were about to be featured in *Tomato Monthly*. But if her plants were propagated and couldn't be eaten—why, she'd poison half the world's population!

"Dr. Marc, this is awful! Make Caleb promise not to let anyone else eat a single tomato!"

The doctor laughed. "Oh, don't worry. Once this news

leaks out no one will go within a hundred yards of those plants."

Annie groaned. "I'm so sorry. I've never eaten one myself."

"I'm sure you never imagined this kind of result. No one would."

"Please, please tell everybody how sorry I am."

"I will. And I'm sorry, dear. I know this was your big dream."

They spoke a few minutes more, then the doctor hung up.

Annie hung her head and dropped the phone back into the cradle. Another experiment down the tubes. Another failure. But . . . at least no one had been seriously injured this time. She hadn't blown up any buildings, and in the course of the great tomato experiment she had managed to meet one of the most charming men in the world.

She'd been knocked down before, and she always got up again. Sheer, dogged persistence (Olympia would call it stubbornness) was probably her best quality.

She blew upward to dislodge a wisp of hair from her eyes, then grinned. Even after devastating news about killer tomatoes, any girl dating Dr. Alex Hayes couldn't be totally depressed.

Chapter Eleven

A before-church quiet filled the bed-and-breakfast when Cleta came in and sat down at her desk. Since she had a few minutes before Floyd would rise and begin clamoring for his Sunday breakfast of French toast and cheesy eggs, she picked up a pen and thoughtfully chewed the end of it, then began to write:

> Dear Angel,
>
> Could you help me with a problem? My daughter and I have always been close. I've loved and protected her since she was born, through scraped knees, colds, and first boyfriends. She has always turned to me for advice and shared her heart with me. I could always count on her being as close as my shadow. But now things have changed, and my heart is broken. It's not that I resent her having married a good man. He treats her well, and I shouldn't complain. But he doesn't understand how precious my relationship with my daughter has been. He's taking her away from me and that hurts me deeply. I don't know how to feel anymore, I don't know how to make things right. Please give me wisdom and guidance about what I should do.
>
> Hurting Mom

Dropping her pen, Cleta read the letter through one more time, then quietly ripped it into little pieces. She couldn't mail it. Bea or one of her helpers would read it, and though angel mail came to Heavenly Daze from all over the world, they'd know who'd written this one.

Still, it felt good to pour out her feelings in writing. And it would feel better still to lift them to the Lord.

She bowed her head. "Please help me," she prayed. "I'm so confused."

≈

After lunch, obeying a prompting of the Spirit, Micah went into the front room and stood at Cleta's desk. The blotter was clean and dust-free, the leather pencil holder loaded with an odd assortment of pens, pencils, and a pair of scissors. A stack of ivory envelopes stood in a compartment in the small hutch, each etched in the upper left corner with a pen-and-ink rendering of the Baskahegan Bed and Breakfast . . .

His eyes fell upon a tidy little pile of paper. Sitting at the desk, he held his hand over the shredded bits of ivory, then closed his eyes.

Information flowed into his brain, borne by the Spirit of God. Cleta was in pain, and she had written a letter . . . to the Heavenly Daze angels. Her words filled his ears, ringing with a mother's anguish, fear, and loss.

Nodding, Micah opened his eyes. "I'll find her, Lord." Moving to the kitchen, he poured two cups of coffee and went in search of Cleta. He'd noticed that she hadn't sung a word of the hymns in church that morning, neither had she sat next to Barbara as she usually did. The cold war had gone on long enough; it was time to call a truce and make peace.

He found Cleta on her knees in the dirt, pulling weeds as if she was on a deadline. He scratched at his beard. There weren't any real weeds to pull, just the dead stalks from last summer. Even a mortal human would have understood that Cleta had to have something serious on her mind to come out and abuse a dead garden.

He stooped to tap her on the shoulder. "That's my job, isn't it?"

"Sorry. I have to keep busy."

Ah, yes. If she didn't keep busy, her agony would devour her.

"It's cold out here," he said. "I brought you a cup of coffee. Thought you could use some warming up."

Cleta brushed dirt from her hands and knees, then perched on a stone at the garden's edge.

"Thank you, Micah." She took one of the mugs. "That's some thoughtful of you."

Micah sat on a small bench at the edge of the flower bed that would be a colorful paradise of roses come summer. He sipped at his own mug, then lowered it to look at the woman in his watchcare. "It's strange, isn't it?"

Cleta's thoughts seemed faraway. "What is?"

"How our lives are like this garden, brimming with potential, but cluttered with a lot of things we need to weed out, prune, and sweep away from time to time. Human prejudices, guilt, unforgiveness, and fears can grow up like weeds. Without being aware of it, many men let them choke out their God-given potential."

He took another sip and let his words sink in. "Remember how pretty this garden was last summer?"

"Lovely," Cleta echoed.

"But if I hadn't vigilantly pruned, pulled, and trimmed, the new plants wouldn't have taken a firm hold in the soil. They'd have grown, ayuh, but they wouldn't have been nearly as strong and beautiful."

Cleta stared at the dead foliage. "I suppose."

Micah nodded toward a dark and leafless rosebush against a trellis. "See that old climbing rose? Roses aren't going to bloom on the old woody vine. They're going to bloom at the end, where the stems are fresh and green. But if you cut back the woody vine, the flowers will bloom closer to the ground where we can enjoy them." He bent forward, watching her face. "But first, you've got to prune the plant back, let go of the old so the new can bloom and grow."

A smile crept across her lined face. "I'm not dense, Micah," she said, her voice wry. "I understand what you're trying to tell me. But I'm not sure you know how it hurts to prune away that old vine. The pruning shears are sharp, and they sting."

He stood, then reached down to touch her shoulder. "Weeping endures only for the night, Cleta. Joy comes in the morning."

Cleta stared at the choppy Atlantic, tears rolling down her cheeks. Micah looked down at his empty mug, knowing his words had fallen on fertile, broken soil.

"Don't stay out too long," he called as he turned away. "It's warm inside where you belong."

Chapter Twelve

January stopped playing coy the next day. A nor'easter tore up the coast and buried the island of Heavenly Daze in fifteen inches of snow and ice. Folks had expected a blast of winter weather to hit eventually, but it didn't make their comments any friendlier.

Stanley waded through hip-deep snow to fetch a box of chocolates for Vernie in Ogunquit. When he showed up that afternoon with a box of Shari's Berries under his arm, she stared at him as if he'd become unhinged.

"Have you lost your mind, Stanley Bidderman? Traipsing around outside in this kind of weather?"

"I have lost my mind. Over you." Silently, he pleaded with her. "Can we sit down and share a cup of coffee before you tell me to get lost again?"

Vernie studied the box of chocolates, then glanced at the old ragged robe she was wearing. He wanted to tell her he didn't care what she had on, he'd seen her looking worse.

It was good he kept his mouth shut.

"All right," she finally said. "I've got a fresh pot of coffee."

Stanley stomped snow off his boots and followed her into the warmth of the little kitchen at the back of the store. When they reached the table, he shrugged out of his coat and hung it near the stove to dry.

Vernie got a cup from the cupboard and poured coffee. "There's no need to bring me chocolates, Stanley. Not on a blustery day like this."

The room smelled warm and cinnamony, as if she'd baked his favorite fresh cinnamon rolls. Smiling, he watched as she dropped two on a plate and set it in front of him.

"Did you make these for me?"

"No."

He bit into the warm buns. "No matter. They're delicious."

Vernie grunted and sank into the empty chair beside him.

They sat in the warm kitchen listening to the howling wind. Snow fell in gusty sheets outside the window.

Vernie clapped her hands and looked at him. "Guess you won't be eating any more of those tomatoes?"

Stanley felt his stomach drop. "I don't think so. Will Annie stop her experiments?"

"Annie, quit?" Vernie snorted. "Not if I know her."

"Persistence is an admirable thing in a woman," Stanley said. "Though it's akin to stubbornness, I think."

He braced himself, but she didn't punch him. When he finished his coffee and rolls, Vernie brought out a Monopoly board.

She shrugged at his look of surprise. "It's been a good long time since I beat you senseless in Monopoly." She gave him a sheepish smile. "Thought since you were here and we had nothing better to do, we might play a game."

He nodded. "Not likely that Winslow will be working on his bathroom today. He's still waiting for the tiles to arrive."

"Let's play. But don't get your hopes up." She looked at him with challenge in her eyes. "I'm undefeated."

He bit back a satisfied grin, bending to unbuckle his galoshes. "Bring it on, woman."

She set the board on the table and put the race car at GO. She took the iron.

Stanley eyed the colorful paper bills. "Want me to be the banker?"

"Go for it."

Vernie flexed her fingers, brought them up to hover over the board. Pausing, she looked Stanley in the eye. "OK."

"OK what?"

"OK, I baked the rolls especially for you."

His eyes warmed with affection. "Well. That's real nice, Veronica."

"Shut up and roll the dice. Then hand me that box of chocolates."

Though a storm raged outside, Stanley thought he might feel a thaw coming on. Progress was progress, even if he had to let Vernie win at Monopoly again.

&

Micah opened his eyes when he heard a rap at his front porch. He had been meditating and praying for the people in his care, and now he knew without being told that one of them stood outside his apartment.

He blinked as his eyes adjusted to the light of earth, so dim after the glory of heaven, then stood and answered the door. Barbara stood there, with a forlorn expression on her face.

"Micah?"

"Come in, child. It's colder than creek water out there."

Barbara shuffled in, then pulled out a chair at his small kitchen table. He leaned against the counter, and hid a smile behind his fingertips. Though Barbara Higgs was a woman grown, in some ways she was a small child. She had accepted the Lord in her seventh year on earth, but spiritually she was still toddling along . . .

"What's wrong, Barbara?"

She burst into tears. Micah said nothing, but pulled out a box of tissue he kept on the counter for visits just like this. Barbara had been stopping by for years—after her first date with Russell, when she'd been so certain he found her unattractive and uninteresting; after their first fight (when Russell left his socks on the floor and she was convinced he'd done it to spite her); and the night Russell's ship had to ride out to sea to escape a gale and Barbara just knew his ship had capsized. Each time Micah had heard her out, then gently led her to the throne room of heaven in prayer.

She accepted the tissue with a bleary smile, then blew her nose. "I thought I was all cried out, but I guess I'm not."

"It's okay." He folded his arms and stared at the streaming tracks upon her cheeks. Though as an angel he possessed emotions, will, and an intellect sharper than any human's, he rarely wept. The process fascinated him. Perhaps, he mused, tears bubbled up inside these humans when they experienced emotions they could not put into words . . .

"It's . . . a baby," Barbara blubbered. "I think I want one—but it's causing trouble between me and Mom, and between me and Russell. And I'm scared, Micah. If I'm to get pregnant, I'll have to have surgery." She squinted at him. "But you're always telling me God can do the impossible. Maybe he could make me pregnant without the surgery if I pray hard enough?"

Micah sank into the chair opposite her. "So—you want God to do all the work? He can do anything, that is true. But He asks that you have faith."

Barbara shook her head. "I sometimes think I should just give up on the idea and concentrate on adoption. Dr. Marc said that even with surgery I might not get pregnant. So why should I bother to try?"

"Adoption is a wonderful thing." Micah gave her a smile. "Jesus was adopted by Joseph. Esther was adopted by her uncle; Moses was adopted by Pharaoh's daughter—"

"Really?"

Micah nodded. "But you're not being honest, Barbara, with yourself, with me, or with God. You're talking about giving up and begging for miracles because . . ." He lifted a brow, silently urging her to dig deeper.

"Because . . ." Barbara's gaze drifted toward the window. "I don't want to have the surgery because . . . I'm afraid. I've always been terrified of doctors."

"Ayuh." Micah smiled in relief. "Some of the modern psychologists would say you must face your fears, but I will tell you that there is no fear in love. Perfect love casts out fear, Barbara, and if you have Jesus, you have perfect love. God told the prophet Isaiah to tell his people, 'But now, O Israel, the LORD who created you says: "Do not be afraid, for I have ransomed you. I have called you by name; you are mine."'"

Micah reached across the table and tapped Barbara's trembling hand. "God created you, Barbara, and he calls you by name. You have no reason to fear anything on earth, under the earth, or above the earth. The Mighty God who keeps you will sustain your soul. You have only to trust him."

The corners of Barbara's mouth were still tight with distress, and her eyes slightly shiny. "Trust him?"

"Ayuh." Micah leaned back in his chair. "Just like a little child."

✒

Barbara lay in a cloud of pink cotton candy as she watched television. A character on the show was having a baby, panting and pushing, sweating and screaming, until—ta da! A squawking bundle of joy popped out beneath a drape and landed in the masked doctor's hands.

Tears rolled down Barbara's cheeks as she brought a chocolate to her mouth. Life wasn't fair. The women of her favorite television drama were beautiful, rich, and fertile. By next week, this character would be thin too.

Across the room, Russell sat stocking-footed in a chair, the classified ads in his hands. Laying the paper aside, Russell stood. "I think I'll make me a bedtime snack. Want a sandwich or something?"

Sniffling, she fumbled for a caramel nougat. "No, thank you. I don't have any appetite."

"You sure?'

"Positive."

Russell left the room, closing the door behind him as Barbara's fingers encountered nothing but empty wrappers. She pulled the box closer, ruffled through the frilled papers, then cast the container aside. Snuggling down into pink sheets, she tried to sleep, but her brain would not rest. Dr. Marc's words kept running through her mind: *The sooner we do it, the sooner your body will have a chance to heal and prepare for a child.*

A baby. A child of her own. Was that what she wanted? Sometimes the thought thrilled her, but at other moments her mother's warnings overshadowed the thrill. A child was a terribly serious responsibility, kids could break your heart, and they did grow up to be teenagers . . .

Rolling over, she picked up the remote and clicked to The Learning Channel. Groan. "A Baby Story" was playing. Her finger was about to hit the channel button again when the screen filled with a shot of a pregnant couple walking down a corridor into the birthing room.

For the next fifteen minutes she watched, alternating between tears and laughter. Barbara joined the chorus of reverent oohs and ahhhs as air filled those tiny lungs and the infant released its first kittenish cries.

Grandparents and siblings entered the birthing room after the new arrival appeared. Barbara had never seen such excitement and joy on any faces. She reached for a clean tissue, picturing Russell as the new daddy, Cleta and Floyd as the new grandparents.

They would be happy with a new baby, she knew it. Cleta was only afraid of losing her daughter. But you couldn't lose what you didn't really own, and, if the truth be told, nobody owned their kids. Babies didn't drop off trees; God sent them . . . and never before had Barbara realized how significant that fact was. God had entrusted her to her mother, and in the future he might entrust a child or two into her care . . . if she could overcome her fear.

Micah's image played in her mind like a movie, his words echoing along a quiet soundtrack: *Perfect love casts out fear, Barbara, and if you have Jesus, you have perfect love.*

A few minutes later Russell returned with a large glass of soda and a Dagwood sandwich on a plate piled high with corn chips. He sat down in his TV chair, arranged his plate and drink, then turned and reached for the classified ads.

"Russell?"

His eyes were intent on the newspaper. "Hmm?"

"I want a baby."

"Uh huh. Let me finish my snack, then we'll talk." He took a large bite of his sandwich.

Barbara crawled out from beneath the covers and perched on the edge of the bed, then propped her elbows on her knees and stared at him.

He glanced up, holding up a wedge of sandwich. "Want a bite?"

"No, thank you. I'm going to find Mom, OK?"

He quirked a brow, then smiled. "OK."

Downstairs, Barbara searched the living room, then peeked into her parents' bedroom. Floyd lay in bed propped up on a stack of pillows watching *Emergency 911,* but Mom was nowhere in sight.

She found Cleta in the kitchen, sitting at the table with a cup of hot tea. Barbara sat down next to her.

Cleta looked up. "Want a cup of tea?"

"No. I want a baby, Mom."

Cleta snorted. "Best talk to your husband about that."

"I want to talk to you about it." She reached for Cleta's

hand. "I love you, Mom, and I love Russell. I'm sorry I didn't ask you to share in my decision about seeing Dr. Marc, but as hard as it's going to be for you to accept this, I'm a married woman now. My first allegiance is to my husband. Even the Bible says a man must leave his father and mother and be joined to his wife, and the two are united into one."

"The Bible says the man leaves," Cleta argued. "It doesn't say anything about the woman—"

"It works both ways, Mom. Besides, in Bible times, the groom always went to fetch the bride away from her home. Pastor Winslow mentions that often when he talks about the Minor Prophets."

Tears swelled to Cleta's eyes. She dropped her head. "I've been acting like an old fool."

Barbara leaned in to hug her. "You've been acting like a mother who has suddenly realized her daughter isn't a baby anymore. I don't know how that feels, Mom, but I will someday, if God gives us a daughter. I'd like to be your baby forever, but I can't. It's time I grew up and faced my own responsibilities. I need to discover what kind of woman God wants me to be."

She softened her voice. "I'll always need and want you, Mom. Nothing will ever change that." Holding out her hand, she motioned for Cleta to take hers. "Come on. We're going to start right now thinking more about the future than the past. The best is yet to come—isn't that what they say? The Bible says perfect love casts out fear . . . and we know Christ's perfect love, so the future can't harm us."

She leaned over and kissed Cleta's cheek. "Now—I'm

going upstairs to talk to my husband, then I'm calling Dr. Marc. If the Lord wills, I'm going to have that surgery as soon as possible."

Cleta patted her hand, her eyes bright with unshed tears. "Go ahead, honey."

Russell looked up when Barbara came back into the room. "Come here, hon," she said, pointing to the phone. "You'll want to hear this conversation."

Russell frowned. "Who are you calling at this hour?"

Barbara picked up the phone and punched in the number. The phone rang once. Twice. On the third ring, Dr. Marc answered.

"Sorry to disturb you so late, Dr. Marc."

"Barbara?" The doctor chuckled. "You haven't disturbed me. I've been expecting your call."

She sighed in relief. "You have?"

"You bet. I knew a lovely young couple like you and Russell would eventually be eager to discover the joys and agonies of parenthood. And I can assure you, a child is more precious than gold. Of course, your gold will be refined in those teenage years . . ."

Barbara laughed, wiping a tear from the corner of her eye. She grinned at Russell and squeezed his hand.

"So—you want me to schedule the surgery?"

"Yes, please. As soon as possible."

"I'll do it. I'll call Dr. Comeaux tomorrow morning."

She hung up, then looked at her husband. Russell stood beside her, an incredulous look on his face.

"What changed your mind?" he whispered.

"You," she said, stepping into the circle of his arms. "And God. And Micah. And perfect love. I'm beginning to realize I have everything I need, and not a single reason to be afraid of the unknown."

Nuzzling her neck, Russell said, "You watched 'A Baby Story,' didn't you?"

Her throat was too clogged with emotion to respond.

He laughed. "That's all right. I always cry when I watch that stupid thing."

She giggled at the thought of her big, tough lobster-man watching "A Baby Story." And crying!

Holding each other tight, they swayed in each other's arms. Barbara closed her eyes, relishing the moment. Tomorrow, no matter what it brought, was going to be bright. Tomorrow would be better for her parents too. Life brought change with every turn of the hourglass, but the important things remained. Love was forever.

Chapter Thirteen

On Thursday, the twenty-fourth, a special package arrived at the mercantile. Vernie pulled it from the wrapper, then weighed it on her palms. Land o' Goshen, there really was such a thing as monkey biscuits!

Tucking the container under her arm, she lowered her head and charged back to the storeroom, then slammed the door. Deftly lifting the edge of the plastic container with a fingernail, she pulled out one of the round nuggets and sniffed it.

Didn't smell like much.

She read the label. "Contains dehulled soybean meal, corn flour, ground soybean hulls, ground oats, corn gluten meal, fructose, soybean oil, and added calcium."

Nothing that'd hurt a body . . . even Buddy Franklin.

Her eyes darted toward the door. She concentrated, listening for sounds. Elezar was cleaning behind the counter, so he wouldn't be likely to snoop if she wanted to give these things a nibble . . .

She brought the nugget to her lips. Texture was OK. She touched the tip of her tongue to its dusty surface. Hmm. Not bad, but a little grassy for her taste.

She put it between her teeth, preparing to bite down—

The door flew open. Startled, her tongue shot forward, launching the monkey biscuit across the room. It hit the window, rattled the pane, then ricocheted toward the door, landing with a solid plop in Elezar's extended palm.

The clerk gazed at the unidentified flying object. "What in the world?"

"It's a . . . a new product."

A grin slowly spread over his face. "It's one of those monkey biscuits, isn't it?"

"So what if it is? Buddy says he eats 'em." Lifting her chin, she brushed by him. "You told me to order them, so I did."

Moving to her counter, she poured herself a Coke, then added a double shot of vanilla to cleanse her palate.

She'd said it before, and she'd say it again. Buddy Franklin was the strangest man to ever land on Heavenly Daze.

❧

The week between Basil's call and their lunch appointment passed slowly for Dana. With no students to teach, no house projects to complete, and no husband to keep her company, she had thrown herself into a crash program of self-improvement—fifty sit-ups upon rising, twenty minutes of jumping rope after breakfast, an hour of poetry reading before lunch. She read every volume of poems she could find in the house—Emily Dickinson, Robert Frost, William Wordsworth. Yakov, who had noticed her feverish interest in the rhymed line, found a book of seventeenth-century poets in the attic and brought it to her. Dana fell head over heels in love with Robert Herrick, who wrote,

> Why dost thou wound and break my heart
> As if we would forever part?

Hast thou not heard an oath from me—
After a day or two or three?
I would come back and live with thee.
Take, if thou dost distrust that vow
This second protestation now:
If on thy cheek, that spangled tear
That sits as dew of roses there,
That tear shall scarce be dried before
I'll kiss the threshold of thy door.
Then weep not, sweet, but this much know—
I'm half-returned before I go.

Reading it for the fortieth time, Dana wiped tears from her eyes and pressed the book to her chest. Why couldn't men write verses like that anymore? Why couldn't today's men even quote verses like that?

The sweetest thing Mike said to her these days was, "Great dinner, hon," just before kissing her on the top of the head and rushing back into the dining room to check his eBay auctions. Sometimes he murmured an "I love you," before falling asleep, but Dana wasn't sure if he was talking to her or to his computer.

On Thursday, Dana washed and curled her hair, dressed in one of her nicest dresses, then slipped into her warmest coat, gloves, and boots. Mike was out in the workroom when she left the house for the short walk to the ferry, and as Captain Stroble steered the boat through the feather-white sea toward Ogunquit, she tried not to think of her husband at all.

One thought rode uppermost in her mind: She'd bet

her last dollar that Basil Caldwell would understand her passion for Robert Herrick.

❧

Waving his hand, Mike sprinted to the dock, but the ferry had already pulled away. He shouted, hoping to draw Stroble's attention, but the captain had the roar of the engine in his ears. Mike was left standing alone on the shore.

Russell Higgs stood on the rocks, one hand in his pocket and a crooked smile on his face. "You're gonna catch it when you get home," he said, grinning. "Looks like your wife left without you."

Mike stared at Russell. "Dana was on the ferry?"

"Ayuh. She was all dolled up, so I thought you two were going out together or something. But, like I said, if you've missed her, you're gonna catch it—"

"Russell . . . you weren't needin' to run over to the shore, now, were you?"

"I might." Russell grinned. "For the price of a hot cider on a cold day like this, I might be talked into a run at Perkins Cove."

"What are we waitin' on, then?"

❧

Dana felt her heart leap into her throat when she spied Basil Caldwell. The Oarweed restaurant lay just across the parking lot from the ferry landing, and the wind was whipping across the empty space something fierce. The asphalt under her feet was wet with melted snow, and large drifts, piled high by the plow, bordered the area like a frozen fence. But there Basil stood, waiting in the cold wind like a perfect gentleman, looking every inch as prosperous and handsome as his magazine picture.

She hurried across the frigid parking lot, her hands in her pockets and her heart fluttering.

"Dana Franklin," he said, coming forward to take her gloved hand. "You haven't changed a bit."

Despite the weather, she felt warmth flood her cheeks. "It's Dana Klackenbush now, and I'm afraid more than the name has changed since I left high school."

"You still look like a girl of eighteen."

"That's kind of you, Basil—but I've got to say, you've changed quite a bit. You look much more . . . mature."

Drop-dead gorgeous, she wanted to say, but didn't.

"Nice of you to say 'mature,' instead of 'old.'"

"You're decades away from old."

"Now you're being kind."

Dana stood there, her hand in his, wondering at the miracle of it all. Here she was, standing in front of one of the area's best restaurants, with a handsome man who wore a scarf and overcoat (cashmere, from the looks of it) instead of an overstuffed down jacket and flannel-lined jeans.

"Let's not stand out here and freeze," Basil said, leading her toward the entrance ramp. "There's a blazing fire inside, and I've already reserved the best table."

Speechless with amazement, Dana could only nod and follow.

❧

As the *Barbara Jean* pulled up to the dock, Mike saw his wife and a strange man walk into the Oarweed.

"That's Dana goin' there, isn't it?" Russell asked, pointing toward the pair. "But who's that other fellow?"

Darned if he knew. But Mike couldn't let on.

"An old friend," he said, leaping from the boat to the dock. He touched the brim of his cap and waved at Russell. "Thanks for the lift. I'll buy you that hot cider next time we're at the mercantile."

"Ayuh," Russell answered, then he threw the throttle into reverse and turned the *Barbara Jean* back out to sea.

Though more than a dozen boats bobbed in the harbor at Perkins Cove, a quiet hush covered the place like a down quilt. Summer sun and balmy breezes brought out the locals and tourists alike, but though the sun shone bright today, the wind cut like a sharp knife through Mike's tattered coat. Thrusting his hands into his pockets, he ducked into the wind and jogged toward the restaurant. Upon reaching the ramp, he stopped.

What was he doing? What would Dana think if he burst in and demanded to know what was going on? In three years of marriage she had never given him a moment's worry. He trusted her with his heart, his life, and his checkbook . . . so why shouldn't he trust her in the Oarweed?

Because she'd been awfully distant the last few days . . . and unusually preoccupied. And Mike, who'd always been able to read her like a book, hadn't a clue what had filled her thoughts lately.

Moving away from the ramp, he walked to one of the restaurant windows. Knowing he looked the fool, he bent an evergreen branch on a nearby shrub until it covered his face, then peered through the greenery into the restaurant.

The man, whoever he was, was taking Dana's coat from her shoulders. The sight of his wife in a dress stole Mike's breath—why, she hadn't worn a dress since last fall, and today wasn't even a Sunday! It was a doggone nice dress, too, one that emphasized her creamy complexion and accented her curves . . .

The branch cracked in his hand, snapping Mike to attention. He pulled back, looking askance at the broken greenery, then dropped the branch to the ground and strode away from the restaurant. No sense in getting in trouble with the folks at the Oarweed for manhandlin' their shrubbery . . . and if there was one thing he didn't want, it was to cause a scene in a public place.

He walked toward the ferry office, dazed and shaken, trying to remember why he'd wanted to come to Ogunquit in the first place. Oh, ayuh—he needed another hour, at least, to wrap up his last twenty auctions of the week, and things went so much faster when he used Jodi's cable modem. No question about it, Captain Stroble's granddaughter had been a godsend. The favor she'd done him was worth far more than the five bucks he left on her keyboard every time he visited. Someday, if he ever met her, Mike had half a mind to give her a hug.

The sight of Captain Stroble's ferry office drew Mike like a magnet. Might as well go inside to warm up and calm down. He'd have to call a cab anyway, unless he wanted to walk all the way to Shore Road. Any other month he wouldn't have minded, but January was a terrible time to walk a far piece in the State of Maine.

≈

After taking their orders, the waiter reclaimed the menus and moved away. Beneath the table, Dana rubbed her hands together and reminded herself to act calm no matter how giggly she felt on the inside. Basil Caldwell, after all, was only an old friend from high school, and she was a married woman. Not happily married at the moment, but this unhappiness would pass . . . wouldn't it?

Now she looked into Basil Caldwell's blue eyes and tried to keep the conversation centered on business. "I want to talk to you about the poem." She squeezed her hands together. "I think I should tell you how I found it—"

"I'd rather talk about you." As Basil smiled, a mouthful of teeth glistened like a row of polished pearls. "What have you been up to since high school?"

"Not much," Dana said, distracted by the change of subject. "After graduation, I worked for a while in Wells, then went to college and majored in elementary education. That's where I met Mike, my husband. He bought a house on Heavenly Daze, we got married, and I moved to the island. We've been there three years now, and I run a day-care center during the tourist season. I also run the Heavenly Daze school, and I have three students. We're in the midst of our winter break, but we'll resume classes in April. Then I suspect life will get real busy again when the folks from away start visiting."

Aware that she was babbling, Dana clamped her mouth shut and reached for her water goblet.

Basil lifted his glass in a salute. "That's an unusual schedule. Most people vacation in the summer."

Dana shrugged. "It fits us. The Grahams—their son Georgie is one of my students—need someone to watch him during tourist season, so we hold classes all summer and take our long break in the winter. As long as we're in session 180 days, nobody much cares when we have school."

Basil sipped from his glass, then asked, "You still have family around here?"

"My dad died years ago, and Mom passed away right after I got married." Dana lowered her gaze. "My brother, Buddy, traveled around, did odd jobs, spent some time in the Navy, and then came home. Since my parents' house had been sold, he moved in with me and Mike."

"Is that . . . agreeable?"

Dana made a face. "Mike and I don't mind, because Buddy lives in the carriage house. If Buddy minds—well, I'm never quite sure what Buddy's thinking." She leaned forward. "That's why I was so surprised about the poem."

"I'm sure he'll be proud of you. Now—" Basil leaned toward her— "I was thinking we could hold a small ceremony on Heavenly Daze, complete with the press, though only heaven knows how I'll get them out on the water in late January. We'll have a brief presentation, award the prize to you—"

"Oh! Did my poem win?"

He laughed. "Of course, I thought you knew."

"No, I thought . . ." Her words trailed away. Actually, she thought they were having lunch as old friends. But Buddy would be delighted to know that one of his castoff poems had won such an illustrious contest.

" . . . and you can say a few words to your friends and neighbors," Basil was saying. "Of course, we'll want to print the poem in our next edition of *Northeastern Living.*"

Dana felt her smile droop, and he noticed her less-than-happy expression instantly. "Is something wrong?"

"When would you want to do this?"

Basil reached into his tweed jacket and pulled out an

electronic appointment book. "Next week would be best. We'll need to do it soon if we're to make our deadline for the March issue. How about Wednesday, the thirtieth?"

"Well . . ." Biting her lip, Dana weighed the odds of persuading Buddy to appear at an awards ceremony. Slim to none, she figured. Any man who felt exposed sitting on the back pew at church would flee a flashy awards ceremony like a felon. They'd be lucky if they saw him again before the spring thaw.

Unless, of course, Buddy thought the ceremony was being held to honor someone else . . . like his sister. Then he might be persuaded to attend.

"Basil," she lowered her voice to a conspiratorial whisper. "I didn't write that poem."

He stroked his clipped beard. "You didn't?"

"No. And the person who did—well, let's just say he's a bit shy, so I don't want you to say anything to anyone about his identity. Just come, do whatever you want to do with the ceremony, and when everything's in place, I'll step forward and unmask the actual poet." She arranged her features in an expression of deep concern. "I'm afraid everything will be ruined if word gets out beforehand."

Basil leaned back in his chair, a calculating look on his face. "The real poet is shy, you say."

"Ayuh."

"And maybe her family wouldn't approve of her dabbling in poetry."

"Well . . . if that's what you want to say, OK. It's not exactly true, though."

"Of course it's not." Basil inclined his head in a sympathetic gesture, then reached out and patted Dana's hand.

"Fear not, little lady, your secret is safe with me. We'll proceed, but we'll not release the poet's identity until the day of the ceremony. It's the least I can do for a poetic genius."

"Thank you. And the thirtieth is fine. We'll look forward to it." Giving him a smile of pure relief, Dana unfolded her napkin as the waiter arrived with two steaming bowls of clam chowder.

Basil watched wordlessly as Dana devoured her soup like a woman who hadn't had a restaurant-cooked meal in months. Imagine, a poet of her talent having to write on the sly! Her husband must be some kind of a brute to make Dana recoil from public praise. She probably figured that if she could get him to the ceremony, the significance of the award would dignify her poetry and earn her work a smidgen of respect.

He picked up his spoon, ladled up a bite of the rich chowder, and blew on it while looking at his attractive companion. Dana Franklin had always been shy, he recalled. As a young girl, round blue eyes and long hair had dominated her face, and he could still remember her sitting in a biology classroom, her lips slightly parted as he tried to sell those silly red carnations. She'd been but a child then, but the woman sitting across from him was a lovely rose in full blossom.

And a poet! Who'd have imagined the Franklin family had a single sensitive soul among them! He remembered Buddy, the long-legged, gangly kid who'd played soccer in the youth leagues. Thick as a post and dull as mud, Buddy Franklin had the personality of an oil gusher: dark and unrefined. Reading between the lines of what Dana had said today, Basil sensed that Buddy hadn't done anything to clean up his act during the years between high school and the present.

The husband was an unknown factor, but he had to be some kind of loser if he'd found it necessary to retreat to Heavenly Daze. Basil remembered reading an article about the island several years ago—the writer had described the island as a charming collection of old houses and old people. Any young man who chose to exile himself there had to be a fool . . . and the way Dana smiled when he promised to keep her secret proved it.

He sampled the chowder, then nodded his approval as Dana caught his eye. Perhaps, if this husband didn't appreciate his wife's talents, Dana would see what a jerk she had married. Perhaps she'd be willing to leave Heavenly Daze in search of greener pastures . . . and a more supportive spouse.

One never knew.

❧

After lunch, Dana said farewell to Basil, who walked her to the ferry landing, then drove away in a late-model BMW equipped with snow chains. Dana checked her watch. The ferry wouldn't head back to Heavenly Daze until six, so unless she could catch a ride with a passing fisherman, she could either stand outside and freeze or see if Captain Stroble minded a little company in his office.

She tapped on the window, then grinned when he motioned her into the warmth of his small space. "Hello, Dana," he said, creaking the seat of his stool as he swiveled to face her. "Did you know your hubby was just here?"

Dana barely managed to mask her surprise. "Oh . . . of course. Mike must have caught a ride."

"Ayuh, he did. With Russell Higgs."

In an effort to appear casual, Dana walked toward the small space heater and lifted her hands to warm them. "Did Mike happen to say where he was headed? I've got to do a little shopping before you take the ferry back over, but I don't want to go to the market if that's where he was going."

"He didn't say much of anything. Just sat here, looking out the window, then he called a cab. I think he was going to Jodi's."

Dana stared. "Jodi Standish?"

"Ayuh. That seems to be working out real fine. I'm glad I hooked those two up."

"You . . . hooked my husband up with Jodi Standish?"

The captain's brows drew downward in a frown. "And what was wrong with that? They both had needs . . . and I figured I could help 'em out. Jodi's a fine girl, one of the best."

Numb with shock, Dana staggered to the window. Was the entire world aligned against her? Captain Stroble, whom she'd always considered a friend, had set her husband up with a husband stealer . . . and was *bragging* about it?

But maybe the captain didn't know Jodi was a husband stealer. Maybe he thought Mike's involvement with that woman was completely innocent . . . but he hadn't heard Mike's guilty whispering on the phone. He hadn't lived with her distant, distracted husband these last few weeks.

Maybe what she was experiencing was paranoia run amuck. But she could check things out while she was here.

If her husband was having an affair, she'd have to see the proof with her own eyes.

"It's some stuffy in here." Afraid the old captain would see the tears brimming in her eyes, she gestured out the window without looking at him. "Do you still have your bicycle out back? Since you're not going to take the ferry back for a while, seems to me the least you could do is let me borrow your bike. I promise I'll have it back before six."

Captain Stroble laughed. "I haven't ridden that bike since summer, but you're welcome to it. It's parked between the hedge and the building."

"Thanks." Dana slipped out of the office and found the old Schwinn bicycle exactly where the captain had said it would be. A cab would have been easier, and she wouldn't really have minded paying the fare, but the sound of an approaching car might tip Mike and his lady friend off, and Dana wanted to catch them by surprise. One chance encounter would finally settle her doubts and prove her point.

Her teeth chattering, she looped her purse over a handlebar, then straddled the center bar. Riding a bike over ice in a dress and long coat wouldn't be the easiest thing in the world, but she'd manage. Fortunately, the dress and coat were long enough to protect her from the wind, but not so long that the fabric would get caught in the chain.

Gritting her teeth, she pushed off and pedaled over the wet parking lot. The front tire was low, though not exactly flat, and required a great deal of straining . . .

Then she came to the hill. Dana lowered her head and stood on the pedals, propelling the bike up the incline by the sheer force of her will.

Right. Left. Right. Left. Right.

Pedaling became easier as she left Perkins Cove and settled onto a flat stretch of Shore Road, but by the time she found the Standish woman's name on a mailbox, Dana had worked up a July sweat beneath her clothes.

Puffing from exertion, she dropped the bike onto the sidewalk, then ducked behind a broad oak tree in the front lawn. Jodi Standish's house was downright cozy, yellow clapboard walls trimmed with blue shutters and a bright white door. A cheery Christmas wreath still hung on the front window, and red vinyl ribbons adorned the two porch pillars like stripes on a candy cane.

Hunching into her coat, Dana darted down the length of the empty driveway, then plastered herself to the side of the house. She hunkered beside a window, through which she could see a pair of lace curtains edging the glass. If she could only elevate herself a little, she could peek inside.

She looked around. The flower bed was bare, strewn with winter mulch and half a dozen empty clay flowerpots. Picking up two of the pots, Dana stood them upside down beneath the window, then planted one foot on each and crouched. She placed her fingertips on the sill, then slowly raised her head to peek through the window.

Her effort paid off. The space beyond was a dining room, where a lovely antique table stood draped in a lace cloth. Beyond the dining room she could see the entrance hallway, and beyond that another room, where she could see just a sliver of Mike's head. He appeared to be sitting in a chair, his head nodding at something she couldn't see . . .

As one of the flowerpots suddenly crumbled beneath her weight, Dana shrieked and tumbled into the mulch.

"Gevalt!" She didn't know what the word meant, but Yakov always said it when he was surprised by the unexpected, and it felt appropriate now.

Afraid she had drawn Mike's attention, she skittered to the back of the house and crouched behind a scraggly boxwood hedge. While she hid there, inhaling the scent of spoiling garbage from the plastic bags stacked on the porch, she glanced toward the detached garage. Miss Standish's car—probably a Lexus, or maybe a Porsche—had to be tucked inside, safe and warm, while she, Mike's lawful wife, had been reduced to sneaking around on a nearly flat-tired bicycle and squatting over dingy snowdrifts.

A creaking sound split the air. For a moment Dana was tempted to forget everything and run, but the noise came from the front of the house. After a moment of trepidation, she inched forward and turned the corner, then crouched by a skeletal mass of winter-bare shrubbery near the front porch. Mike stood by the door, his attention on the lock. He was struggling to turn a key, and after a moment he pulled it free, then bent to slide it under the welcome mat.

He had this woman's key. Or at least knew where she kept it.

How close were he and Jodi Standish?

Her heart sinking, Dana waited until a cab appeared and Mike jogged toward it, his jacket collar high around his ears. He paid no attention to the bike on the sidewalk, but pointed the driver toward Perkins Cove.

As the cab pulled away, Dana picked herself up and trudged to the bike, then hoisted her leg over it and wearily began to pedal back to the ferry office.

Was her marriage in such dire straits that even Captain Stroble had decided to point Mike toward greener pastures? The idea made no sense, but nothing in her life had made sense lately.

Nothing at all.

Chapter Fourteen

On Sunday night, at the angels' regular weekly meeting, Yakov took his place at the table and smiled a welcome to his brothers. Gavriel was present and in fine form, his long white hair glowing with reflected glory. Kindness radiated from the lines around his mouth, and wisdom shone in his eyes. His height commanded the attention of every angel in the room, but for all his power, Gavriel's soul was gentle, bent to serve and minister to the angelic squadron he supervised. True leaders, he often reminded the others, were servants first.

Gavriel called the meeting to order, then stood and offered a word of encouragement for his brothers:

> *"The LORD has made the heavens his throne;*
> *from there he rules over everything.*
> *Praise the LORD, you angels of his,*
> *you mighty creatures who carry out his plans,*
> *listening for each of his commands.*
> *Yes, praise the LORD, you armies of angels who serve*
> *him and do his will!*
> *Praise the LORD, everything he has created, everywhere*
> *in his kingdom.*
> *As for me—I, too, will praise the LORD."*

Yakov loved all his angel brothers, but he held a special respect for Gavriel, who had ministered to the people of Heavenly Daze longer than any of the others. A human might have been jealous of Gavriel's unique position, but when one's will was completely wedded to the Father's, jealousy was impossible. Yakov could no more envy Gavriel than he could tell a lie.

Gavriel had been able to remain in service on the island because he appeared so rarely. While the others inhabited bodies of flesh that appeared to age and suffer various mortal weakness (Abner kept complaining that his body was too prone to growth around the waistline), Gavriel's physical manifestation most closely resembled the angels' supernatural bodies.

Yakov had never minded inhabiting mortal flesh. It was merely a shell, and though it wrinkled and sagged and sometimes grew hair in the most inconvenient places (last week, he'd found long hairs growing in his ears!), it could not diminish his strength, his intellect, or his willingness to serve the Lord.

In order to keep the human population from marveling that some residents seemed immune to death, the Father allowed the angels to rotate off the island after a certain span of human years. They did not die, of course, for angels are eternal. When they had finished their task, they simply said their farewells and left the island, usually on the ferry or another boat, and ascended to the third heaven from a secluded spot on the mainland. Their mortal bodies vaporized into the dust and water from which they'd been created, and within hours, a new angel would appear at the angel-less house and offer his services to the inhabitants. Never in two hundred years had an angel been refused.

Immediately following Jacques de Cuvier's prayer, Yakov had served in the Klackenbush house as a manservant to a retired sea captain. Fifty years later he was recalled to the halls of heaven, and as time on earth passed he found himself ministering to the saints in China, Africa, and England. In the second Great War, Yakov sorrowed as evil swept over much of the earth, cutting short the mortal lives of so many of God's chosen people. The Almighty sent him to minister in Holland, where he sought to alleviate suffering and bring comfort according to the will of the sovereign Lord. It was in Holland that he picked up the Yiddish language and a unique admiration for the descendants of Abraham, Isaac, and Jacob.

During that dark time, when so many people feared that God had deserted his people, Yakov realized the significance of what the Lord had spoken to his prophet Isaiah: "I form the light and create darkness, bring prosperity and create disaster; I, the Lord, do all these things." The Almighty God, Yakov learned, was not only more powerful than any evildoer, but he could take the worst evil and use it for the highest good.

Because one evil man had murdered so many of Abraham's descendants, other men rallied around their cause and established the state called Israel. And now, as God moved men and nations according to his sovereign plan for the ages, Yakov was thrilled to be ministering again in the small community known as Heavenly Daze.

For God's boundless love was never intended only for nations and kings, but for men, women, and children. The spiritual growth of Dana Klackenbush was as important to the Almighty God as the spiritual growth of a president, and millions of angels watched and waited for news of Buddy Franklin's salvation.

As the wind whistled around the windows of the Heavenly Daze church basement, Gavriel paused for a special announcement. "The Father has told me that next month, one of you will be transferring to another branch of service."

Yakov felt a stirring in his soul. As much as he loved his duty on Heavenly Daze, the thought of serving the Lord Almighty in another venue sent a thrill shivering down his mortal spine.

The angels looked at each other, each one silently asking, "Will it be you?"

Yakov looked at Gavriel. "No further word?"

The angel captain shook his head. "Nothing yet. The Lord will reveal His will in His timing."

After another round of musical praise, the angels relaxed for refreshment and their weekly reports. Gavriel paused before Yakov, a tray of pizza rolls in his hand. "I thought you might like these, brother. They're a nice change from our usual dinner."

Yakov picked up one of the snacks and held it to the light. "I don't know. It doesn't seem quite as filling as the round pizza pie."

"Take two," Gavriel suggested. "I can make more."

"I think," Zuriel called from his place at the table, "that pepperoni pizza is our favorite. It's warm, it fills the belly, and Abner can bring the dough from the bakery."

"It's my pleasure," Abner added, taking one of the bite-size treats from the tray. "Birdie never minds me taking a pinch of dough, though she would never believe how such a little bit manages to expand to feed seven hungry angels."

The others laughed, and Yakov knew they were all

remembering how the Lord fed over five thousand men with two loaves of bread and five fishes. They had watched that miracle from the balconies of heaven, but it wasn't the last time they had witnessed miracles of provision.

"I'm anxious to hear your reports," Gavriel said, sinking into a chair at the head of the unadorned table. "Abner, how are Birdie and Bea?"

Abner paused to swallow a last bite of pizza roll, then smiled. "They are well. Bea continues to answer the incoming angel mail as best she can, though it has slowed a bit in recent weeks. Birdie continues to minister to Salt and the children. Bobby and Brittany are looking forward to school, and when the weather is nice, little Georgie Graham fellowships with them. They are no longer lonely—and neither is Salt."

Murmurs of "Praise the Lord" filled the air, then Zuriel lifted a hand. "Speaking of the Grahams, I've good news to report. Charles has begun to paint with new passion, and Babette hopes to sell quite a few paintings when the tourist season begins. And—" he leaned forward, "though Babette herself doesn't know it yet, new life has been conceived in her womb. By next fall, little Georgie will have three new sisters!"

"Triplets?" Caleb's lined face lit with joy. "Glory be to the Father, who does all things well!"

"I'm looking forward to new avenues of service," Zuriel added, "and hoping to brush up on my diapering skills. I haven't diapered a baby in eighty-three years."

"It's very different now," Elezar said, nodding. "I watched a woman diaper her baby at the mercantile last summer. It's all done with plastic and adhesive tape."

"Really?" Zuriel's eyes grew thoughtful. "I suppose I shall have to pay closer attention to the television commercials."

"I see them all the time," Micah inserted. "You'll want to watch the ones for Huggies. Nine out of ten new mothers prefer them. They change colors when they are soiled."

Zuriel stroked his beard. "Amazing."

"Vernie's heart is softening," Elezar volunteered. "She and Stanley are actually eating meals together now. Stanley's still occupying the guest room, but I daresay Vernie is beginning to consider him a friend and not a foe."

"Love is a powerful thing," Zuriel observed, smiling. "It can soften even the hardest heart."

"And the Lansdowns?" Gavriel asked, gently leading the conversation around the table. "Are Barbara and Russell learning to walk by faith?"

"Ayuh." Micah beamed. "Barbara is learning to face her fears with the name of Jesus. She has scheduled a surgery for tomorrow, and will be checking into York Hospital tonight."

"We will remember her to the Father," Gavriel promised. "And he will send a special detachment of angelic ministers to remain by her side while she is away from our watchcare."

"Olympia is learning to rest in the Lord," Caleb offered. "She still misses Edmund, of course, but I think his home-going has caused her to envision heaven as a real place, just beyond a mortal breath. The other day I caught her staring off into space. When I asked if she was OK, she said, 'I can almost hear them, Caleb—the sound of angels' wings.'" The angel smiled. "Indeed, she can."

"Pastor Wickam," Gavriel added, "has settled into his people's hearts as a minister should. They see him as a man, which he is, but as a man who loves God, which he does. And lately he has been praying for wisdom to lead his little flock."

"Amen," the angels chorused.

"What about his bathroom?" Abner asked.

Gavriel grinned. "I am happy to report that the bathroom project has been handed over to a professional crew which will complete repairs by the end of the month. And during this trial, not once did Winslow fall prey to his fleshly impulses. During the complications he was tempted to lose his temper, quit, curse, and snap at his wife, but on each of these occasions the Lord offered grace enough to resist . . . and Winslow chose grace. The parsonage will soon have a fully functioning bathroom once again."

Micah waved his arms. "Praise the Lord!"

Gavriel abruptly lifted his head, raising his hands in reverent awe. For a moment he closed his eyes, and when he opened them again, Yakov knew from their bright gleam that his captain had been communing with the Almighty.

"Your place of service, Yakov," Gavriel said, his voice resonating within his mortal frame, "is filled with confusion and fear. You must help all of them—Mike, Dana, and Buddy—return to their first love."

Yakov spread his hands. "How?"

"Your assignment is simple," Gavriel said. "Make sure Buddy attends the ceremony Dana is planning."

Yakov acknowledged his task with a nod. The job seemed too easy, almost trivial, but every command of the Lord was supremely important.

Chapter Fifteen

The sound of neoprene soles squeaking against waxed floors made Barbara tense. She sat in a narrow hospital bed, her eyes open, her arms at her sides. Cool as it was in the room, she felt a bead of perspiration trace a cold path from her armpit to her rib.

Perfect love casts out fear.

She mentally repeated the phrase over and over, her fingernails clicking on the bed railing in the rhythm of the words. From outside her room, foreign sounds drifted through the cracked door: a baby's cry. The gentle tink of the elevator. Heavy footfalls down the long corridor.

How odd, to be perfectly healthy and in the hospital. Russell had borrowed a car from a friend in Ogunquit; he had driven Barbara and her parents to York after church. He, not Cleta, had signed her into the hospital, and he, not Cleta, had taken Barbara to her room and helped her slip into the cotton gown. Dr. Phyllis Comeaux had dropped by to meet them, and Barbara had instinctively liked the professional, pleasant woman—and she found it oddly reassuring that she'd have a female surgeon. Then her parents and Russell left to take a hotel room near the hospital, but not before promising to be back before Barbara went into surgery the next morning.

Barbara shifted her gaze from the door to the window, through which she could see nothing but darkness. Dr. Marc said the 7 AM procedure shouldn't take more than an hour, but he warned her that the surgeon wouldn't know what she'd find during the laparoscopy. The surgery could take all morning.

Her mouth felt dry from the sedative the nurse had administered earlier. She reached for the water pitcher by her bed and heard the sound of ice cubes jostling against the side of the plastic container. She wasn't allowed to eat or drink anything, not even water, after midnight, but that was hours away. When she asked the reason for the prohibition, the nurse said they didn't want anything on her stomach in the morning because anesthesia nauseated some people.

Barbara winced. She had thrown up only once in her life, the day she drank some of Annie Cuvier's experimental soda pop. She supposed she was lucky to be alive—later the concoction blew a portion of the roof off Olympia's garage.

She sloshed some water into a paper cup, then lifted it to her lips. She drank thirstily, then dropped the cup back to the bedside table and leaned back on her pillows.

She missed Russell. She missed her mom and dad. She even missed Micah, for the gardener had comforted her on more occasions than she could remember. And if he were here, he'd be telling her to take her worries to the Lord.

She closed her eyes. "Thank you, Father, for giving me a wonderful husband who's been patient when he had every reason to want to strangle my family. I'm unworthy of him, but I'm going to work harder at being a good wife, and, if it's your will, a good mother. I've been selfish, but I'm going to work on that too. Teach me how to be a daughter without sacrificing the attention I should give my husband and children. I'll be walking a thin rope, so grant me shoes that grip."

A tap sounded at the door. Barbara opened her eyes to see a crown of graying hair appear in the crack.

"Mama?"

"Shh!" Cleta held her forefinger to her lips. "I'm not supposed to be here." She eased through the doorway and quietly closed the door. Hurrying to the bedside, she hugged Barbara. "Are you OK?"

Barbara wriggled out of the bear hold. "Of course I'm fine. You just left an hour ago."

"I know, but things can go wrong so quickly." Pulling a vinyl-upholstered chair closer to the bed, Cleta settled in.

Barbara pressed her lips together. Part of her wanted to be annoyed at her mother's continued overprotectiveness, but it was good to see a family face. "Where's Russell?"

"Sound asleep at the hotel. So is your daddy. I couldn't sleep, so I grabbed a cab and came back."

"You slipped out without them knowing?"

Cleta shrugged. "I suppose. Alst I know is that I wasn't doing a bit of good just lyin' there."

"Mama." Barbara leaned over and took her mother's hand. "Someone's going to be here to run you out in a few minutes. Visiting hours ended at eight."

"I'll take my chances. If they make me go, I'll sleep in the waiting room." Her eyes softened. "I won't leave you."

Barbara patted her hand, then lifted it to place a kiss on the brown-speckled knuckles. "I love you, Mom."

"I love you too, Doodles." They sat in silence a moment, their hands linked. Then Cleta drew a deep breath. "Now there's nothing to be afraid of. This is a simple procedure done every day. 'Course it is surgery and anything could go wrong, but it won't."

Barbara laughed at the halfhearted reassurance. "I'm not afraid. Not now."

Now that she'd settled her mind, she was anxious to proceed. And Russell was as excited as a kid at Christmas. "A boy," he told her as they packed her bag for the hospital. "Let's have a boy first. I want a son to help me on the boat."

"It could be a girl, you know."

He grinned. "That'd be fine, too. She can bait traps."

Barbara laughed and warned him they didn't get to pick. "We take what we get."

"Maybe you'll have twins."

That comment had left Barbara feeling a little weak-kneed.

The hospital settled down for the night. Outside her window, a cold rain fell on the mounds of dirty snow.

"Are you sleepy?"

"A little woozy."

"Well, you go to sleep, darlin'. I'm right here if you need me."

Barbara squeezed her mother's hand before releasing it. "Thanks, Mom."

She closed her eyes and relaxed, and for a while she drifted in a shallow doze. Once she thought she heard Cleta talking to a nurse. The nurse said visiting hours were over, but Cleta refused to budge. The nurse finally left with a warning about breaking rules.

"Been breaking 'em all my life," Cleta muttered as the door closed.

᷿

As Barbara slept, her breaths coming deep and even, Cleta stood and gently tucked the blanket around her child's shoulders. She'd been performing the task for years. Bedtime was always a special hour of the day, an hour that accented the closeness between a mother and child.

Leaning close, she whispered: "I know I have to let you go." A tear dropped onto the blanket. "When you become a mother, you'll find out that letting go is the hardest thing a parent can do. But I'm going to do it, Barbara. For your sake, for Russell's, and for mine.

"I'll always be here if you need me. I'll always love you as much or more as the day I brought you home from the hospital. Just allow me to be your friend. I vow to you tonight that I'll never again tell you how to run your life, how to wear your hair, or beg you to share your private thoughts unless it's what you want to do."

Resting her head on the side of the bed, Cleta made a heartful of promises, and meant every one.

Chapter Sixteen

The lights in the hospital room snapped on at five-thirty. Barbara had been awake, afraid to make a sound for fear of disturbing her mother. When the lights came on Cleta sat straight up, blinking at the harsh glare. "What's wrong? What's happened? Barbara? Floyd! Something's wrong with Barbara!"

Barbara slid out of bed. "I'm right here, Mom. And don't have a cow, but I'm going into the bathroom."

She moved into the adjoining rest room as the nurse faced Cleta.

Through the bathroom door, Barbara heard the nurse explain. "We're here to get your daughter ready for surgery."

Cleta sounded sheepish. "Oh my—I was in a deep sleep."

"They'll be down to get your daughter in forty minutes or so."

Barbara splashed water on her face, then ran a comb through her hair. Though it was probably silly, she pulled out a tube of lip gloss, then rubbed some over her chapped lips. Russell would be coming to the hospital, and she wanted to look nice for him.

She stepped back into the hospital room, smiled at her mother, and because there was nothing else to do, crawled back into bed.

"You look pretty, Doodles."

"Thanks, Mom."

Soon a nurse came with a pair of green paper slippers. Wiggling her toes in the flimsy footwear, Barbara giggled. "I won't be wading through much snow with these."

"Wait until you get into the surgery," the nurse teased. "You'll be grateful to have something to keep your toes warm."

Barbara consulted the clock on her bed stand. "I was hoping Russell would—"

At that moment Russell walked through the doorway with Floyd following. Russell bent and kissed Barbara. When he pulled away, his dark eyes were serious. "Are we ready for this?"

She nodded. "Let's do it!"

Her gaze shifted to her dad, who looked grumpy and out of sorts. His frustration flared when he saw Cleta.

"Woman," he said, "we spent half the night looking for you. I was going to call the State Patrol until Russell thought to call the hospital."

Cleta gave him a guilty look. "I'm sorry, Floyd. I know I promised, but I had to be with her. Just this one last time."

He grunted. "Can't say I blame you. I wanted to do the same, but I figured you were the only one who could pull it off without getting thrown out."

Cleta squeezed his hand. "It's going to be OK, Floyd. I know my place now."

He winked at her. "Well, it better be by my side."

"Forever," she promised, leaning into his warmth.

Pastor Winslow arrived at 6:50, then family and their shepherd held hands in prayer. "Father," Winslow prayed, "we ask that you guide the surgeon's hands this morning. May she be an extension of your wisdom and grace. Amen."

At six o'clock the babies in the nursery rode out for their breakfasts. Barbara and her family watched as nurses wheeled cart after cart of newborns down the hall to their waiting mothers.

Leaning close to Barbara's ear, Russell whispered, "Next year, one of those could be ours."

Sleepy now from a shot the nurse had administered, Barbara squeezed his hand. "A girl, you said?"

"Boy," he reminded. "Or girl," he added when a pink-hatted little cherub rolled by.

A pair of smiling orderlies came into the room and helped Barbara onto the gurney, then the family walked beside her to a large bank of elevators where they each were allowed to speak a word of encouragement.

Cleta took Barbara's hand. "Be brave, baby. Mama's right outside the door. Everything will be fine."

With tears shining behind his glasses, Floyd planted a quick kiss on his daughter's forehead. "You're still my little girl, no matter how sassy you get."

Pastor Wickam patted her arm. "God's peace be with you, Barbara."

"Thank you, Pastor."

Russell gave her a long kiss. "I love you, honey—and I'll be waiting for you in the recovery room." Their hands touched as long as they could until the orderlies wheeled Barbara into the elevator.

～

Cleta finished the last of the roast beef sandwich Floyd had brought her for lunch, then rose to check Barbara's IV drip. All was well. Sighing, she sat back down in her chair, idly wondering if the vinyl of the chair would mold itself to her old bones by the time she left.

Floyd and Russell had gone down to the cafeteria for lunch; Winslow had returned to the island. The hospital sounds seemed muted now, or perhaps her hearing wasn't as acute because her nerves weren't so edgy.

She glanced at the sleeping form in the hospital bed. Her daughter.

Her beautiful Barbara.

Pale, sleeping, unaware that the surgery had been blessedly successful. *Thank you, precious Lord.*

Cleta knew she didn't need to remind God that it hurt to see one's child in pain.

Tears pricked her eyes as she remembered the day Barbara had been born, the moment she'd known they had a daughter, the first startled cry, the wrinkled little face peering up from a pink blanket. What an exhilarating and frightening moment that was! She had been given a baby to hold and love, a child to nurture and teach. And after that beautiful first day had come the first laugh, first tooth, first steps, first day of school. Graduation. And a wedding.

Her life had been rich with hopes, dreams, and promises . . . all fulfilled in Barbara. How unfair she'd been to try to deny Barbara those same gifts.

"Mom?" Barbara's eyes were unfocused, barely open.

"I'm here."

Cleta brushed her daughter's hair and kissed her cheek. "Everything went well. The surgery was a success."

"Good." Barbara closed her eyes again. "Is Russell here?"

"He's right down the hall," she said, "with your dad.

And the phone's been ringing off the hook—in fact, I turned off the ringer so you could get some rest. You know how Heavenly Daze is. Everyone cares about everyone else's business."

"Send Russ in—I want him with me."

"Sure. I'll visit with you later."

Cleta smiled as an indefinable feeling of rightness flowed through her. See? That wasn't so hard. With a little practice the words would come automatically.

"Mom?"

"Yes, sweetheart?"

"I love you."

"Love you too, baby."

Cleta walked to the waiting area, caught Russell's attention, and pointed him toward Barbara's room. He rose and went instantly, and Cleta blinked back tears as her eyes sought Floyd.

Floyd had been right. Russell didn't deserve a cotton candy–pink bedroom. What had she been thinking?

She'd have to change it—maybe she ought to put the old spread back on, the one Russell liked. After all, they'd be moving soon, that much was evident. And in a year or two or three there'd be grandchildren, either biologically or through the miracle of adoption. Either way, Cleta might find another use for that cotton candy–pink fluff—maybe a little girl's bedroom, with ballerina prints on the wall.

Change. Micah had done his best to point out that pruning did a plant—and a person—good.

When Barbara and Russell moved out, she wouldn't see her Doodles every day, though Barbara might insist they would. Oh, they'd come for Sunday dinners, Christmas,

Mother's Day, and Father's Day. Barbara respected her and Floyd. There never was any doubt of that. But when a baby came, colds and colic and other things would get in the way of coming back to visit Heavenly Daze.

Cleta closed her eyes against the need to cry for the loss of what had been. As Micah said, she had to embrace the new. But what was the new? What would be her new relationship with Barbara? More friend than mother? More mentor than friend? Could she accept that?

Yes, she would accept it—even grow to love it, for if she didn't, she would have no relationship with her daughter. And somewhere in the distance, if God was good, their roles would reverse yet again. When Cleta and Floyd were bent with years, Cleta would be the child and Barbara the caregiver. Barbara would wipe her mother's chin and spoon soup into her mouth.

It was the garden all over again, the circle and cycle of life. As plants bloomed and died, new ones grew up to take their places. Just as people left this earthly garden to move to a heavenly landscape where they would bloom forever.

That thought gave her comfort.

After sitting with Floyd a while, Cleta returned to the hospital room. Russell was occupying the worn vinyl chair, his hand outstretched toward Barbara's, Barbara's fingers resting on his palm.

Cleta walked over and squeezed his shoulder. "The nurse said she'd sleep most of the day."

"I know." Russell's voice sounded thick.

The light on the phone blinked, so Cleta picked it up. "Hello?"

"Cleta?"

"Micah! How are things at the house?"

"Fine, how are things there? I was wondering if there was anything I could do to help."

"We're doing great." Cleta lifted her arm, stretching her stiff joints. Hospital chairs could be murder on a person's bones.

"Are you sure there's nothing I can do?"

"Well—" Cleta looked at her long-suffering son-in-law. "There is one thing, Micah. Will you run over to the mercantile and see if Vernie has a chocolate cake mix and a pound of walnuts? I have an awful strong urge to bake a chocolate fudge cake with walnut icing."

The gardener laughed. "I'll have the ingredients waiting when you get home."

⟿

Stretched out on his bed, Buddy laughed as Roxy nibbled at his big toe. The sun would be down in an hour, and, true to her nature, his little pet was awake and wanting to play.

Outside, snow drifted down like silver fleece shorn from a woolly sky, but the thermometer on the wall of Buddy's room read eighty-six degrees—not quite ninety, but Buddy wasn't worried about Roxy taking a chill. Yesterday, in a brainstorm born of desperation, he'd remembered a box of old toys Dana had stashed away. So, after church, Buddy went into the workroom, burrowed through dozens of dusty boxes, and finally found the mother lode. Inside, tossed together in a jumble of vinyl, hair, and shiny fabrics, was Dana's Barbie-doll collection, complete with accessories.

An hour later, Buddy had designed what he hoped

would be a workable outfit for Roxy—clothing comfortable for the animal, yet warm enough for Buddy to keep the temperature at something less than tropical heat wave. The sugar glider now wore a pink tutu from Barbie's ballet ensemble, featuring a stretchy top and about six inches of netting. Buddy had to trim away three inches of net in the front to keep Roxy from tangling her toenails in the stuff, but the form-fitted top suited the critter just fine. There were even little cap sleeves that slipped over her arms and dangled just below her shoulders—

"Ouch, Roxy! Don't bite so hard!" Buddy jerked his toe out of range of the animal's sharp front teeth. He reached for one of the monkey biscuits he'd picked up at the mercantile. "Eat these, and leave my toe alone!"

Rolling onto his stomach, he buried his face in his pillow as the persistent animal barked for his attention. Who'd have thought that a six-inch marsupial would work him harder than a drill sergeant? From sunrise to well past sundown he worked for Roxy, hauling firewood, searching for driftwood, preparing her food, cleaning her cage, stoking the fire, training her to sleep in her pouch and eat from his hand. And at night, when Buddy was dead tired and ready to hit the rack, that's when Roxy wanted to play. If he turned out the light to go to sleep, she began to bark. In order to silence her barking, he had either to leave the light on or put her in the pouch around his neck. Trouble was, after dark Roxy never wanted to stay in the pouch, she wanted to race up and down his bed, wriggle beneath the covers, sharpen her teeth on his toenails, and peek into Buddy's ears. Though Buddy desperately wanted to sleep, he found himself playing nursemaid and nanny to a fourteen-week-old sugar glider who was only beginning to discover the wonders of the wide, wide world . . .

Yesterday he'd gotten his best sleep in weeks . . . from two to five o'clock in the afternoon, when he should have been out combing the beach for driftwood. When he woke it was too dark to search, and this morning he'd been forced to burn three stacks of his precious Superman comic books just to keep the room at a lukewarm eighty-five degrees.

He loved his pet, honestly he did. Roxy could charm the whiskers off a lobsterman, and the quiet shushing sounds she made as she settled into her pouch each morning were music to his ears. She did keep him company, and since her arrival he didn't feel as lonely as he used to.

But as he lay on his bed and struggled to keep his eyes open, he wondered why he still didn't feel complete.

Chapter Seventeen

On the morning of Basil Caldwell's poetry awards ceremony, Dana's alarm clock woke her at 6:30 AM. Bounding out of bed in the darkness, she shivered her way into the shower where the water took fifteen minutes to heat. After dressing in jeans, wool socks, and her heaviest wool sweater, she tiptoed back through the dark bedroom (where Mike had not budged) and went downstairs to the kitchen. She tuned the small television to *Good Morning, Maine,* then plugged in the coffeepot and made toast while the weatherman predicted a high of twenty-two, low minus fifteen. The snow, thank goodness, had stopped falling.

Dana reached into the refrigerator and shivered at the touch of cold air. Basil and his media crew would freeze their noses off on the ferry—they'd probably all crowd into the cabin with Captain Stroble, who wouldn't have room to turn around. Most Maine folks were tough, but the inland folks didn't know what cold was until they'd spent a little time on the water in winter.

As the radiators in the kitchen clanged and hissed, Dana drank her coffee, ate two slices of buttered toast, then checked her "to-do" list. First on the list was a call to Pastor Wickam, but she waited until the clock struck seven-thirty before she picked up the phone. "Good morning, Pastor," she said when he answered. "Just wanted to remind you that you promised to grill a couple of turkeys for the dinner today."

"Thanks for the reminder, Dana." The pastor's voice was crusty with sleep. "Guess I'll go set up the grill."

"No need to rush, Pastor. We probably won't eat until around two or three, depending upon how long the ceremony lasts. But since Basil and his people won't even arrive until the noon ferry docks, I don't think we'll get started until one."

"Sounds good. Thanks for calling."

"Um, Pastor—" Dana bit her lip. The situation with Mike had not improved in the last week—he'd kept his secret, and she'd kept hers. He'd been cold, distant, and even more devoted to his eBay business, and she'd thrown herself into preparations for the awards ceremony and the celebration dinner to follow.

For the last few days she and Mike had been living like two strangers in one house, conveniently managing to avoid a single honest conversation, and Dana knew the stalemate had to end. She and Mike needed to talk about Jodi Standish, and they needed to be completely honest with one another. But before she confronted her husband, it might be nice to get advice from a man of God.

"Pastor, I'd like to talk to you sometime about me and Mike. Things aren't going as well as they should be, and I . . . well, to be blunt, I think Mike's been seeing a woman in Ogunquit."

A moment of astonished silence rolled over the phone line, then Pastor Wickam cleared his throat. "Perhaps you'd like to talk to Edith. She's up, making a pot of tea, so if you'd like to come over—"

"I can't come today, Pastor. There's too much going on here. But I'll try to stop by later, OK? Maybe tomorrow."

Dana hung up and placed a bold check mark next to the first item on her list. Tomorrow's heartbreak could take care of itself; she had enough to worry about today.

⤝

The sour scent of something funky woke Buddy from a sound sleep. Propping himself on his elbows, he crinkled his nose and looked at Roxy's cage . . . then realized that he'd fed her too much the day before. "Sugar gliders do not usually smell," the glider book had assured him. "If you do notice an odor, you have either fed them too much, or you have fed them the wrong things. Remove the soiled bedding, then cut back on the feeding or change to an approved diet and your little pet will be stink-free once more."

"Roxy!" Buddy held his nose as he sat up. The petite animal curled in her pouch, oblivious to his discomfort.

He glanced at the thermometer on the wall. The temperature in his room had fallen to sixty-nine degrees, which meant the fire in the woodstove had guttered and died during the night. He had to crank up the stove, and quickly . . .

Slipping into his jeans, down jacket, and boots, he ran out to the woodpile, the strings of his boot laces flapping around his ankles. Wincing beneath the sting of the cold air, Buddy used a rock to chip ice away from two split logs at the top of the stack, then scooped them into his arms and jogged back to the carriage house. Dropping the logs on the floor, he slammed the door and bent forward, panting, until he caught his breath.

"I hope you appreciate this," he told Roxy as he stood shivering in his coat. He opened the firebox of the stove, slid the logs onto the glowing coals, then tossed a couple of fire-starter cones on top of the logs. Finally, after the flick of a match, the pine cones burst into flame. Buddy waited until the bark of the logs began to crackle before he shut and sealed the door.

The warmth was welcome, but the smell of wood smoke did nothing to camouflage the sugar-glider stink. Hugging his knees, Buddy made a face, then did some quick computations. A thorough cage cleaning would require him to open and close the door several times, and with the temperature already so low, he couldn't risk Roxy taking a chill.

He searched his room for a moment, then found the little mesh-and-cardboard box under his bed. Taking the pouch from the cage wall, he dropped it through the little doorway, then set the temporary pet carrier on top of the warming wood stove.

There. Roxy would have the warmest spot in the room while he cleaned, and with any luck, he'd be rid of the stinking mess before Dana's intellectual friends descended upon the house. She had expressly told Buddy she wanted him to attend some one o'clock shindig she was throwing, followed by a spectacular lunch buffet. Buddy didn't care much for high-society shindigs, but the buffet sounded promising.

He yawned, overwhelmed by a sudden wave of sleepiness, and then crawled toward his bed. The rumpled pillow and thick comforter looked inviting, but as he lifted himself off the floor a wave of stink assaulted him right between the eyes, knocking the sleepiness clean out of him.

Maybe he'd clean the cage first and catch a nap later.

⌒

Sitting up in bed, Mike listened to Dana banging pots and pans downstairs, then he looked at the clock. Nine o'clock. He'd slept half the morning and Dana hadn't even popped in to see if he was sick or something.

He bent his knees and lowered his head, trying to cast off the lingering fog of sleep. He hadn't rested well; he felt as though he had tossed and turned half the night. A lady in Florida had received the wrong print, and it'd taken him until after midnight to sort out the difficulty. Then he had to send a conciliatory e-mail and promise to set things right, then he'd worried that she would post negative feedback on eBay, ruining his perfect record.

He shook his head in dismay. Not that Dana cared about any of this. His wife was all keyed up about Basil Caldwell and his snooty friends; she'd talked of nothing else for days. She hadn't bothered to discover that he, her husband, had earned his purple star. The purple star on eBay proved at least five hundred people agreed that he was a fair, honest, and efficient merchant, but Dana hadn't bothered to notice, or even ask why he had been putting little purple stars on his mailing labels. Worst of all, he had a sneaking suspicion she wouldn't even appreciate all that a purple star meant.

A man was what he did for a living, and for the first time in his twenty-nine years, Mike felt he had found his niche . . . and his wife didn't have a clue. And what did it profit a man if he sold every last item in his warehouse at 1,000 percent profit and lost his own wife?

Reluctantly leaving the warm cocoon of his bed, Mike rose and slipped into a pair of jeans and his most comfortable sweatshirt, then jammed his feet into his fur-lined moccasins and crept downstairs. Habit nearly drew him to the computer in the dining room, but he resisted the impulse. Pulling his coat from a hook by the door, he shrugged his way into it, then fitted a knitted cap over his tousled hair and strode out the front door.

The day that opened before him offered the intriguing combination of a frigid wind and a warm sun—rather like his wife's mood of the last few days. Dana smiled at the prospect of her party, and frowned at the sight of her husband. Cold waves practically radiated from her, and Mike had instinctively withdrawn, preferring the friendly enthusiasm of his customers to the frosty attitude of his wife.

He didn't know what had happened between them— all he knew was for the first time in his marriage he needed help. Ordinarily he'd have asked Yakov for advice, but now he needed the kind of advice only a married man could give.

Last night's snow still dusted the ground, crunching beneath his moccasins as he skimmed the lawn between his house and the Lansdowns'. He ducked into his coat and lengthened his stride as he crossed the graveled church parking lot. The wind whistled around the steeple and rattled the clapboards, but Mike didn't even look up. A moment later he was climbing the porch steps of the parsonage.

Edith Wickam didn't seem at all surprised to see him.

Dressed in a quilted robe with a kerchief over her curlers, she opened the door and nodded pleasantly. "Winslow's out back," she said, leading Mike through the living room and into the kitchen. Wearing a secretive smile, she pointed to the back door. "He's right out there; you can't miss him."

Mike stepped back out into the cold. "Hello, Pastor."

Winslow nodded, then pointed to a black grill standing on a slab of concrete. "Got a pair of turkeys in there. I figure they'll be ready by one o'clock if they don't freeze first." He forced a laugh, then pointed back toward the stairs. "Come inside, Mike. We'd have to be daft to stand out here and talk. I thought you might be dropping by."

"You did?"

"Ayuh. But let's get warm before we discuss it, shall we?"

A few minutes later, after Edith had served two steaming cups of apple cider and discreetly disappeared, Winslow drew a deep breath and folded his hands on the kitchen table. "Tell me what's on your mind, son."

"It's Dana." Mike fingered the rim of his mug as he sorted his thoughts. "I always thought we had a good marriage, but lately she's been like ice . . . and it has nothing to do with the weather. I saw her in Ogunquit having lunch with that Basil Caldwell fellow last week, and though I know he's just an old friend from high school, well, it still felt strange to look through the restaurant window and see them in there together."

"It may have been completely innocent, Mike. Did you ask her about it?"

"Pastor, she wore a dress."

Winslow whistled softly. "In January? That's something."

Mike nodded. "That's what I thought. I didn't ask her about it because she told us all about it at dinner. Basil Caldwell is having some kind of poetry contest, and somehow Dana got mixed up in it. And she's all worked up about him coming over this afternoon—honestly, I've never seen her so excited. Meanwhile, I'm busting my buns trying to make a living for us, and she acts like she doesn't give a flip."

Winslow lowered his hands. "I don't mean to be intrusive, Mike, but remind me—you guys live mostly off her trust fund, right?"

Mike felt heat creeping up his neck. "Hers and Buddy's, ayuh. But Buddy's money goes mostly to pay off his debts, and most of ours goes to pay for the house— these antique houses are expensive to maintain, you know."

The corner of the pastor's mouth dipped in a chagrined smile. "Oh, I know. My thirty-dollar border idea has mushroomed into a four-thousand-dollar renovation."

Mike plunged ahead. "But this month I earned a purple star on eBay, and for the first time I think I'll be able to bring in a monthly amount equal to her trust fund income. So I finally feel like I'm doing something, being the man—"

Winslow lifted a hand. "Hasn't Dana always made you feel like an equal partner?"

"Ayuh, sure. She's never said anything bad, you know, and she does appreciate all the work I did to get the house in shape." He felt himself flushing again. "I don't mean to brag, Pastor, 'cause Yakov helps a lot, too. He seems to know where everything should be, even where the pipes are hidden in the walls. But Dana runs the school, and that's what our house is—the Kennebunk Kid Kare Center. So, in a way, I feel like we are all about her money, her business—"

"But you're her husband, her partner."

"Ayuh, pastor, but a man is what he does, and until recently I've never found any work I really enjoyed. But now I'm an official Internet merchant . . . and Dana doesn't seem to care."

Winslow silently stroked his chin between his thumb and index finger. Finally he said, "This Internet business of yours—you doing any of it in Ogunquit?"

Mike blinked. "Ogunquit? No. I mean, yes. I sell on the World Wide Web, which means I ship to all kinds of places, but yeah, I have been going to Ogunquit a few times a week. Captain Stroble's granddaughter has a high-speed cable modem, and I use it while she's at work. It shaves a couple of hours off every workday . . . hours I had hoped to spend with Dana."

Winslow closed his eyes and nodded, a knowing smile crossing his face. "Mike, I am quite certain this situation is not as desperate as it seems. What you and Dana need is a good heart-to-heart talk. It sounds like you've both been too wrapped up in your own little worlds to connect with each other."

"But she—"

"Listen to me, son. The Bible says we shouldn't let the sun go down on our wrath. That's another way of saying you shouldn't let the day end without clearing the lines of communication. You need to talk to your wife openly and honestly; the sooner, the better."

"But she's expecting a houseful of company today! The entire town's coming for lunch, so when am I supposed to—"

"You're the man of the house, Mike. You make time for your wife."

≈

Roaming the island in search of enough driftwood to see him through another night, Buddy climbed over the rocks near Puffin Cove and tried to keep his thoughts centered on his task. Overhead, the sun was as weak as yesterday's dreams, and the rising wind chafed at his cheeks. But he couldn't turn back yet.

Fact: Roxy needed warmth. Fact: Roxy was his pet, and he loved her. Fact: In the coldest month of the year, he had purchased a desert animal to live in one of the coldest places in America, so he'd have to become extremely creative before spring blew in and warmed up the island. This meant he might have to confess what he'd done, pay for some extra firewood, and endure a week or so of Dana rolling her eyes at his stupidity.

But he wasn't the only person on Heavenly Daze who'd flirted with folly. Why, he'd just passed Pastor Wickam's house, and everybody was still yakking about how silly he'd been when he went through the toupee phase last October. And the entire island was laughing about his recent bathroom debacle. And Charles Graham, who fancied himself the Great American Novelist, had learned the hard way that sometimes dreams were best reserved for sleeping. And Annie Cuvier, that brainy girl, why, there wasn't a soul on the island now willing to come within a mile of a sandwich made with her miracle tomatoes. In every house on this island, someone had done something silly, so why did he feel like the only one with an albatross around his neck?

Standing at the top of a black granite boulder, he looked across the island's sand dunes and saw the boarded-up Lobster Pot. That was another dream, a far-flung one at best, and he had about as much chance of buying the restaurant as he had at winning Miss America. Success didn't come easily to the Buddy Franklins of this world, and sometimes it didn't come at all.

Why were some people born winners and others losers? Why were some people fast and others slow? Why were some people born beautiful and others so homely people averted their eyes rather than look them in the face? Did God decree who got what? If so, why was the Lord so ticked off at the losers and outcasts?

Tilting his head back, Buddy lifted his gaze to the overcast sky. "What have I ever done to you?" he called, his voice ringing across the empty rocks. "How could you hate me before I was even born?"

⤙

From where he stood beside the church steeple, Gavriel heard the cry of a soul in distress. His supernatural eyes fixed on the source, and instantly his heart leaped at the opportunity to minister.

"Show me, Father," he prayed, keeping his eyes on Buddy Franklin. "Show me what to do."

Then the answer came. This job would not fall to Yakov, for the sight of a familiar face would only silence

Buddy's cry. This was not the time for a supernatural vision, for Buddy would not be able to accept it. This was a time for speaking in the way Buddy understood.

Moving at the speed of light, in invisible supernatural form Gavriel swooped from the rooftop and planted his feet on the rocks beside Buddy. Without using audible words, Gavriel bent down and whispered in Buddy's ear: "Your cry has been heard. Pull out the paper and pencil in your pocket."

For a moment Buddy hesitated, then he obeyed. As his eyes watered in the stinging wind, he reached into his coat pocket and pulled out a stubby pencil from the Pitch and Putt golf course in Wells and a long grocery receipt from the mercantile.

"Now sit," Gavriel whispered again, "and write the words I will speak to you."

After settling onto the rock, Buddy pressed the pencil to the paper and began to write.

≈

Dana stopped drumming her nails on the mantel long enough to check her watch. Twelve-fifteen, and no Buddy. Basil and his crew would arrive at any moment, and she'd told her neighbors to be at her house by twelve-thirty. She had planned to serve punch and cookies while people mingled until one, then they'd hold the ceremony and surprise the entire town with Buddy's brilliance.

But where was the boy?

She moved to the stairs and tilted her face upward. "Yakov!" Something in her cringed at the whiny sound of her voice, but she couldn't help it. Mike's trusty assistant had been upstairs in his room all morning, not lifting a finger to assist. She had baked three cakes, tossed a fruit salad, baked two loaves of shredded wheat bread, and put a huge pot of hot cider on the stove to simmer—and she'd done everything herself.

A moment later Yakov appeared at the head of the stairs. "Ayuh?"

"What are you doing up there? I need your help."

The slender man nodded as he jogged down the steps. "Sorry, Dana. I was praying for your event this afternoon."

Dana looked away, her face growing hot as guilt smote her. How could she be irritated with a man who'd been praying for her? But right now she needed help with feet on it, not wings.

Yakov touched her shoulder and gave her an open and eager smile. "How can I help?"

She raked a hand through her hair. "I need Buddy. I don't know where he is, and it's really important that he be here when Basil Caldwell arrives."

A shadow of concern flitted through Yakov's dark eyes. "Buddy is not here?"

"No. I went to the carriage house and knocked on his door, but he didn't answer and the door was locked. He wasn't in the workroom, either."

"Has Mike seen him?"

"Mike has made himself scarce, too." Dana bit her lip, trying to curb her desperation. "If you find either one of them, you can wring their necks for me—after the ceremony. I'm so frustrated with both of them I could scream. I wanted Mike to rearrange the furniture so there's an open space in the front of the classroom."

Without even stopping to grab his coat, Yakov moved toward the front door. "I'll send someone to help, then I will find Buddy. Don't you worry."

Before she could say another word, he left the house. Through the window, she saw him moving across the front porch, his tread so light he barely creaked the old floorboards.

Dana had one cogent thought before she hurried back to the kitchen: All the men in her life had proved utterly undependable on the day she needed them most.

<hr />

Sitting on the rocks with his head resting on his bent knees, Buddy opened his eyes when he heard the soft scrunch of shoes against the scree on the rocks. Yakov stood beside him wearing only a sweatshirt and jeans, yet the man didn't even shiver.

"Your sister is quite concerned about you." A smile hovered in Yakov's eyes. "She is a little frantic about this afternoon's hoo-ha."

The sun seemed suddenly bright; Buddy shaded his eyes with his hand as he looked up to meet the other man's gaze. "Whatever."

"You are not concerned about your sister?"

"Dana's always a little frantic."

Yakov shrugged. "She will be OK now. I summoned Caleb, Zuriel, Elezar, Micah, and Abner to help her. But you, boychik, are my responsibility."

Laughing, Buddy turned his gaze out to sea. "I'm nobody's responsibility, Yakov-my-man. Nobody wants me hanging around their neck, especially not Dana."

"You are wrong. She loves you very much."

Slowly, Buddy shook his head. "I don't think so. She's only trying to be responsible. She and Mike probably wish I'd clear out and let them get on with their lives. Truth is, Dana's been covering for me ever since grade school. She kept the other kids from picking on me when we rode the bus home from Wells; she helped me finish the math papers I never could finish. And now she's tired. I see it in her eyes."

The silence between them stretched for a moment, then Yakov slipped his hands in his pockets and nodded toward the slip of paper tucked beneath Buddy's boot. "What is that you have there?"

"This? It's junk. Just a cash-register receipt."

"Somehow I think it is something more."

Shrugging, Buddy pulled the paper free. "Ayuh, maybe it's something. Maybe it's nothing. It's just some stuff that came to me a few minutes ago. Sometimes I have thoughts, you know, and I like to write them down. But they never amount to anything."

He lifted his hand until the paper caught the breeze and fluttered toward the ocean like the tail of a kite. He released the paper, watched it do a loop-de-loop in a sudden updraft and disappear into a white mist hovering above the water.

"I have not seen your little pet today," Yakov said, his eyes crinkling with concern. "How is the little creature?"

"Roxy's fine." Reminded of his former task, Buddy stood and brushed sand from the back of his jeans. "I was out here trying to get some wood, but I think I've picked this part of the beach clean. I had to clean out her cage this morning, so I built the fire up nice and high so the cold air from the door wouldn't bother her—"

He stopped suddenly. The breeze carried a scent from the south end of the island, the definite aroma of roasting meat.

"Buddy," Yakov's eyes narrowed in concentration, "where did you leave Roxy?"

Buddy's stomach dropped as he met Yakov's gaze. Hoarsely he whispered, "On top of the woodstove. Where a hot fire was burning."

"Hot enough to bake—"

Buddy didn't wait to hear the end of the sentence. He took off at a sprint, running for home.

⁂

Dana was on her way to the carriage house when Buddy tore around the corner, followed an instant later by Yakov.

"No!" Buddy roared, digging in his pocket for his key. He fumbled with the lock, then thrust his head into his apartment. He turned an instant later, his long face flushed. "Not here!" He stared at Yakov. "Not roasted. Gone!"

Yakov seemed to find meaning in this gibberish. "Then where?"

"Don't know! But Butch—"

Yakov shook his head. "Surely he would not."

"How do we know? He likes to catch squirrels!"

Dana propped her hands on her hips. "Yakov," she injected a note of steel into her voice. "Tell me, this instant, who you are talking about. Who's gone?"

"My pet," Buddy interrupted, lifting his hands in a

don't-shoot pose. "I have a pet. It's a sugar glider, a little animal that looks something like a squirrel. But she has to stay warm, and I needed wood, so I put her on the wood-stove, and I was afraid she was roasting, but now she's gone—"

Dana pressed her hand to her forehead. "I don't care about a runaway squirrel. I have some very important people on their way from the ferry right now. I need you to make yourself presentable and come into the schoolroom for the ceremony. It'll only take a few minutes, then we'll have a late lunch. OK?"

Buddy grimaced as though she had struck him across the face. "But Roxy could freeze! She has to stay warm!"

"Animals have a sixth sense about these things; she's probably curled up in a warm place somewhere. After the party, we'll help you look for her, OK?" Softening her tone, she walked forward and placed a hand against her brother's chest. "I don't mean to sound insensitive. I guess it's OK for you to have a pet as long as I don't have to take care of it. But I don't have time right now to stop and look for a rodent."

"A marsupial," Buddy answered, his voice flat. "She would carry her babies in a pouch, like a kangaroo."

"And possums," Yakov added. "Possums come from the same family."

Dana resisted the urge to roll her eyes. "Whatever. Just get yourselves cleaned up and come inside, will you? Don't disappoint me, either of you, or I'll make sure you never forget it."

Buddy opened his mouth as if he'd protest again, but something in her eyes must have convinced him she meant business. He clamped his mouth shut, went back into his apartment, and slammed the door.

≈

Half an hour later, Dana sat on the front row of her classroom, staring at the blackboard and Basil Caldwell's imposing figure. The other chairs, most of them kid-sized, had been filled by the citizens of Heavenly Daze, for Basil had not been able to find any members of the media willing to brave the ferry ride across the frigid feather white waters. Instead of a photographer, Basil had brought a camera, which Vernie Bidderman now held, her lips flattened in a frown as she peered through the viewfinder.

"If I take the picture," she was asking Basil in a none-too-subtle stage whisper, "will they put my name in the magazine? I always did want to get my name in *Northeastern Living*. Since I sell it at the mercantile, seems only fair."

Ignoring Vernie, Basil stood with his hands folded and his head lowered, an almost reverent posture, but Dana knew he was only killing time. Mike had finally arrived—and taken a seat on the far side of the room—and so had Yakov. They were waiting for Buddy, but Yakov assured Dana her brother was on his way.

While they waited, Dana scanned the room. Barbara Higgs was still in the hospital, and Russell was with her, but Bea, Vernie, Olympia, Charles, Babette, Dr. Marc, and Cleta occupied kiddie chairs in the front row while Salt, Floyd, Stanley, Yakov and Mike lounged on two of the kid-sized tables behind the chairs. Birdie, who wore a pretty wool dress with a low-cut lace collar, sat primly beside Salt, now her official beau. The Smith men, with the exception of Yakov, had stationed themselves in the doorway between the schoolroom and the bountiful buffet spread on the kitchen table. (Dana had mentally cursed the computer a hundred times as she set out the food—the buffet would have looked a hundred times better in her formal dining room, but noooooooooo, Mike had to put his beloved computer on her grandmother's antique dining table.)

Bobby, Brittany, and Georgie were occupying themselves by coloring puffin pictures at the table right behind Dana's seat, while Winslow and Edith Wickam oversaw their efforts from another kiddie table. Winslow had winked at Dana when he came in, and while she wasn't sure what the wink meant, she took comfort from it. Perhaps something good would yet come out of this disastrous day.

Her heart settled to a more normal rhythm when the clunk of heavy boots announced Buddy's presence in the classroom. From the disheveled look of his clothes and hair, and the streak of soot across his cheek, she knew he hadn't taken time to clean up, but had kept looking for that creature. By the defeated look on his face, she surmised that he hadn't found it.

Maybe her surprise would take the sting out of his loss.

Sighing in relief, she nodded to Basil, who had agreed to wait for Buddy only when she explained that the ceremony would mean nothing without her entire family present.

"If we may begin," Basil said, lifting a brow in Dana's direction, "we are gathered here today on behalf of *Northeastern Living* to recognize a superb new talent. A talent that has been long buried, long ignored—"

He grimaced as Vernie flashed the camera in his face.

"Um," Basil widened his eyes in an apparent effort to focus, "as I was saying, we are here to recognize a new talent. A few weeks ago, you see, *Northeastern Living* decided to run a poetry contest. Poetry, as you know, is the language of the gods—"

"Really?"

Dana lowered her head onto her hand when she recognized the voice. Why was Yakov interrupting?

"There is only one God and one mediator who can reconcile God and people," Yakov said, looking around the room. "He is the man Christ Jesus."

Winslow Wickam and several of the Smith men applauded.

Dana looked at Basil and made a little hurry-up motion with her hand.

Basil tipped his chin back and studied Yakov through lowered lids. "May I continue?"

"Please do." Yakov resumed his seat.

"As I was saying," Basil said, pressing his hand to his chest, "imagine my surprise when one entry proved to be not only from Heavenly Daze, but from a woman of my previous acquaintance, Dana Franklin Klackenbush."

Dana felt her cheeks burn as her neighbors, in unison, applauded lightly.

Vernie advanced with her weapon. "Say cheese, Dana!"

The camera flashed.

Blinding spots clouded Dana's vision as Basil continued. "I'd like to read the poem Dana sent us, but before I do, let me assure you that we found it deserving of our highest honor. We have declared it the first prize winner!"

"What's the prize?" Georgie Graham sang out.

Babette Graham perked up. "Does she win money?"

"She wins—" Basil paused for dramatic effect. "Ten free copies of *Northeastern Living!*"

Dana felt her hopes fall. She hadn't been expecting much, but a cash prize would have done a lot to encourage Buddy.

"Well, there never has been any money in poetry." Charles Graham nodded sagely. "Fine art, yes. Novels can be lucrative. But poetry, never."

"Ten copies is barely enough for all of us," Birdie groused. "Cheap magazine."

Basil cleared his throat. "And now, if I may read the poem."

With a great flourish, he pulled a sheet of paper from a leather portfolio. After settling a pair of half-glasses on the end of his nose, he tipped his head back and began to read:

> "My joy cannot be contained in words or song or
>   expression.
> Letters, juxtaposed puzzles, are rife with discretion,
> But boundless joy, the rarest fruit of my heart,
> Is far more an elixir of life than mere art."

From the back of the room, Buddy began to chant with Basil:

> "Two black velvet eyes, a tip-tilted gaze,
> Have launched me round this sphere in a daze."

Basil stopped reading, obviously annoyed, and Buddy finished the poem.

"My heart doth pound in rapturous beat
Because your love makes my poor life complete."

As Basil frowned, Dana stood and turned to face her brother. "I told Basil the poem wasn't mine, Buddy. I knew you'd never send your poem to a magazine, even though you're a good poet."

"A darn good poet," Floyd seconded, slapping his knee for emphasis.

"A love poem," Birdie said, her hand at her throat. "Gets me all choked up."

Bea leaned forward to see around Cleta and narrowed her eyes at Buddy. "What woman inspired your poem, Buddy? Somebody you met on that Internet?"

Buddy shook his head. "It wasn't a woman at all. It was—"

Basil Caldwell exploded without waiting to hear Buddy's explanation. "Impossible!" he roared. He glared around the room, his face darkening dangerously. "I don't know what you folks think you're pulling here, but I will not let a major magazine like *Northeastern Living* be shanghaied by local yokels. I know Buddy Franklin; I grew up with him. And there was never anyone on God's earth less poetic, less intelligent, and less inclined to the sensitivities a true poet must possess—"

"Still waters run deep . . . or have you not heard that poetic witticism, Mr. Caldwell?"

The voice was Yakov's. He stood from his place and came forward, a long slip of paper trailing from his hand. Dana stared, bewildered, but something in his confident countenance made her heart leap.

Yakov walked to the front of the room and turned to face the gathering. "Earlier this morning I found Buddy Franklin out on the rocks by Puffin Cove, where he had just composed this piece. I would like to read it to you now."

Basil stamped his foot. "I protest!"

"This is my home, Mr. Caldwell." Crossing her arms, Dana gave him a cool stare. "And I would like to hear this."

Yakov stretched out the scribbled grocery receipt and began to read:

"Who is like the Lord God?
All the people of the earth
Are nothing compared to Him.
He has the power to do as He pleases
Among the angels of heaven
And with those who live on earth.
No one can stop him or challenge Him,
Saying, 'What do you mean by doing these things?'
Should the thing that was created
Say to the One who made it,
'Why have You made me like this?'
You are worthy, O Lord our God,
To receive glory and honor and power.
For You created everything,
And it is for your pleasure that they exist and were
     created . . .
Such words seem to come from far above me,
Yet in this hour they rose in my heart—
Can it be that the God who made and loves me
Has breached the gap that kept us apart?
If so, I am found; if so, I know.

I understand why I sought Him so.
For only in finding the One who created,
Will my longing for completeness and home be
        sated."

Yakov lowered the page, and for a moment the room echoed with the sound of silence. Then Dana whispered, "That was beautiful, Buddy."

"You'll never convince me Buddy Franklin even knows the meaning of *sated,*" Basil snapped, lifting his chin. "Furthermore, it's a clear case of plagiarism. I don't know where I've heard that, but I've heard most of it before. The prize will not be awarded."

"I'm sure you have heard those words before," Winslow said, standing, "for many of them come from Scripture." He shot Buddy a twisted smile, and something in the look touched Dana's heart. She knew the pastor had been praying for Buddy ever since his arrival on Heavenly Daze.

"Buddy, it was like you took some of the words right out of God's mouth," Winslow said, his smile spreading. "But it was beautiful—and every word was true. God created us, designed us, to have fellowship with Him."

Buddy had gone as red as a turkey's wattle. "I don't know the Bible." He lowered his gaze to the floor. "So I don't know where those words came from. Sometimes things just . . . come out of me." He looked up to glare at Basil. "By the way, *sated* means 'fully satisfied.' I do know a few things."

"You've been coming to church with your sister for a while now," Pastor Wickam said. "And we've all been praying for you. And what goes in your ears can remain in your brain, particularly when supported by the power of prayer."

"You see, Buddy," the warmth of Yakov's voice filled the room, "you reached out for Roxy because your heart was lonely for fellowship. Even though you are surrounded by family and friends who love you, you yearned for something more. And that something is God—the One who designed you according to a unique blueprint, the One who knows your strengths and weaknesses and quirks better than anyone on earth. And He loves you. Enough to provide a way to heaven through the sacrifice of His Son, Jesus Christ."

As her vision blurred with tears, Dana heard a murmuring sound from behind her. When she turned, she saw the Smith men gathered in a semicircle behind Buddy. Their eyes were closed, their hands clasped in a display of unity, and as they prayed softly their faces were . . . glowing.

Dana shook her head. The camera flash must still be affecting her eyes.

"Alst I know," Buddy said, his voice breaking as he looked up and caught Dana's gaze, "is I'm tired of not belonging. If God wants me, He can have me, lock, stock, and barrel. I want to come home."

Dana ran to her brother and drew him into an embrace. As Pastor Wickam followed to clasp Buddy in a brotherly hug, Dana stepped back, dashed tears from her eyes, and walked toward Basil Caldwell.

"I'm sorry," she said. "I didn't mean to mislead you, but I knew Buddy would never come out for this if he thought we were going to make a big deal about one of his poems."

Basil grunted as he thrust his papers back into his briefcase.

Dana tapped him on the arm. "Please, Basil, give the prize to the second place winner. I will look forward to reading the other poem in your magazine."

"Can't do that," he snapped.

"Why not?"

"Because. No one else entered the contest."

"Oh." Dana stepped back, her perception of the scholar crumbling into dust. So—the mighty Basil Caldwell, poet laureate and pompous snob, had only succeeded in inspiring one nostalgic housewife. And if she hadn't been bored and feeling neglected, she wouldn't have given his portentous poetry contest a second thought.

"Thank you," she murmured, dropping her hand.

He scowled at her. "What for?"

Dana smiled. Would he understand how his pretentiousness had helped her appreciate her ordinary lifestyle? Doubtful.

"You'll never know what you've done for me," she said, catching her husband's eye. "Have a nice life."

Birdie tugged on her sleeve. "Who in tarnation is Roxy?"

That's when Georgie Graham, who'd been happily drawing a picture of a squirrel in a pink dress, suddenly giggled. "Look!" he called, holding his picture up for everyone to see. "It's a good picture, isn't it?"

Babette smiled at her precocious son. "What is it supposed to be, honey?"

Georgie pointed toward the overhead light fixture. "That!"

Dana lifted her gaze . . . and felt a sudden weakness in her knees. There, perched on the edge of the glass plate light fixture, a squirrel-like creature in a pink ball gown and tiny puffed sleeves stared down at them with a strange little grin on its striped face. Audible gasps echoed through the room, then Buddy yelled, "Roxy!"

At the sound of his voice the creature barked, then launched itself in his direction . . . but fell short by a good five feet, landing on the collar of Birdie's dress. When she shrieked and stood, the animal dove beneath the collar, apparently trying to bury itself in her décolletage.

"Salt! Sister!" Birdie hopped on the balls of her feet, her hands flapping uselessly at the lace on her collar. "Somebody help me!"

The men, paralyzed by the fear of impropriety, retreated in unison while Bea and Edith rushed to the rescue. They succeeded in wresting the bewildered creature from its hiding place just as Vernie yelled, "Say 'cheese!'" and flashed them all blind.

Lost in a happy daze, Dana sank into her teacher's chair and smiled as Yakov caught the squirrelly animal, then held it for the children to examine. As the women comforted Birdie, Pastor Wickam slipped his arm around Buddy and led him toward the hallway. Babette and Charles were studying their son's drawing, while Basil Caldwell stood in a corner and fumed.

Dana grinned. Let him pout.

"Dana." Mike's voice broke into her thoughts. "We need to talk, honey."

She looked up at her handsome husband, overjoyed to see a calm face in the hubbub. "Indeed, we do," she said, taking his hands. "But before you say anything, I need to know—why would Captain Stroble set you up with Jodi Standish?"

"His granddaughter?" Mike blinked. "Because she needed extra income, and said I could rent her cable modem while she's at work. I've been going over there to free up more time for you, but lately you haven't exactly been with me, if you know what I mean. It's like you're living on a different planet."

Dana acknowledged his comment with a rueful smile. "I'm sorry. I jumped to a wrong conclusion about you, Mike."

He squeezed her hand. "I realize I've been focusing on my eBay business, but you've got to understand that this work is important to me." He lifted one shoulder in a shrug. "I suppose we need to find a balance, huh?"

Dana smiled as a wave of relief swept through her. "Come on, babe," she said, standing and pulling him toward the kitchen. "We can talk about compromise while we eat. I'm starving."

And as she walked by Birdie, who sat in one of the kiddie chairs with her knees together, her feet spraddled, and a flush on her face, Dana noticed that little Georgie Graham was peering intently at the cleavage into which the sugar glider had disappeared. "Mama," he asked, his childish voice ringing through the schoolroom, "why is Miss Birdie's backside on the wrong side?"

Dana pressed her face against Mike's shoulder in an attempt to smother her giggles.

Kids!

Epilogue

January is, by definition, a cold month on the island of Heavenly Daze, but I'm pleased to know there were more than a few heart fires burning as the month drew to a close. Mike and Dana Klackenbush renewed their commitment to one another, and I've heard that Mike is giving Dana first crack at his February calendar—she gets to pencil in his work hours, and make sure he allots time for what she's calling "marital fellowship."

Russell and Barbara Higgs are doing nicely too. Barbara is healing from her surgery, and Dr. Marc holds high hopes that she'll be able to conceive within the coming year. They're praying for a child, but Micah is trying to teach them that the most important thing is finding and following the Father's will. Ah, well. Humans sometimes learn their lessons slowly.

Cleta learned an important lesson this week—children are a gift from the Lord, and gifts are never to be esteemed more highly than the Giver. By surrendering her right to occupy the primary position in her daughter's life, Cleta will give Barbara the freedom to become the wife, daughter, and child of God she was intended to be. Cleta will discover new purpose for her own life, as well. God never leaves his people in a vacuum.

Floyd is still studying his mechanics lessons . . . and praying for new tires on the fire truck.

Roxy? That little varmint has temporarily gone to live with Babette and Charles Graham, whose house is more efficiently heated than Buddy's apartment. Vernie has promised to permanently stock monkey biscuits at the mercantile, and Georgie is thrilled with his part-time pet. Babette is thinking of launching a line of designer rodent wear to help bring in a little extra income. If Roxy will become only a little more compliant, they might feature her in a booth at the spring bazaar. If you visit Heavenly Daze in April, two bucks will buy a Polaroid shot of you holding the town's resident marsupial in a stunning silk ensemble.

Things have calmed down in the parsonage; Bea is continuing her ministry with the angel mail, and Birdie is quietly planning her spring wedding to Salt Gribbon. Charles and Babette Graham have no idea what a surprise the Lord has in store for them next September.

Vernie and Stanley are becoming friends. Perhaps, given a bit more time, they will rediscover the perfect love they once had for each other . . . and they can have again, if they are willing to let the One who loves them love through them.

Annie has gone back to the tomato drawing board, and A. J. flew down from New York to comfort her. Only the Lord knows if a special love is sprouting between those two, though I suspect it might be so . . .

Time will tell. Until next month, I am wishing you warm nights and heavenly days. May you discover the power of God's perfect love.

Until we meet again,

—Gavriel

If You Want to Know More About . . .

- Angels having their own language: 1 Corinthians 13:1

- Angels as servants and messengers: Genesis 24:7, Exodus 23:20, Hebrews 1:14

- Angels are as "swift as the wind" and "servants made of flaming fire:" Hebrews 1:7

- Angels' special care for children: Matthew 18:10

- Angels as protectors: Psalm 91:11–12

- The heavenly throne room: 2 Chronicles 18:18, Psalm 89:14, Psalm 11:4, Rev. 4:1–6

- Angels' limited knowledge: Matthew 24:36

- Angels eagerly watching humans: 1 Peter 1:12

- The third, or highest, heaven: 2 Corinthians 12:2, Deuteronomy 10:14, 1 Kings 8:27, Psalm 115:16

- The reference to God creating evil: Isaiah 45:7

- A man should leave his father and mother and cleave to his wife: Ephesians 5:31

- Gavriel's song of encouragement: Psalm 103:19–22

- Sugar gliders: http://skinhorse.net/gliders

About the Authors

LORI COPELAND is the author of more than 95 books. She lives in the beautiful Ozarks with her husband Lance. They are very involved in their church and active in supporting mission work in Mali, West Africa. Lance and Lori have three sons, two daughters-in-law, and five wonderful grandchildren.

ANGELA HUNT is the best-selling author of *The Tale of Three Trees, The Debt, The Note,* and *The Nativity Story,* with over three million copies of her books sold worldwide. Her book *The Novelist* won gold in ForeWord Magazine's 2007 Book of the Year award. *The Note* was a Hallmark Christmas movie in December 2007. Romantic Times Book Club presented Angela with a Lifetime Achievement Award in 2006. She and her husband make their home in Florida with two mastiffs.

$\mathcal{V}$isit us on the web at

www.heavenlydazeME.com

Read all of the books in the
Heavenly Daze series

The Island
of Heavenly
Daze

Grace in
Autumn

A Warmth
in Winter

A Perfect Love

Hearts at Home